KING'S HARLOTS SERIES: BOOK 5

NUMB

J.M. WALKER

ISBN: 978-1-989782-60-6

DEDICATION

Tammi Plummer
Angie Stanton
Joanne Thompson

ACKNOWLEDGEMENTS

This book was the hardest book I have ever written. Due to personal reasons, it was more difficult to write than I thought it would be. But thanx to an amazing team, I got through it.

First, I have to thank Angie, Joanne and Tammi for all of their hard work when reading this story for me. Without the three of you, Numb wouldn't be what it is today.

Tammi Plummer: You are the best PA a girl could ask for. Thank you for all of your help. #semicolon

My review team: You girls are everything. You don't even know how much you mean to me. Your comments and messages about this book have blown me away. I have no words.

My Jems!! Girls, you all are my rocks! I wouldn't be able to finish this series if it wasn't for your love of these books. Thank you so very much for your never-ending support.

To all of the authors and blogs: Thank you for everything. Thank you for sharing my posts, reading my books, commenting, liking and more. Thank you doesn't even begin to describe how much I appreciate your support.

Christine Stanley with The Hype PR. My Poopy!! Girl, you have been with me since Brett! Can you believe I'm on my 25th book? Love you!!

Jennifer Scarn and TD Ross. My "haters". I love you both and thank you for reading an ARC of Numb even though I destroyed your heart and made you feel all the feels.

My readers. I can't even with you all right now. You make my heart happy. You fill my soul with your messages and comments. When I started this series, I never expected it to take this turn and I thank you for being with me 100% of the way.

And of course my hubby. He never wants recognition but I'm thanking him anyway. Love you my hunni!!

And lastly, to all of YOU! Every single one of you. Whether you have read my books or not, I appreciate you.

JM
XX

NUMB
PLAYLIST

https://open.spotify.com/user/jmwlkr/playlist/3DX4IEbgEh79Rx3y7sOXQ8

SUPPORT INFORMATION

Several people close to me have dealt with infant loss in some way. I invite you to find support through these links and please know that you are not alone.

Hand of the Peninsula -
http://handsupport.org/services
Now I Lay Me Down To Sleep -
https://tinyurl.com/ydd4pbtw

Australia

Stillbirth Foundation -
http://stillbirthfoundation.org.au/about-us/

UK

Sands - https://www.sands.org.uk
Support website to purchase memorial pictures:
http://carlymarieprojectheal.com

Support group:
http://www.thetearsfoundation.org/page.php?id=25

PROLOGUE

Max

FROM THE MOMENT I found out I was pregnant, I was in love with her. But almost as fast as that love formed, she was taken from me. Now as I looked down at my daughter, lying in my arms with her eyes closed, I only imagined she would open them for me. *Just give me a breath. Anything. Wake up for me, baby girl.*

When my lips touched her forehead, I prayed with everything in me that she would cry. But she didn't. She couldn't. It wasn't fair. None of this was fair. The man I loved wanted nothing to do with me, and the daughter I didn't know was stolen from my very body.

I begged to anyone who would listen, *Let her stay with me. Take me instead. She didn't deserve this. She didn't deserve any of it.*

With tears rolling down my cheeks, my sobs of anguish ripped through me. They took hold and strangled me, sucking the air from my very lungs.

NUMB

"I love you, baby girl." I kissed her softly on her perfect mouth. "I love you, and I don't even know you," I said through my tears. Brushing my thumb over her full cheek, I kept my lips against her forehead. "Lord, give me strength. Help me move on from this." My breath hitched. "Help me learn to live without her."

"Maxine."

I didn't look up at the gentle voice, knowing the person had come to take my baby away.

"It's time, dear." The nurse reached a hand out, placing it gently on my baby's head. "I'm sorry."

A sob tore from my throat. "It's not fair," I screamed, my soul shattering around me. "It's not fair. I need more time. Please."

The older nurse nodded, leaving me alone with my daughter.

Lying down on the bed, I kept her by my side, holding her close.

It never should have been like this. We were supposed to be happy. Just her and me.

When my baby girl was taken from my arms, the last bit of light inside of me went with her. My world would forever be clouded in a sea of darkness.

Because of this, a part of me died.

Because of *him*, I would never be the same.

CHAPTER ONE

Max

I HATED HIM.
As I stared down at his still body lying in the hospital bed, I hated him.

When I lay beside him, curling against his warm body, I hated him.

And when I lost his baby, I *loathed* him.

Dale Michaels was everything to me and nothing at the same time. He cracked open my ribs, ripped out my heart, and forced me to fall. I had been sucked into the pits of hell, clawing and digging, trying to find my way out. But the demons of my misery only pulled me deeper. I had fought against them for so long that now I stood beside them and smiled.

Life sucked.

Straight up.

Dale was the beginning of my suffering and there wasn't a damn thing I could do about it. I loved him. No matter how much of an asshole he was, I couldn't help but love him. The heart wants what it wants and shit.

It was a week into his coma, maybe longer; I couldn't remember and I tortured myself by visiting him every damn day. Maybe a part of me had hoped he would wake up, realize he loved me, and we would finally have our happy ever after.

The doctors kept him safe, comfortable, doing everything they could in preparation that he would eventually wake up. The doctor had told me Dale was lucky to still be alive—the bullet he had been shot with missing a vital part of his head.

I remembered when Vice-One came back from their mission. The Navy SEALs I had come to know over the past couple of months looked everywhere but directly at me. And that was when I heard the words. Coby had been the one to tell me. He was Dale's best friend. All of them were close but those two were the epitome of brotherhood. Dale was the youngest and Coby was the oldest. It was like he took Dale under his wing. A slight twinge settled deep in the middle of my chest over my reaction to his words.

"Dale is in a coma."

I broke. I screamed. I cursed. I cried. And then nothing. I had beat my fists against Coby as his words washed over me. He didn't react. He had stood there like a stone wall while I unleashed my wrath on him.

All my feelings over the past couple of months were pulled from me as they shredded my soul. But I no longer cried for Dale.

From the research I had done, they say if you talked to a coma patient, they could hear, maybe even react to a person's voice. It had been weeks, and I still didn't talk to him. No words could leave my mouth as much as I tried. As much as the voice screamed inside of my head for me to give him everything I felt and show him the pain he had caused me. I wanted Dale to feel what I felt. I wanted to break him like he broke me. I wanted his bones to shatter as he begged at my feet, pleading for me to forgive him. I wanted everything from him but nothing at the same time. He didn't deserve me. All of these thoughts rushing through my mind only made me feel guiltier.

I *loved* him.

I *hated* him.

I *needed* him.

I *pushed* him.

When I first told Dale I was falling in love with him, he laughed in my face. I laughed as well because I was surprised at how stupid I had been. Dale was a slut. How could I ever think he would settle down with someone like me? Well I had. And then I got pregnant. That conversation didn't go over well no matter how many times I had rehearsed it in my head. He was young. Scared. We only just met. *Blah. Blah. Blah.*

But now we were in the hospital. With him in bed and me beside him. I wondered if maybe him falling into a coma and me losing the baby at the same time was a sign.

I sat on the edge of the bed, letting my head fall into my hands. The tears had dried up, but I knew it was only because he couldn't talk back to me. As soon as I heard his voice, I would break, crumbling to the ground because I was weak. So damn weak.

I had no baby.

I had no boyfriend.

Depression had settled in, and I let it, not caring in the least how it had affected me or those around me.

"You did this to me," I whispered, finally able to speak to Dale after all this time.

He didn't stir.

I cupped his cheek, the rough stubble scratching my fingers. "You did this to me," I repeated on a whisper. My heart raced, pounding hard behind the walls of my rib cage.

He looked at peace while inside I was a raging inferno of despair.

Rubbing my hands up and down my legs, I pushed and pushed until a sob escaped me. I shook my head, the tears rolling down my cheeks and dripped off my chin. "You. It's your fault," I croaked, my heart thumping hard in my ears.

As each day passed with Dale still being in a coma, my soul crushed with the added weight. As much as I hated him, I would never wish him harm. Unless *I* was the one doing it. I wanted to beat my fists against his chest. To yell and scream at him. For him to shout back. And then I wanted his arms to wrap around me and tell me everything would be okay and that he loved me. But none of that happened. It would *never* happen.

I rose from the bed, staring down at him just as a nurse came into the room.

She didn't say anything while checking his vitals. She didn't look my way. She didn't ask me how I was because the fuck if I knew. She learned from the last time. She knew better. The staff had come to know that I could be a raging bitch so they ignored me.

When the nurse left, I glanced back down at Dale's unmoving form. He was intoxicatingly beautiful; I couldn't resist him from the first moment he smiled at me. With that delicious dimple that popped out of his cheek when he smirked. The flick of his tongue as it slid along his full bottom lip. The heat in his eyes, reminding me what he could do to me. As much as I hated him, I missed him even more. Even though the past couple of months involved only us fighting, I needed it. I needed *him*. I needed *more*.

"There isn't any change," the nurse said and left the room. Nothing more. Nothing less. She didn't give me any sign that Dale would pull out of this. That he would come back to me.

My chest constricted. It wouldn't be me he was coming back to.

With a heavy heart, I curled my fingers around his, falling to my knees. It had been the same thing every damn day since the first. I would beg. Plead for God to wake him up. But no tears came. Not for him. Not for our baby. Not until now. The only sounds leaving me were screams. Violent tremors tore at my soul, shredding the last bit of hope I had. Terrorizing nightmares left me stripped bare, only to remind me what had happened.

I promised myself that when he woke up he would feel my wrath. My slap against his cheek for hurting me. My fists beating against his chest for leaving me.

My throat tightened. No. I would not cry. He didn't deserve my tears. Not anymore. Not ever again.

I still held his hand. I still prayed he would wake up. I would continue to beg until his beautiful blue eyes opened for me. How could I fall in love with a man who wanted nothing but sex? Delicious, life-altering sex. But he had been selfish, only worrying about himself. And yet, I still crawled back to him like some bitch in heat.

My body hummed, images of our time together melting into my mind.

I swallowed hard, pushing them back.

The alarm clock on my phone dinged, alerting me it was time to go back to the gallery before I was missed.

Placing a soft kiss on Dale's cheek, my lips tingled under the scratchiness of his beard, mentally promising him that I would be back the next day.

As I left the hospital, the further I got away from Dale, the heavier my body felt. It didn't make sense for me to spend time with him day in and day out. I got that. And as much as I hated him, I couldn't pull myself away. I needed to make sure he was okay, not that my presence would mean anything.

I wasn't sure what bothered me most. That the man I loved was in a coma or that I lost his baby. I already regretted the day I would have to tell him. But maybe he wouldn't even care. It wasn't like he wanted anything to do with us.

Wind whipped around me, brushing under the hair at my nape and sent a shiver down my spine. Much like the way Dale used to touch me while he held me during our passion.

With my body heavy and my muscles aching and vibrating over my bones, I trudged to my bike. The beauty sat by the curb, shining and bright. The only light in my life. Before Dale's accident, I loved riding but something kept me from it. Now, I was driven with a need, a want so hard, that I had to ride it out for fear of losing myself. The open wind in my hair curbed the darkness that had settled deep on my heart.

Once I straddled my bike and turned her on, the rumble between my legs sent a shiver down my spine. A part of me was thankful Dale was at the hospital in the city. I could then enjoy the drive back to town. It wasn't long, but it was enough.

My phone vibrated in the pocket on the inside of my leather jacket, but I ignored it and kicked off from the curb. I knew who was texting me. It had been the same person since Dale fell into a coma.

Jay Gold, my best friend and president of the King's Harlots, was worried about me. But I was fine. She had no reason to be concerned. I scoffed. Even *I* didn't believe that.

Pulling out of the hospital parking lot, I felt a piece of me had been left back with Dale. Since the moment I had heard about him being in a coma, some part of me had followed him into that darkness. Maybe he was better off. The shit storm that had gone down with the human trafficking organization we were trying to shut down only kept getting more difficult to stop.

Once I reached the edge of the city, I glanced in my side mirror, wondering if Dale would wake up when I wasn't there. It had been the same battle of thoughts in my mind day in and day out.

My phone rang, the jarring sound screeching in the ear piece hooked up to my helmet. Letting out a hard sigh, I tapped the screen on my phone resting on the mount. The speedometer caught my eye, forcing a small smile tugging at my lips. Speeding up at the same time I grunted a greeting into the phone, I let the open road guide me home.

"Don't you sound fucking chipper."

"Always," I mumbled. "What's up, Jay?"

She sighed. "Listen, I'm just going to come out and say it. I'm worried for you."

"*For* me or *about* me?"

"Same thing, isn't it?"

Maybe. "I'm driving."

"You have a hands-free, Max. I'm talking to you until you get home."

"I'm heading to the gallery. I need to paint." Painting had been my only solace. It was the one true way I could escape and leave the hell of my mind behind.

"Are you sure that's a good idea?"

"Why wouldn't it be?"

"You know why."

I swallowed hard. "Nothing is going to happen."

"Did you get the image of Zane?"

"Yeah, the fucker is gorgeous," I muttered, remembering the photo of Zane Birtch. The man we were told was behind this organization of trafficking but I had a feeling it was someone else. Someone on the inside. Someone we knew.

"Well, maybe, but remember, if you see him, call it in."

"I'll do that." We talked until I reached town. Which consisted more of Jay talking and me grunting answers. It used to be the other way around. But since Jay had found her one true love, engaged to be married, and now pregnant with his child, I had become the bitter one. I was happy for her, but I was also jealous. It was the most honest emotion I had allowed myself to feel in weeks.

"Max?"

"I'm almost at the gallery. I'll talk to you soon, Jay." I hung up the phone before she even had a chance to respond.

Pulling my bike into the narrow alleyway beside the gallery, I shut her off and waited. The wind whipped around me, brushing over my skin like the touch of a lover's kiss.

A shiver rippled down my spine, and before I could allow my mind to drift to that pain, I slid off my bike and headed into the gallery.

It was midafternoon on a Thursday. The gallery would open in a couple of hours and go well into the late evening. Artists from our small town and the surrounding cities would come out to see my work or try and get their own art into my space.

It had been the same old routine ever since I started working there a couple years ago. I never went into painting expecting to sell anything. I also didn't go into it to make a quick buck. I did it so people could see my work if they wanted to and hopefully become inspired in the meantime.

Rounding the corner of the building, I unlocked the front door and headed to the back where my home away from home was.

As soon as I reached my office, my heart stuttered. Blank canvases sat against one wall. A table lined with paint, brushes, and pencils sat against another. And the easel stood in the middle of the room, holding another blank canvas I hadn't been able to touch since … I swallowed hard and shook myself.

Although Dale was in a coma, I wouldn't give him the reprieve of shattering. It was unfair of me. I knew that. It wasn't like he knew what had happened.

Our baby. Our sweet, precious baby girl.

NUMB

Tears streamed down my cheeks.
Fuck.

CHAPTER TWO

Max

"WE NEED SOMETHING new from you. Something fresh. Something not so damn painful," Josee Ross stated, rummaging through canvas after canvas. She was the manager of the gallery after I met her at a showing a couple of years before. Although she owned the gallery and was my boss, we had become fast friends. She had come highly recommended and I loved her no bullshit attitude, even though she was royally pissing me off now.

"I don't know what you want from me, Jo," I mumbled, staring at the sea of white in front of me.

"Max, baby." Jo sighed, turning to me, and blew her red curls off her forehead before pulling her hair into a messy bun. "I love you. I think you're fucking brilliant but you have to get your shit together."

"My shit is just fine." It was. It was peachy-fucking-keen.

"You may lie to yourself and your fucking friends but you can't fucking lie to me." Josee continued looking through the canvases lined against the wall. "These are intense as *fuck*."

My lips pulled up into a smile at her overuse of the F word.

"Have you started anything new?" she asked, all joking set aside.

"No." I rubbed the back of my neck, stretching my arms above my head, and shivered at the crack rippling down my spine. "I'm not inspired." I hadn't been inspired for weeks.

"Well, get inspired." She pointed at me. "We have some big names coming here next month. They're expecting something new from you."

"I can't force it, Josee." I pointed the brush at her. "You know that."

"Take a vacation. Go to a damn graveyard for all I fucking care. Just paint something new."

I sighed, pinching the bridge of my nose, and focused back on the blank canvas in front of me. I thought about what I should paint, what I *wanted* to paint, but even my mind was blank. *What the hell was wrong with me?*

After a couple of minutes of trying to think of something to paint, a sharp pain pierced into the side of my head. The impending headache wouldn't help so I took a couple deep breaths and placed the brush back on the table.

"Max," Jo barked.

My eyes snapped to hers.

"Don't give me that look," she said, her voice firm but gentle. "Don't strain that artistic brain of yours. Just let the paint flow. Which is what you usually always do. I've never seen you actually think about what you want to paint before you paint it. It's not how you roll. Why is it hard this time?"

She was right. I never outlined my paintings beforehand or even thought about them until I sat in front of an empty canvas. Sometimes, something inspired me and I just had to paint it but not usually. I flew by the seat of my pants and it had always worked. Until now.

I let out another heavy sigh, dipped my brush in some paint, and lifted it to the canvas. But again, nothing. Absolutely fucking nothing. I waited. I paused. I begged for something to come out of me and pour itself onto the bare board in front of me. But nothing happened. I needed to go for a walk or … see her. That could help.

Josee sat beside me, placing a gentle hand on my shoulder. "Give it time. I know I ride you hard but it's only because I'm proud of you. You're the best in this area but I want you to be the best you can be. For yourself. Not to make money. Not for fame or popularity. For *you*."

I nodded, a hard lump forming in my throat.

She sighed, pulled her curls loose, then redid the messy bun. It was her signature move when she was either nervous or stressed. This time being the latter. "How long have we been working together?"

"A couple of years." I shrugged. "Why?"

"I know nothing about you," she said, pushing her black-rimmed glasses higher up the bridge of her nose. "Tell me something about you."

"There's nothing to know." There wasn't. I was boring. Besides being the vice-president of an all-female motorcycle club, there was nothing to tell.

"As fucking if, Max." Jo clucked her tongue. "You hang out with that motorcycle club and those other men."

"I don't want to talk about my life." I rose from the stool, cutting her off. "If we're done here, I'd like to get back to painting. Or try to."

"Tell me one thing about you that has nothing to do with painting and I'll leave you alone," she insisted.

"Fine." I thought a moment. "I'm the girliest of my sisters."

She laughed. "I already knew that."

"Is it obvious?"

"Little bit." She smiled. "Tell me something else."

"I go see Dale at the hospital even though I know I shouldn't," I confessed, the words pouring from my lips unexpectedly.

She stared at me. "I've never been in a relationship."

"Tit for tat?" I asked, sitting back on the stool.

"Something like that." Josee didn't push further. "Take care of yourself, Max." She squeezed my arm gently and left the room. "Feel better?" she called out.

"Yeah," I mumbled, I did feel a little bit better.

But once I was alone, the dam of my demons broke. The sobs left me, shaking through my core, and split me wide open. I tried forcing them back but they took control and forced me to submit.

Slender arms wrapped around me. "Shhh …" Josee rubbed my back. She was the only person who didn't know every singled detail about my life. Even before shit went down, I didn't say much. She knew about Dale and that was it. I was a private person but the need to tell someone who would be unbiased was on the tip of my tongue. I needed to talk about the baby but the words wouldn't leave me so I just reveled in her hug.

"I don't know what's going on but I want you to know I'm here if you ever need to talk," she said, her voice soothing.

I nodded, wiping my cheeks roughly.

"Do you want to talk about it?" she asked, grabbing hold of my hand.

Yes. "No."

"Okay." She tapped my hand. "Back to work?"

I stared at the blank canvas. "I guess."

***

"You're here," Jay said, leaving the clubhouse and coming toward me.

I slid off my bike and pulled off the helmet before pulling my hair back into a ponytail. "I am." It had been months since I had been to the clubhouse. Nothing had changed, really, just that it became bigger after Vice-One had reconstructed it.

"How are you doing?" she asked, her gaze moving back and forth over my face.

My chest tightened. She wasn't one to worry over things but since getting kidnapped months ago, add to the fact she was pregnant, she worried over everything. Especially when it came to me.

"Jay," I grit out, clenching my jaw. "I'm fine."

"Are you? I'm only asking because you didn't come back to the house last night. Where did you sleep?"

Home. I didn't have a fucking home. "I slept at the gallery."

"Seriously?" she raised an eyebrow. "Why the hell would you do that?"

"Because," I snapped. "This place is no longer my home. Your home isn't mine. It belongs to you and Angel. I appreciate what you've done for me. I really do. But the gallery is all I have right now."

Jay crossed her arms under her chest, resting them on the pronounced bump she was now sporting and stared at me.

"What?" I frowned.

"That's the first time I've seen any emotion from you since …" She waved a hand out in front of her. "You know."

"Yeah, well, you get on my nerves," I muttered.

"And you're back to being a bitch." She sighed. "I thought I was the only one allowed to be a bitch."

"Not long now," I said, ignoring her comment and pointed at her very swollen belly.

"Yeah." She rubbed the bump. "I *am* sorry."

"Don't." I shook my head. "Don't go there. Not right now. I can't take it."

She nodded. "Fine. Let's go inside. The guys are getting antsy and I know the girls want to see you." She hooked her arm through mine, leading us into the building.

"*Max*," Brogan exclaimed, jumping off the stool by the bar, and ran toward me. "I haven't seen you in weeks." She wrapped her arms around my middle.

I pulled back, leaned down, and gave her a proper hug. She was several inches shorter than I but, man, could she pack a bite. I had seen her dark and sadistic work. It made sense now, seeing as I felt that same darkness.

"I'm here," she whispered in my ear.

Swallowing hard, I gave her a squeeze and released her. "How's your wrist?" I asked, nodding toward the cast on her arm.

She shrugged. "It's getting there," she answered, looking over her shoulder at Coby. He met her gaze, his eyes filling with a warmth that was envious.

I cleared my throat. "Did you accept the vice-president role yet?"

"I have." She grinned and pointed at Jay. "Not like I had a choice in the matter, really. She's kind of a hard ass."

I smiled softly. "She is."

Jay scoffed. "Whatever. You bitches love me."

"Not as much as I love you," Angel Rodriguez said, walking toward his fiancée, and handed her a bottle of water.

She sighed, taking it from him. "I really wish this was alcohol."

He chuckled, kissing her forehead.

"You two are disgusting." Brogan scrunched up her nose.

"She thinks *we're* disgusting." Jay barked a laugh. "I know your ways."

Brogan stuck her tongue out and went back to her boyfriend sitting at the bar. Their relationship intrigued me. Something disturbing happened over a month ago and it brought them closer.

I watched as Brogan slipped between Coby Porter's legs, cupped his cheek, and kissed him softly.

The warmth and love in his dark gaze made my own heart stutter.

Before they caught me staring, I headed to the meeting room. It had felt like a lifetime since I had been in this room.

After everything that had happened, I found I just couldn't cope with life and being in a motorcycle club.

"Max?"

I jumped, spun around, and found Creena Chan standing in the doorway.

Her brows narrowed in the center, her concerned gaze zeroing in on me so hard it felt like she was reaching into my chest attempting to make my heart beat again.

But no one could give it the life it needed to pump. Except for one person. And he no longer existed in my life.

"Do you have plans tonight?" she asked, crossing her arms under her chest. "We can hang out at Asher and Meeka's. Please. I'm not taking no for an answer, either."

Funny, neither had he. "I have to work."

"Yeah, right. You've been working nonstop for the past couple of weeks, Max. We need to do something tonight."

"And just what are we going to do?"

She winked. "Don't you worry that beautiful brain of yours. I got your back." She started whistling to herself and sat in one of the leather chairs around the large oval table.

Just when I was going to ask her what the hell she was talking about, everyone filed into the room.

"Max?" Jay sat her swollen body at the head of the table. "You good?"

"Yup," I muttered.

She winced, breathing deep and even.

Angel cupped her shoulder, whispering in her ear.

"I'm fine," she told him, patting his hand. "Don't worry so damn much."

"Woman, I'll worry about you all the fuck I want," he said, smacking a hard kiss on her mouth.

My chest tightened, the air in my lungs coming out in short shattered breaths. I would not break. I was strong. I got this.

"I …" I blurted, my cheeks heating.

All eyes landed on me, the sudden stare down sucking the breath right out of me.

"I need some air," I said quickly and ran out of the room. Once I was outside, I ran around the building and collapsed to the ground. Taking deep painful breaths, I chanted over and over that I was okay. I was fine. I would get through this.

I needed to go see Dale. It was the only way I could ease this anxiety in my chest. It didn't make sense. None of it did. Not when I hated him. *But he was the only one who could make me feel better.*

"Max?"

My head snapped up. "What?" I bit out as Creena approached me. I was getting sick and fucking tired of the pity. Just let me be and let me deal. I could handle this on my own.

"Listen" —she leaned against the wall beside me— "I was going to take you out, but maybe being around other people might not be the best idea right now."

I scoffed. "No kidding."

"Where are you staying?"

My brows narrowed in the center. "You're the first person to ask me that." Jay had meant well but she always assumed I would stay with her and Angel. I knew the guys didn't want us to be alone but the security at my gallery had been newly updated since the last show down with that damn organization.

"Well, it is a reasonable question." She shrugged. "I figure there's three places you could be. Jay's, here, or your gallery. Unless you're staying somewhere else."

"No," I sighed. "I haven't even bothered to look for a new place."

"I understand." Creena pulled away from the wall. "Text me where you'll be later. I'll bring by beer and junk food."

"Thank you," I whispered as she walked around the corner, leaving me alone to wallow in my own self-pity.

Letting out a heavy sigh, I went to head back into the building when the door leading to the basement caught my eye.

Brogan had spent many hours in the dark damp area, doing what she did best when it came to getting information out of informants.

I unlocked the door, closing it quietly behind me, and slowly made my way down the staircase. I had never been in this room without my sisters before but something about the empty space called out to me. With everything that had happened, was the darkness washing around me finally pulling me in deeper? I had no idea but it was frustrating and exciting as hell.

Once I reached the basement floor, I turned on the light and swallowed hard. The room was clean but what I noticed first were the tools lined up on a table against the far wall. I had seen Brogan use them before when trying to get information or when she just wanted to have some fun and scare the bastards who sat in her chair.

I always had respect for her. Anyone who could do what she did and not let it mess them up was strong.

"Max?"

I jumped, spinning on my heel, and saw Brogan standing a few feet away from me.

"What are you doing in here?" she asked, tentatively taking a step toward me.

"I ..." I looked around me, wrapping my arms around myself. "I'm not sure."

"You just needed to get away?" she asked, running her fingers over the back of the chair in the middle of the cool damp room.

"Yeah." I leaned against the table opposite her. "How do you do it?"

"Do what?" She raised an eyebrow, crossing her arms under chest.

"How do you do this" —I waved a hand toward the table lined with tools— "and not lose yourself in the process?"

Brogan shrugged. "Having Coby now helps but I've always craved this ... darkness. It hasn't been easy to deal with, Max. Whatever you're thinking, I'm not that woman. I'm not a killer. I do what I need to do to survive and protect those I love. That's it. I'm just ... me."

"I know." I nodded. "I know that. Do you ever regret it?" I needed to direct the conversation elsewhere. I didn't want to talk about myself.

"Sometimes," she paused. "Is something going on, Max?"

NUMB

I hesitated, wringing my hands in front of me. "I don't know." I took a deep breath. "I shouldn't be down here. I'm sorry." I rushed past her and up the stairs before she could ask me any more questions. I didn't know what I was doing or what my purpose was anymore.

Dale was in a coma.

My friends were getting partnered off, and I was alone. Always alone. All I had was my painting, and even that was proving to be difficult.

CHAPTER THREE

Max

THE WORDS ENGRAVED in stone stared up at me.
me.
Laughing. Taunting.
They egged me on until I broke and shattered like glass, breaking into tiny pieces only never to be put back together again.

I wasn't sure how I ended up at the graveyard, but after leaving Brogan in the basement, I hopped on my bike and the world fell away from around me.

My baby, tiny and fragile, never stood a chance. She was never given the right to breathe or make it in this world. She was taken away from me before I ever got a chance to hear her cry or feel her heart beat. She was gone before I could stare into the eyes I knew would belong to her father.

As soon as I found out I was pregnant, I was in love. It was a different sort of love than what I felt for Dale. It was a love I knew I would get in return. I didn't have to worry about my baby breaking my heart or laughing in my face when I first told her I loved her. I didn't have to hold back my feelings for fear she would think I was crazy. I could protect her and let her be her. And if it would have been a boy, I would show him how to treat women. How to be the man of the house without being a complete asshole like his father. I would … I would show him or her, the good things about their father. I would never bad talk him in front of our baby.

But I was never given the chance. The only thing her death didn't take from me was the love I had for her. *Nothing* could take that away.

Screams sounded in my head, forcing me to my knees when I realized they were coming from my mouth. The pain was worse than anything I had ever felt. It was like a part of me was ripped from my soul. I had begged God to take *me* knowing I wasn't strong enough to deal with this on my own, but he took my daughter instead.

I had pleaded with the doctors to save her. To wake Dale up so he could be with me. But nothing. They probably thought I had gone mad.

I tried forcing those memories from my mind, not wanting to taint the soil with my anger. "Oh, baby girl," I sobbed, brushing my fingers over the words staring up at me. No matter how much the doctors and nurses told me I should give her a name, I couldn't. Instead, I provided the funeral home with both my last name and Dale's.

Baby girl Stanton Michaels was good enough. It was perfect. I just wished Dale could be there with me. To hold me. To tell me it would be okay and I would get through this. That no matter what, our baby was in a better place. Maybe she was a little girl now instead of a newborn. With blonde curls framing her round face and bright blue eyes like sapphire gem stones. I imagined her playing with dolls. Or maybe she was a tomboy. Maybe she liked to play with cars and trucks instead. Wherever she was, I just prayed she was happy. I didn't believe in life after death, but at that moment, I would give anything to know she was safe and happy instead of just stuck beneath the soil.

My fingers dug into the earth, my tears streaming down my cheeks and landing on the grass. Bone crushing sobs wracked through my body, tearing my soul apart.

"I'm sorry. I'm sorry I wasn't strong enough to keep you safe. I'm sorry I couldn't protect you. It should have been me." I inhaled a shaky breath. "I'm sorry," I repeated, my whispered words falling like leaves from a tree only to rot away in the earth. Like my sanity.

***

Every time I left the gravesite, I felt naked and vulnerable. Stripped bare and completely exposed for the world to see and judge.

It was the next morning, and after passing out from diving deep within a bottle of vodka, I was hungover and grumpy as hell. Alcohol didn't solve shit but it made me forget, even if it was just for a couple of hours. It was a dangerous game I was playing, and I knew without a doubt the vodka would surely win. It was the true master, and I was just a lowly pawn.

With coffee in hand, I stood outside the room leading to my destruction.

Taking a breath, I pushed open the door, my gaze instantly landing on Dale. His eyes remained closed much like they had done for the past few weeks.

"He hasn't woken," the nurse had told me.

My chest pained, my heart thumping hard against my rib cage like it was trying to escape.

Walking into the room, I shut the door behind me and made my way to the end of his bed. The scruff on his jaw had grown in some more.

Since the first time I met him, he finally looked at peace. But I wanted to yell and scream at him for it. *He shouldn't be at peace. He should be awake and begging for my forgiveness. He should be standing in front of me and holding me as I shatter in his arms.*

My throat became raw after each hard swallow.

I didn't wish any harm on Dale but I also didn't wish him happiness. I wanted him to suffer just as much as I had over the past couple of months. He had no idea how he made me feel. He probably didn't even care.

Walking to the side of the bed, I placed my coffee on the end table and grabbed hold of Dale's hand. Linking my fingers between his, I reveled in the feel of his calloused and scarred hand in mine. The tiny marks on his knuckles and palm proved how much of a hard worker he had been for most of his life. Those hands had also given me an intense amount of pleasure in the short time I knew him. I wasn't sure if I could ever feel the same way toward another man. Or that I even wanted to. Being with someone else would never be the same. Dale had his moments of being a selfish lover but something inside me was drawn to the asshole side of him.

I had tried hard not to fall in love with him, knowing what we had was only for fun. It wasn't supposed to be anything serious but I couldn't stop my heart from beating for him.

My chest tightened. Before I completely lost it again, I loosened my grip and his fingers tightened around mine.

My eyes widened at the sudden movement. "Dale?"

He remained still but he wouldn't release me.

I squeezed his hand, hinting, waiting, *needing* something from him that he was in fact waking up.

His fingers squeezed mine again. The movement was so soft, I wasn't sure if I was dreaming it or not.

When he gave my fingers another squeeze, I gasped. "Nurse," I cried. "Nurse!"

She rushed in, asking questions and demanding answers but all I could focus on was Dale possibly waking up. I prayed he was. *Please.* As much as I was pissed at him and hated him with everything I was worth, he didn't deserve this. No one did.

"He squeezed my fingers," I finally said.

The nurse checked his vitals before rushing out of the room only to bring the doctor back with her.

While everyone continued working on him, I slowly released his hand and backed out of the room. I couldn't let him see that I was there. It wasn't time. I wasn't ready.

NUMB

No one called out to me. No one asked me to stay. So many questions bounced around in my mind.

What if he didn't remember me? What if he had no idea who anyone was? What if he didn't remember himself?

I couldn't bring myself to question further on what he could or couldn't remember. It would only drive me insane.

Once I left his room, I called Angel. No one knew I visited Dale while he had been in a coma. No one would understand because hell, I wasn't even sure *I* did.

"Max," Jay answered after the first ring.

"Tell Angel that Dale is awake." Before she could question how I knew, I hung up. It wasn't fair of me to expect judgment from my friends but I couldn't control these raging thoughts taking over everything I believed in.

As I left the hospital, I decided to call the one person who would be unbiased through everything I had to say.

"Hello, Maxine."

I smiled at the sound of my grandmother's voice. "Hi, Gammie."

"What's wrong?"

I sighed, my eyes burning. My grandma knew me well. "Everything."

"Talk to me, dear. Your brothers don't talk to me. They always say they're fine and tell me not to worry. Talk to me. Tell this old woman what's on that beautiful mind of yours."

I laughed, brushing away the lonely tear rolling down my cheek. My chest ached for my siblings. The men in my life who had taken care of me when our grandmother couldn't. But with all five of them being enlisted in the Army and several years older than me, I didn't see them. And that made the tears fall even harder. "What isn't on my mind?"

"I know, sweetheart. Your brothers ask about you."

"I miss them," I whispered.

"And they miss you but fighting for our country … your grandfather would be proud. Now tell me, what's gotten you so upset?"

"I just … the guy I was telling you about, Dale, he's awake."

"Oh, that's wonderful news."

I agreed with her. Kind of. We had many things to talk about, but the one I dreaded the most was telling him his daughter had passed away.

"You're strong, Maxine. You can do this."

When I reached my bike sitting by the curb, I finally commented, "If I was as strong as you, it wouldn't matter."

My grandma scoffed. "Your grandfather was a controlling asshole. But I still loved him. That love is what made me strong. But we can't fix all of them, dear. You have to remember that."

"I know." Sliding onto my bike, I gripped the phone tight in my hand. "We got along when it wasn't serious. But I can't control my heart. I shouldn't have told him how I felt but I never expected him to react the way he did."

"Dale will come around."

"What if he doesn't remember?" I asked, revealing my biggest fear.

"He will. After everything you have told me, I would bet my house that he does in fact love you."

That time I was the one who scoffed. "I love you, Gammie, but you're wrong."

"Either way. Just don't push him. But also know he might not remember every little detail. Be his friend first. Worry about everything else later."

"He doesn't deserve my friendship," I muttered.

"I know but *you* have to be the one to tell him about his daughter. Before it's too late."

I knew that too. I just didn't know how it would be seeing him again. When all was said and done, could we be civil?

***

(Dale)

I was awake.

Although everything in me was saying to keep sleeping, my eyes opened on their own accord.

People barked orders back and forth. I frowned, not exactly sure where I was, but what I really wanted was to go home. I wasn't sure what had happened or how long I had been out but it felt like a damn lifetime.

"Hi there," a feminine voice said. "I'm Dr. Andrews. Can you open your eyes for me?"

My eyelids were heavy as if they were stapled shut but after a couple blinks, they finally remained open.

An older woman smiled down at me. "It's nice to see you awake. Do you know your name?"

"Dale," I croaked, clearing my throat and tried again. "Dale Michaels."

"Good." Her smile widened. "I'm just going to check your vitals and then you can rest."

The blinding light of the room pierced into my retinas, but all I could do was nod. My throat was parched, my lips dry like a desert heat. But no one I knew was in the room with me. Did they not know I was awake?

A lingering scent suddenly filled the air. My body stirred, parts of me reacting to the unknown source. It smelled of vanilla and roses and damn if it wasn't delicious.

"Dale," Dr. Andrews said, interrupting the torture the intoxicating scent was causing. "You have been in a coma for three weeks. We will do some tests to see how much memory loss you've endured but I'm quite certain it won't be anything too drastic. Do you understand?"

I nodded, swallowing past the dry lump in my throat.

A coma. Well, that fucking sucked. "What happened?"

"You were shot in active duty." She placed a hand on my shoulder. "I just want to say, thank you for what you have done for our country."

My chest tightened. *Don't thank me. I didn't do shit. I got fucking shot.*

"Get him some water." Dr. Andrews continued checking me for signs I'd need more medical assistance but all I could focus on was that damn smell.

"That smell," I said, my voice rough like I had gargled with broken glass.

"Shhh …" Dr. Andrews barked some more orders.

"No." I tried sitting up, my arms shaking beneath me at the added weight.

"Dale, lay back. You're not ready yet." A nurse pushed my shoulders, lying me back in the bed.

I huffed, giving up, but I was still determined to find the source of that smell. I needed to know what caused it. The scent calmed me. I couldn't remember everything that had happened, but I remembered enough that I had come to crave the roses and vanilla mixture.

"We've called your next of kin," Dr. Andrews told me. "He brought several people with him." Her eyes warmed. "You're very loved, Dale."

"Is there a Maxine Stanton waiting?" I croaked.

Dr. Andrews frowned. "I'll check."

A nurse left the room, coming back a moment later only to tell me what I already knew. Max wasn't in the waiting room.

I let out a soft curse. For the life of me, I couldn't understand why Max wasn't waiting with everyone else. Everything had been good between us. Hadn't it? I couldn't remember. Everything was black. I had no memory but I knew I had been with her. My heart started racing, the air in my chest becoming tight. Why couldn't I remember?

Beeping sounded around me, the machines becoming crazy with noise much like the anxiety I was feeling.

"Dale," one of the nurses said. "You need to calm down."

"I can't remember." I tried. I tried so fucking hard to remember everything I had shared with Max. Every touch. Every kiss. Every single moment. But most of those memories came out blank. Like a dark hole. All my moments with her were lost. They were a jumbled mess, and I knew the only way to help myself remember was by contacting her. "Max."

"Dale …" The doctor touched my arm gently. "You need to rest. I'll inform your friends."

A sudden rush of drowsiness took over. My eyelids became heavy, my body feeling like it was falling into an abyss of peace and calm.

"Max," I whispered, her name being the last thing on my tongue as I gave in to the control of slumber.

CHAPTER FOUR

Max

"JOSEE, DO YOU know where Max is?" I heard Jay ask.

"She's in the back."

Shit. Way to have my back, Josee. I braced myself, trying with everything in me not to fall back inside the darkness of my mind. Excuses pounded through my head but none of them would go over well with Jay. She knew better. She knew *me* better then to put up with my shit.

"Max?" Jay came into the room and stood just inside the door.

I turned, a soft gasp leaving my mouth. I looked away, the sting of the tears threatening to escape. It wasn't her fault. None of it was her fault but I was damn envious it was ruining our friendship.

Her pregnant stomach had become more pronounced since I saw her last. It had only been a couple of days and yet every day her belly swelled even more.

I tried not letting the pain stabbing me in the chest show on my face but by the deep frown suddenly setting between her eyes, I knew I had lost.

Choosing to ignore my feelings like usual, I pasted a smile on my face. "What's up?"

"We're going to see Dale," she said, taking a cautious step toward me. "We went yesterday but they wouldn't let all of us in." She paused. "Dale's asking for you."

"Yeah." I laughed. "Okay."

"He is," she insisted. "He's been asking since he woke up a week ago."

"I love you, Jay, but please don't try and make me feel better." I turned back to the blank canvas, letting out a frustrated sigh. There was no way he would be asking for me. I made sure not to leave anything behind indicating I had been there in the first place.

"You need to plan a party," Jay suggested. "It will make you feel better."

"Maybe," I mumbled.

"Plan it for next week. Dale should be out by then. He's been doing physical therapy, and the doctors are impressed with his progress."

My heart jumped. I was happy he was finally awake but I knew when we were finally able to confront each other, I would close up. But he had no issues telling me exactly how *he* felt.

"Well, I'm going to head out." Jay paused at the door. "You sure you want to just stay here?"

"Yes." *Abso-fucking-lutely.* There was no way I could see Dale without it causing a scene. We had so many things to say to each other; a hospital was not the place for it.

When Jay left, I went back to the blank canvas and stared. And stared some more. The canvas was mocking me. Laughing and teasing me that I had no inspiration because a man broke my heart.

Letting out a scream, I threw the canvas against the wall.

Josee charged into the room and headed right for me. "Don't." She grabbed my shoulders, spinning me around to face her. "Don't you dare trash this room."

I let out a hard cry, covering my face.

"I know, honey." She wrapped her arms around my shoulders, holding me tight. She gave me a squeeze, probably making sure I wouldn't snap, push her away, and trash everything I had worked hard to create.

I knew I couldn't keep doing this to myself. The doctor at the hospital had told me to start talking. *Like a counselor would be able to help me.* I bit back a scoff.

"You good?" Josee held me at arm's length.

I nodded, rubbing my hand up and down my arm. I let out a slow breath and another. "How did you know I was about to snap?"

"I've dealt with it in my family." She shrugged, giving me a soft smile. "No big deal."

"Thank you," I whispered. "I think I'm going to head back to the club and ..."

"Get some rest." She gave me another hug. "And take care of *you*."

***

(Dale)

"Dale, open those pretty baby blues for me."

I frowned. "Fuck you. I'm trying to sleep."

"Yup. Nothing changed."

I slowly opened my eyes and found Angel, Coby, Asher, and Stone standing around the bed. My brothers. Vice-One. The men I had fought beside for years.

"Nice to see that you're awake." Angel clapped a hand on my shoulder. "You gave us quite the scare, brother."

"It wasn't planned." I sat up higher in the bed, my body stiff. I was miserable and ready to leave this damn place. "Where are the girls?"

"In the waiting room." Stone squeezed my other shoulder. "Glad you're okay, brother." His gaze took on a faraway look like he was remembering something from his past. Clearing his throat, he left the room, shutting the door quietly behind him.

"So … how are things?" I asked, needing to get the subject off me. The elephant in the room was big enough to strangle me, and I didn't want to talk about it.

"We'll talk about everything later." Angel sat on the chair beside the bed, the metal creaking beneath his weight. "Do you remember what happened?"

"I remember raiding the bunker and that's about it. But I don't even know if there is other shit I can't remember." I pinched the bridge of my nose, attempting to ward off the impending headache. "Everything is fine physically even though the doctors won't let me fucking leave yet." I winced at the pounding in my head.

"The doctor said those headaches should go away in time," Coby explained, crossing his arms under his chest. He winced at the movement, taking a breath before meeting my gaze.

"What was that?" I asked, sitting forward.

"Nothing," his gaze locked with mine. "I'm fine."

"You may be able to fool others with your lying bullshit but you can't fool me, Coby. What the fuck gives?" I looked between Asher and Angel. "Someone tell me what the hell is going on. Coby looks like shit. You two look stressed the fuck out. And Stone looks like the rage is going to tear through him. Someone. Talk. *Now.*"

Asher leaned against the wall.

Angel shifted in his seat.

Coby stared at me.

My heart started pounding in my ears. "If someone—"

"Fine." Angel took a breath. "I'll talk."

"No," Coby said. "*I* will talk."

Stone took that moment to enter the room, followed by Jay.

I shook my head.

He nodded, ushering Jay back out of the room and closed the door. Standing guard, he leaned against the far wall, waiting.

"No. Stone, come over here too. You're our brother," I told him.

Stone, or Vincent, if he let you use his first name, pulled up a chair at the foot of the bed. But he didn't say anything. His silence was almost as unnerving as Coby's, if not more so.

"Dale," Coby said, pulling me from my thoughts. "After you got shot, we all ended up back here but some shit went down with the Organization."

"Is that what we're still calling them?" I grumbled.

"It's what they're going by now," Asher added.

A fucking sex ring stealing women. *Our* women. And we called it an organization. Fuck, a lot had changed.

"What-the-fuck-ever. Someone needs to tell me what the hell is going on." I waited. The impending headache piercing the back of my brain started pounding harder.

"Leave us," Coby barked.

A round of grumbling erupted from my brothers but I kept my gaze locked with my best friend. His face was impassive, no emotion showing how he was feeling. The guy was a vault, and that woman of his was the only one who held the key.

When the guys left, Coby sat on the metal chair beside my bed. With his hands folded in his lap, he told me what had happened.

Nothing could have prepared me for what Coby told me next. It was as if I was living a nightmare. *His* nightmare. Every secret. Every feeling. Every dark and dirty inch of the last couple of weeks.

He fucked another woman. He had no choice. He was fucking *raped*.

"Shit, man," I rubbed the back of my neck. "How are you doing?"

He looked away, down at his hands but not at me. "I don't give a shit about myself. As long as Brogan is happy, that's all I care about." His dark gaze met mine.

"It'll take some time but we will get through this. I'll make sure of it."

"It's not your fault. None of it is."

"I was raped," he said slowly, almost as if he was hearing the words for the first time.

"It wasn't your fault," I repeated. "It could have happened to any of us."

"You see, I hear you saying that. I hear everyone saying it but it doesn't help. I feel guilty. I feel like I cheated on her even though I didn't. I know I had no control over the situation and you know what? That's what pisses me off the most."

"I … I have no fucking idea what to say to you right now," I told him, my chest tightening. *Fuck.*

"Brogan and I have taken it upon ourselves to lay low."

"You have to do what's good for you two." I sat up straighter. "But tell me she took her out. Tell me Tina is fucking dead."

Coby's lips twitched. "My girl took her out." His face darkened. "But we have to worry about Zane and Charles. Something is off and I'm itching for another fucking fight. Shit's gonna go down, Dale. We need you strong enough to handle it."

"I will be." I *needed* to be but, first, there was someone I needed to confront. Max and I had unfinished business. I couldn't do anything until she and I sorted out our own shit.

"Have you heard from Max?" Coby asked, changing the subject.

I swallowed hard. "No."

"She's changed. You need to approach her before she loses herself completely."

I scoffed. "How the hell am I supposed to do that if I have no idea where the hell she is?"

"She's throwing a party next week. The doctor said you should be out by then." Coby pointed at me. "Don't tell Angel I told you this shit. He's being protective, especially now that Jay is due in the next couple of weeks."

"How's Max doing? With the baby and all? Do you know how far along she is?"

Coby searched my face. "You ... Shit ... *Fuck.*"

My heart jumped. "What? What happened? Is the baby okay? Is Max fine? Tell me. Tell me why she hasn't been here to see me."

"Dale ..." Coby hesitated, rubbing the back of his neck which I had come to know was his signature move whenever he was uncomfortable.

"What's going on?" I laughed. "You're making me nervous."

"Dale," Coby repeated slowly. "You and Max can't stand each other. That's why she hasn't been here. You don't remember?"

"I ... I remember fighting with her." I thought back to the past couple of months. Hurtful words, hate, so much damn pain but the worst was when we ignored each other. "She loves me," I muttered.

"She did. But you haven't spoken in months. I don't know how she feels anymore."

"What?" That damn headache started pounding. "What's going on?" I was confused. I tried remembering but it all came out fuzzy. I only got snippets from what had happened between us and, even then, I wasn't sure if it was just my mind playing tricks on me or if it was making up some shit to protect me from truly losing it.

Coby rose from his chair and sat beside me on the bed. "Dale, I shouldn't be the one to tell you this but I don't know when you'll see Max again ..." He took a breath and put his hand on my shoulder.

"No." I shrugged him off. "Tell me."

"Max lost the baby."

"Like fuck she did." I pulled away like his touch burned me. "Don't fucking lie to me. She was far along. I remember seeing her. She was fine."

"She wasn't, Dale. She was sick. The baby was stressed. Max couldn't carry it to term. I don't know all of the details but I do know the baby was ..." His gaze searched my face before he let out a hard sigh. "The baby was stillborn."

My mouth opened on a scream but no sound came out. Of all the shit I had done in my life, this was the worst. The person who shot me should have just killed me because death would be better than what I was feeling.

Coby pulled me into his arms, wrapping himself around me.

And that was when I broke.

CHAPTER FIVE

Max

"YOU NEED TO go see him."

I jumped at the deep voice sounding in the silence of my office. Coby stood in the doorway, his gaze moving around the room. The man was light on his feet for being so big.

"What are you doing here?" I asked, my heartbeat slowing back to a normal rhythm.

"We all went to see Dale today. You never showed." Coby came further into the room, taking in everything around him.

"I didn't think anyone would notice."

"Dale noticed." Coby leaned against the wall beside me. "I didn't tell him that you went to see him before he woke up."

My head whipped around. "You knew?"

"Every time I went to visit him, you were there." Coby rubbed his jaw. "Why?"

"That's none of your business." I didn't care that they were best friends. "It doesn't matter anyway."

"Of course it fucking matters. He thinks you didn't go see him, Max."

"I don't have to explain my actions to you, Coby," I snapped. I went back to staring at the blank canvas. This lack of creativity was really starting to piss me off.

"You don't have to explain shit to me but when I was the one who had to tell my best friend that his baby fucking died, that shit doesn't sit well with me."

I winced, not needing this right now. I got it. I did. I understood the tension between Dale and me was not just between us. Everyone was feeling it. But I couldn't control the asshat and how he treated me. So, fuck him. He dished it out? I was going to throw it right the fuck back.

"What are you doing here, Coby? Want me to feel worse? Are you trying to make it so I never forgive myself for the shit that's happened?" Tears burned my eyes, but I swallowed past them. I would not cry, it was only a sign of weakness. And Dale didn't deserve any more of my tears. "I never told you to tell him."

"He fucking asked me," Coby said, his voice raising. "He thought you were fine. That you were one big happy fucking family."

My heart jumped. "That's not my fault."

"Don't let people in, Maxie Girl," my granddaddy had told me as a child. *"They'll only disappoint you in the long run."*

He had been right but I still never listened to him. Stupid, stupid heart.

"Listen, Dale is a dick," Coby continued, forcing me back to the present, "I get it. But he's my brother. I love him like my own but I refuse to stand by and watch you two kill each other."

"You haven't seen anything yet, sweetheart." I laughed. "We haven't talked in months." I glared at Coby over my shoulder. "How do you think it will be when we confront each other? Especially now that you told him our baby died."

"You blaming me for that shit?"

"I …" I sighed. "No." My shoulders slumped. "It's not your fault. I should have told him."

"Yeah, you should have but I also know that Dale can be difficult to talk to. Especially when he gets something into his head. He fights for it first and asks questions later."

But he never fought for me.

"He'll come around."

"You really don't believe that, do you? The only thing he'll ever want from me again, and that's if he can't find someone else to curb his cravings, is sex. You're not stupid, Coby."

His brows narrowed in the center. "You are a challenge, girl. No wonder he likes you."

"*Liked.* Big difference. He hasn't wanted anything to do with me in a long time, Coby." I shrugged. "It's done."

"If you believe that, you're not as smart as you make yourself out to be." Coby inhaled a sharp breath.

"You need to go see him. Whatever else you do is up to you." And with that, Coby left.

My muscles quivered. Fuck him. Fuck them all. And fuck the fact that Coby was right. I *did* need to see Dale, but what could I say? What could I possibly tell him to make everything right? And why did *I* have to be the one to approach him? Why was it all me? But now Dale knew about the baby, *our* baby, our first meeting would not go over well. He would blame me for not telling him. I knew, because I did as well.

"Max?"

I turned around on the stool, finding Josee standing at the doorway.

"Everything okay?" she asked, looking behind her.

"I have no idea." I roughly picked up a paint brush. Fuck it. If I couldn't get inspired, I was just going to paint the first thing that came to mind. Dabbing the brush into a pool of black paint, I brushed it along the canvas.

"Are you sure?" Josee asked, coming toward me.

"Yup. I'm fucking fine and dandy." The brush moved along the canvas on its own accord. "I feel great." Repeating my movements, I stroked black onto the canvas, followed by a deep red. Eventually, the two colors flowed together. They created the look of a woman weeping. It was dark, dreary, and exactly how I felt at the moment.

"Max," Josee breathed. She stood behind me, placing a hand on my shoulder. "Wow ... this is fucking stunning."

My throat closed, the lump that had been permanently lodged there since Dale hurt me months ago growing. My chest ached when I looked at the canvas. Never before had an image come out of me so quickly.

"This will sell instantly," she said, giving my shoulder a light squeeze.

I didn't care about it selling. "I'm not selling it."

"Excuse me?"

"It's not for sale. I'll make another one but this one I'm keeping for myself."

"Max."

"No." I spun on her. "I'm *not* selling it." I rose from the stool and grabbed the canvas, placing it against the wall to dry. "I'll work on something else."

"But this one is raw. Real. People will be able to feel the emotion coming off of it."

"I'm not arguing over this." I grabbed another blank canvas, praying an image came out of me as fast as the first one. "I'll work on some more."

"Don't stress yourself out."

"Thanks, but I kind of need to," I told her. "You need some product from me, don't you?"

Josee headed to the doorway, glancing back at me over her shoulder. "I'm worried about you." She left before I could give her a reply.

Yeah, well, she wasn't the only one.

***

(Dale)

Physical therapy sucked hairy, sweaty balls.

It hurt like hell, and the only thing I wanted to do was go home, have a beer, and find Max.

I had been out of the hospital for a couple of days, taking up solace in my shithole of an apartment. I really needed to move. As soon as I had stepped over the threshold, memories came back of what I had done. I couldn't remember them in detail but I knew I had brought woman after woman home. Max had spent many nights with me there and because I was a dick, I never changed the sheets. I wanted them to smell her.

Fuck. What kind of man was I?

After Coby told me what happened to the baby, I couldn't wrap my head around what I had done. My mind played tricks on me. I knew we had our problems and that we weren't talking in the end but I never realized it had been that bad. But I couldn't remember the words we said. I only remembered the emotions and that gut out my fucking heart.

Squeezing the bridge of my nose, I took a deep breath, trying to ward off the impending migraine.

The physical therapist wanted me to start working out again so I went to the best person I knew to train with.

Coby handed me a bottle of water. "Take a drink."

I did as I was told, the cool liquid soothing my parched throat. When I was done, he took the empty bottle and threw it in the recycling bin.

"Look at me," he demanded.

I met his gaze and waited.

When he circled his hands around the back of my head and started massaging, I almost fell into him. A tingle shot up my back. It felt good. Damn good.

He chuckled. "Don't get a fucking hard on for me, brother."

I laughed which came out more as a groan. "No wonder Brogan loves you. Your fingers are magic."

He laughed even harder. "Lots of practice dealing with the migraines she gets. Although, if you were her, this would turn into me fucking the migraine out of her."

I grunted. "Thank you for the image."

"Anytime." His fingers continued to move over the back of my head, down to my neck and back up again. The pressure of his hands released some of the tension building up in my head since waking up. "Better?" he asked, gripping my shoulders.

No. "Yes."

"Liar." Coby took a swig of his bottle of water before heading to the weight rack. "How come you're not working out at the club?"

"This gym is bigger. Gives us more options to work with."

He raised an eyebrow, glancing at me in the reflection of the mirror. "That the only reason?"

"Yes."

He shook his head. "You're lying again."

"You know why I can't go to the club."

"I do." He glanced at me over his shoulder. "I just wanted to hear you say it."

"Max could be there and I don't want to deal with that shit yet," I blurted. *Fuck.* The guy had some voodoo Jedi mind shit. I had never meant to let that admission leave my mouth.

Coby nodded once, his dark eyes turning black. "You two need to talk."

"About what? How I caused her so much fucking stress, she lost our baby? That she confessed her feelings for me and I treated her like shit and fucked woman after woman trying to get her out of my skin?"

"Do you remember the other women?" he asked, stretching his arms above his head.

"No," I mumbled. "Just that I was a dick about it."

"Whatever happened then, stays there. You two need to talk about now."

"And say what?"

He shrugged. "Doesn't matter what you talk about." He lifted a dumbbell off the rack. "You just need to talk."

"And what exactly is that going to do?"

"You talk to me, don't you?" he asked, sitting on the bench.

"You're different."

"How?" he asked, doing several reps of bicep curls before looking my way. "Dale?"

"How the fuck should I know?" I snapped. "You just are."

Coby repeated the movements with his other arm, placing the heavy weight on the mat in front of him when he was done. "I've learned in the time I've been with Brogan that life is too damn short. Make the most of today because you don't know if you'll get a tomorrow."

"Are you writing greeting cards for Hallmark or some shit now?" I crossed my arms under my chest, leaning against the wall. I had no drive. No motivation to even work out. I needed to fuck this frustration out of me but just the thought of being inside another woman made my dick go limp as a fucking noodle.

"I'm just stating the truth, Dale." After a couple more sets, Coby rose from the bench and stretched out his arms.

"I need to talk to her but I know it won't start off well. We can't talk without it turning into a fight." But fuck me if I didn't enjoy fighting with Max.

"Maybe it's what you need," Coby suggested.

"What do you mean?"

"Max is not who she used to be. The girls are worried for her and when my girl is upset over one of her sisters, that doesn't make me a very happy man. Angel is on edge because he doesn't need any more stress. They have enough with the baby coming." Coby came toward me. "You two have to get this sorted or at least find some way where you can be civil."

"I don't know how," I confessed, feeling like the smallest motherfucking person alive.

Coby sighed, his eyes warming. "All you can do is find her alone and approach her," he said, his voice gentle.

"Since when have you become the relationship expert?" I teased.

"Since I had to fuck a stranger to save mine," he muttered, rubbing the back of his neck.

"Shit, man. I … fuck. How are you two doing?" If I could go back in time and kill Tina Birtch myself over the shit she caused for my friends, I would.

"We're getting there." He leaned against the wall beside me. "But it will never be the same."

"Brogan loves you. Shit, man. I would cut off my balls to have Max look at me like Brogan looks at you."

Coby chuckled, shaking his head. "She does, Dale. You just haven't noticed."

"Like fucking hell she has."

Coby pushed away from the wall. "Brogan and I have an appointment but I want you to remember what I said."

"All right," I mumbled, watching him leave the gym.

Max was having a party on the weekend. Looked like I would have to make my appearance be known. I knew she wouldn't go down without a fight, and that was a battle I looked forward to starting.

CHAPTER SIX

Max

BLOOD DRIPPED FROM my fingers while agonizing pain ripped through my abdomen. I hunched over, wrapping my arms around myself, my mouth opening in a silent scream. The pain couldn't be helped. No matter what I did, it only became worse. Please God, make it stop. Make the agony go away. It was like someone stabbed me repeatedly, not stopping even though I begged. Pleaded. The desperate cry for help on the tip of my tongue.

"Your baby is dead."

"You need to give birth to it."

Her, damn it. She was a girl. My baby girl.

NUMB

My thoughts were jumbled as the nightmare took over. It had been the same dream for the past couple of weeks. No matter how hard I tried, I couldn't get out of it. I knew I was dreaming but I was stuck. Until something drastic happened, I couldn't wake up.

The dream switched suddenly. I was in a hospital bed. I had something in my arms. Warmth spread through me and I looked down and saw her. My chest constricted. Her eyes were open, her irises white and no longer seeing. Her skin pale with lack of life. A sob tore from my throat.

Why did God take her away from me?

The baby in my arms giggled.

A scream escaped me. I shot up from the couch and fell off the edge, landing hard on the ground. A cold sweat coated my body. My chest rose and fell. I glanced around my office. I was no longer dreaming. I was safe. Breathing deeply, I calmed my racing heart and pushed from the floor onto shaky legs.

My gaze glanced to the pill bottle sitting on the table beside the couch. As much as I needed sleep, I didn't need to medicate. Or maybe I did. Maybe it would help me forget if I stayed in a constant drug induced state. I was confused and shaken by the remnants from my never-ending nightmare.

Even though it was in the middle of the night, I decided to start planning the party for the weekend and texted everyone. It only took a matter of minutes before my phone started dinging with replies. I left my phone on the table and went to the easel in the middle of the room. It was the same thing every time. I only texted them when there was a party. Most of them didn't even know who we were. They heard our name and that was it.

King's Harlots.

Women.

They ignored the motorcycle club part, attempting to get into our pants the first time around. Only when Brogan stabbed a guy in the dick did the other clubs take us more seriously. But there had always been a straggler or two.

I wish I could have been as strong as my sister.

Having friended both Jay and her twin sister back in school, I thought it would be fun to join them. Little did I know at the time how serious Jay took it. And how different women were treated in this world.

I sat on the stool and rubbed the grit from my eyes. Hoping I could get inspired again, even if it was dark, I sat in front of the canvas and took a deep breath. With the empty tray in hand, I squeezed some black and red paint onto it and began pouring my emotions onto the blank canvas.

What eventually stared back at me forced new tears to pierce the back of my eyes. All my emotions. Fear. Anger. Pain. Suffering. All of it. They bled onto the white canvas until I looked into a reflection of myself. No one would know it was me. Hell, I didn't even know it until I looked into the eyes of my demons.

All I wanted was this pain to go away. Painting canvas after canvas didn't help my mood but after each image was done, I felt a little lighter. Like I was literally painting my feelings onto the blank space.

The phone in my office rang, making me jump. I snatched the portable off the table, taking a breath to ease my racing heart before answering the phone. "Hello?" I croaked, my voice still thick with sleep.

"What are you doing up this late?" Jay asked.

I frowned. "What do you mean?"

"It's almost four in the morning and you decide to text everyone about the party now?"

Shit. I had forgotten my sisters would have been included in the mass text I had sent out. "I had a nightmare." No point lying about it. Jay would find out eventually anyway.

"Do you want to talk about it?" she asked, worry coating her tired voice.

"It's the same shit, different night. Every time I close my eyes, I see her." I stabbed my brush against the canvas. "There's nothing I can do about it. I thought painting would help."

"That's why you slept at the gallery?"

"It was late when I finished and I didn't feel like driving."

"I need to ask," she paused. "Have you talked to Dale?"

"No." I swallowed hard. "Is he out of the hospital?"

"Yeah, he is. He's been training with Coby. But, Max, he doesn't remember everything."

"What do you mean?" I asked, gripping the phone tight in my hand.

"Coby told Angel that Dale didn't remember that you two are no longer talking."

"Oh." I rubbed the tight spot that had taken up residence between my breasts. "Now he knows everything I guess."

Jay hesitated before she gave me the answer I didn't want to hear. "Yes, Max. He does."

Fuck.

***

(Dale)

Every time I closed my eyes, I thought of her. Max had engrained herself in my skin without even knowing it. I was the fool who pushed her away all because I was scared. No one wanted me as a kid, how the hell could a woman want me as a man?

I wasn't sure what was different this time around or why. It didn't make sense and the need to find out what the hell was going on was drilling a hole in my brain. From what Coby had told me, we had our problems but I didn't remember half of it.

Working out was the only way I could ignore the voices in my head telling me how worthless I was and how much of a dick I had been. I didn't deserve her. And I damn well didn't deserve the baby she was unable to give birth to.

I needed answers. I needed to know what had happened and why she didn't tell me herself.

It was Saturday night, and I was standing outside of the club, staring at her through a window like a fucking creeper. She was with Angel and Jay, laughing at what they said but the smile never reached her eyes. She was beautiful. So damn breathtaking and she didn't even know it. Her dark, wavy hair was pulled back into a messy braid. Her curves had filled out, clearly not losing the weight from the pregnancy, but she was perfect. She was everything I was not. She was the light in my darkness. The innocence to my madness. I wracked my brain with memories of her but I only got snippets. I wasn't even sure what was real anymore. The only thing I knew for certain was that I could still feel her. Every inch. Every breath. Every ripple as I forced the pleasure from her body.

My cock stirred, jumping in my pants. Adjusting myself, I leaned my head from side to side. The slight crack in my neck sent a wave of heat rushing over my skin.

This was it. It was time. I would confront her and demand answers. I needed to know where our baby was buried. I needed to know if Max missed me like I had missed her. I also needed to apologize for whatever pain I had caused.

"Dale?" Coby stepped around the corner with Brogan at his side. Her cheeks were flushed, her curly hair a mess on top of her head. She had that just-fucked glow and it only strengthened the madness inside of me.

Brogan smiled, whispering something to Coby.

He nodded, placing a kiss on her forehead.

"It's good to see you, Dale," she said, her eyes warming. "Be nice to my girl."

"Sure," I grunted.

Brogan headed into the club, the music inside the building becoming loud when she opened the door. "All right, bitches. Who's having a drink with me?" she yelled, slamming the door shut behind her.

Coby shook his head before his gaze locked with mine. "She doesn't even drink."

"Looks like she'll be getting trashed on water." I chuckled even though the laugh did nothing for my mood.

"You need to go in there sooner or later," Coby said, coming up beside me.

I would rather just watch Max. I knew as soon I approached her, she would close up and become withdrawn. Maybe even shut down until I had to force the thoughts out of her.

"Talk to her when Angel isn't nearby," Coby suggested.

My head whipped around. "Why?"

"Because the fucker is pissed at you." Coby rubbed the back of his neck. "Listen, I refuse to be in the middle of this shit so I'm only going to tell you this once. I won't protect you against Angel."

"He won't do anything." But even I didn't believe those words when they left my mouth.

"Not unless it has to do with Jay. He loves you but her and their baby come first."

"I wouldn't do anything to harm them." What kind of man did they think I was?

"Not directly you wouldn't. Upset Max? Jay gets upset. If she gets upset, so does the unborn baby she's carrying."

"Oh," I mumbled, looking down at the ground.

"Exactly. Whatever you have to say to Max, do it quick."

I already knew this meeting would not go over well. But I found that I craved her wrath. I wanted the bite of her anger as it slid over my skin. I wanted to suffer like she did. And until then, I refused to forgive myself.

SEVEN

MAX

Max

THE HAIRS ON the back of my neck rose. My breathing became labored, my chest tight. I didn't have to turn around to know that Dale was right behind me.

I didn't need to look at him to know he had a scowl on his face and that he was enraged. I didn't need to turn around to know he was still gorgeous and affected me in the most sinful ways imaginable.

I didn't want to face him at the party. I didn't even want him there but needing to be civil, I gave in when Jay asked that he be invited. Not that he would have listened anyway. But I did make her promise she would help keep him away from me. I wasn't ready for the confrontation we were about to have. This wasn't the time or the place. But God, I could feel him. All over me. Inside me. My mind took me back to our first time. It had been hot, fast, and so damn satisfying, I became addicted. Dale Michaels had become the drug I craved. He was a player, an asshole, but the innocent part of me needed him. I had always been the good girl and when the bad boy finally started showing interest in me even in my twenties, I couldn't say no. Stupid me.

Jay peered over my head.

Angel came up beside her and kissed her cheek before meeting my gaze. "You good?"

"I can't talk to him here," I confessed, raising my voice over the loud music.

Angel nodded once, kissed Jay again, and walked past us.

"He *will* confront you, Max," Jay told me.

"I know." I looked over my shoulder and swallowed hard.

Dale moved with ease, talking to people, accepting their hugs, but still kept his gaze trained on me. Only when people stood in front of him, did his eyes deter from mine.

My heart pounded in my chest at the sheer intensity in his eyes. He had filled out some, clearly working out hard before the mission that involved the attack. My body came alive at the idea of him even just talking to me and hearing his deep gravelly voice.

But I couldn't do it. *Not here. Not now. Maybe not ever.*

Before Dale went into a coma, I could handle being in the same room as him. We were civil. Sort of. We mostly ignored each other. But now, something changed. I could feel it. I couldn't place exactly what *it* was but something was there hidden deep within my soul. It was so close, but yet so far away at the same time. I knew the only way I would reach it is with Dale standing at my side.

"I … I need some space," I told Jay and rushed to the bedroom at the back of the club. It had been mine for years. Although the club had been blown to shit a couple months back by Charles Brian, one of the douche bags from the Organization, our clubhouse had been rebuilt. But it wasn't the same.

Sick of feeling sorry for myself, I went in search of the spare set of paints I kept in the room. I let out a sigh of relief when I found them stashed in the corner of the room between the dresser and the wall. I didn't have a blank canvas with me when I moved into this room, so I started painting a mural on the wall behind the bed. The image of the map stared back at me. It was always my dream to travel the world but only making it as far as California—where my grandmother lived— seeing the map would have to do. Much to my sister's delight, they liked when I painted. I wasn't feeling the image but kept painting it anyway.

The sound of the door closing made me jump.

I spun on my heels, finding Dale standing inside the room. *My* room. A place I had called my own since the club had been rebuilt. A club *he* helped put back together. But now, he was invading the space like he owned the fucking world. He took up so much room; it sucked the air right from my lungs.

No words left me as I watched him lean against the door with his thick arms crossed under his broad chest. A chest I had seen bare so many times I lost count. Under normal circumstances, I would have run into his arms and kiss him until we couldn't breathe, happy and elated he was out of a coma. But this wasn't normal. Not even remotely close. Our situation was fucked up. It was his fault. And it was *my* fault for letting him affect me the way he did.

He didn't say anything as he watched me. The more he stared, the faster my heart beat. His eyes roamed down the length of my body and back up until they landed on my chest. His nostrils flared, the deep blue of his eyes twinkling in the light of the room. "You didn't come see me," he finally bit out as he reached behind him and locked the door.

I swallowed hard but stood my ground. He would not break me. Not again. "I don't know what you're talking about."

"You didn't come see me," he repeated, slower that time. "Not when I woke up."

"Why would I?" I placed my paints on the dresser. "You had everyone else there."

"But not you," he said, taking a step toward me. "I knew you were there though. Before."

"What are you talking about?" My heart jumped.

"I could smell you." He took another step in my direction. "I'm right, aren't I? You did come see me."

Shit. I looked anywhere but at him.

"Tell me you were there. Say it," he demanded. "Tell me you visited me."

"*Fine,*" I shouted. "I was there. By your side. From the moment Coby told me you were in a coma to the day you woke up. I visited you. I was there. Are you fucking happy now?"

"Max," he said gently.

"No." I raised my hand. "You should leave. You can't be in here anyway. If the girls find out—"

"What, Maxine? What will they do if they find out I'm in your room? A room I have spent many hours balls deep inside of that beautiful fucking body of yours. Four walls holding screams of pleasure and nights filled with passion." He took another step in my direction. "What exactly will they do?"

I shivered at his words, erotic memories of our time together filling the void in my mind. "We … we haven't done anything in here since it was rebuilt. You know that," I pointed out. "Or do you? What exactly do you remember, Dale?" I took a step to the side but now I was trapped, the only way to get far from him was to jump over the bed.

His brows narrowed in the center. "It doesn't matter what I remember or not because I can still feel you. Every single inch of your skin. Whether we fucked before or after the club was blown to shit, this room is still in the same location as before. You know *that*." His mouth set in a firm line, the strength of his gait powerful and domineering. Nothing like before.

This man standing before me was no longer the man I had fallen in love with months ago. I realized that now as a wicked grin grew on his handsome face.

"You checking me out, kitten?"

I looked away at the term of endearment he had given me when we first started sleeping together. He had said I was feisty and small. I wasn't as short as Brogan but I was the youngest out of our group so in his mind, *kitten* fit perfectly.

"Don't you dare take your eyes off of me," he demanded, closing the distance between us. His hands reached my hair before I could stop him. He pulled my head back before I could run away. "I told you. Never take your eyes off of me." He leaned down to my ear.

"You remember, don't you? You remember every word, every stroke of my tongue, every thrust of my cock."

My heart raced, thumping in tune with each syllable leaving his mouth.

"Let go of me," I pleaded, shoving against him, but it only made his hold on me tighten.

"You remember the conversations we had." He licked up the length of my neck. "You begging for me to control you. You submitting to me. You giving all of you. To me." He tugged my head back, forcing me to meet his gaze. "Tell me you remember. Tell me how much you miss it."

"Fuck you," I whispered, slapping my hands against his chest.

He growled, the rough sound mixing with the desire I couldn't ignore.

"Do *you* remember, Dale?" I pushed him back, my chest rising and falling with the ragged breath. "Do you remember when you laughed at me? When you told me to get the fuck out of your bed like some cheap whore? You made me feel worthless. Is that what you want to hear? You want to hear that every night since then, I have nightmares of you laughing at me. Of … of … our …" My voice cracked. I couldn't do this. I didn't like confrontation.

"Tell me about her." He reached for me.

I slapped his hand away, glaring at him.

"Tell me," he said, the twinkle of amusement fading from his eyes. "I deserve to know. Especially when it was Coby who told me that my daughter is fucking dead."

"Your daughter? *Your daughter!*" I screamed punching him in the chest. "You don't deserve to call her yours. You never claimed her as such. Are you feeling guilty, Dale? Is that it?"

"I deserve to know," he said through clenched teeth.

"You deserve to know?" I laughed. "You deserve shit." I pushed him back. "You should be groveling at my feet for the hell you put me through. And for me not telling you about her? Fine. I'll own up to that, but when did you expect me to tell you? We can't talk without fighting. Look at us now. So, tell me, when should I have told you that your daughter died?"

"How about at the fucking hospital, Max," he said, his voice raising. "Tell me about her," he repeated, grabbing my wrists.

He was faster but I was angrier. "Fuck you." I shoved him. "I'm not telling you shit."

"Maxine." He inhaled deeply, breathing it out slowly through his nose before he continued. "Tell me."

"What? Tell you what, Dale?" I pulled myself from his grip and pushed him back, stepping around him. "Tell you that I had to give birth to her after she died inside of me? Tell you that even though she wasn't allowed to take her first breath, I still held her?" My heart started pounding, my voice becoming louder as each question left my mouth. "Tell you how her skin was blue but she was still the most beautiful baby I had ever seen?" I raised my hand when he opened his mouth. "No. You don't deserve to know. My grandmother told me to be your friend. That you needed it and, as much as she'll be disappointed in me, I can't be your friend. I'm done trying to be civil." I turned and went to open the door when a heavy hand slammed it shut.

Letting out a heavy sigh, I roughly wiped the tears falling down my cheeks. Never in my life had a man affected me as much as the one standing behind me. No one hurt me like he did. And no one made me feel this damn alive at the same time.

We stood like that for a while. His front to my back. His hand on the door so I wouldn't run away from my problems. From him. His hot breath slid across the back of my neck, fanning just over my head. He stood several inches taller than me but his body had become bigger over the past couple of weeks. He could crush me if he wanted to, and part of me wished he would.

Placing his other hand against the door, he caged me in. His body was mere inches from mine, not touching me in the least but I still felt him everywhere. Inside and out. I could feel him moving along my skin, taking every waking desire I had for him and unleashing it onto me.

Dale brushed his mouth under my ear, sliding it down the length of my neck until he reached my shoulder.

A gasp escaped me and, as much as I wanted to deny it, I was still attracted to this man. Every nerve ending exploded from his touch.

"Where is she?" Dale asked gently, breaking the silence a moment later.

I bit back a sob at the thickness in his voice, but I wouldn't give in. I wouldn't try and console him when he never did the same for me. It wasn't right, I knew that, but he needed to see he couldn't always get what he wanted. He couldn't be demanding and expect me to fall to my knees. He couldn't kiss me and expect me to submit. I was no longer the woman he met weeks ago.

One look of his baby blues and I was done for. But not this time. "That's none of your concern," I muttered.

Dale grabbed my arms, spun me around, and slammed me up against the door. "Tell me where the *fuck* my daughter is," he yelled.

"Why, Dale? Huh? Tell me one good reason why I should give you that information when you never wanted it before."

"She's my daughter," he shouted, digging his fingers into my arms.

"She was my daughter too. *I* gave birth to her. *I* buried her. *Me.*" I shoved him. "I did all of it by myself. Do you understand what that can do to a person?" I didn't want to show him this side of me. I didn't want anyone to see how broken I was. As soon as the words left my mouth, I clammed up and snapped my mouth shut.

"You did it by yourself?" he asked, taking a step away from me. Rubbing the back of his neck, he bellowed out a curse and punched his fist into the wall. "Why, Max? Why the fuck would you do that?"

"Because I didn't want people looking at me with pity," I screamed, digging my fingers into my hair. "I didn't want everyone ..."

"What?"

"I didn't want them to feel sorry for me." That was only partly the truth. The real reason was I didn't want people to see the darkness that threatened to consume me. I didn't want them to think I was losing my ever-loving mind.

My legs buckled, no longer able to hold my weight. I dropped to my knees, hugging my arms around myself.

Hands touched my shoulders, rubbing down my back.

"Don't touch me," I sobbed, but I no longer had the strength to push Dale away.

****

(Dale)

There was no way in hell I would ever get this woman back in my life. Back to where she looked at me with adoring eyes. Back to where she loved me. I fucked up. I one-hundred percent screwed up any chance I had with this woman. This beautiful, breathtaking woman.

"Don't touch me," she repeated on a whisper but she didn't pull away.

I didn't push her. I already started out this night by doing that. Instead, I rubbed my hands in small circles over her back while she gave me a part of herself that I knew pissed her off. Max was strong. Unlike any other person I had ever met but I was too stupid to see it until right then. She was right in questioning why I wanted to know where our daughter was. It enraged the fuck out of me when she wouldn't tell me but, on the other hand, I understood.

An apology was on the tip of my tongue, but what good would it do? It was only words. Words didn't do shit. Actions spoke louder but I had no idea what the fuck to do to make her forgive me.

Her shoulders shook, her cries only getting harder.

She needed something. Anything. I didn't know what so I did the first thing I thought of. I pulled her into my arms.

"What are you doing?" she cried, struggling against me.

"I'm holding you." I cupped her nape, pulling her head down to my shoulder. "I'm just holding you."

Her struggling ceased but she never hugged me back.

I was fine with that.

She came to visit me at the hospital. I knew before the words left her mouth, but when she admitted to it, it was still like a slap in the face. After everything I had done, she stood by my side. I didn't deserve her. Not one fucking bit.

After a couple of minutes of me rubbing her back and her crying ending, a knock sounded on the door.

Much to my dismay, Max slid off my lap and wiped the tears from her cheeks.

My body ached as I rose to my feet. There was a pain in the back of my throat I had never felt before. Even after all the shitty foster homes I had as a child, nothing compared to this. I was thrown away as a boy and tossed aside as a man. That fact alone tore my heart out. Knowing it was my fault was like a flesh-eating disease as it gnawed away at my soul.

Seeing the hatred in Max's eyes, knowing it was directed toward me affected me in a way I wasn't used to. That light I had after all of these years, that glow I held onto even after going to war, still held on. Until now.

Holding out my hand, I waited.

Max raised an eyebrow, looking at my hand and then back at my face. Tentatively, she placed hers in mine and I pulled her to her feet.

Although she shoved from my grip, she still let me touch her. It was small but I would take it.

She opened the door, revealing her best friend.

"We wanted to make sure you were okay," Jay said from the doorway.

"Have you seen—" Angel's gaze landed on me. He barged into the room, barreling toward me. "What the *fuck* are you doing in here?"

"I don't think it's any of your business," I threw back at him, not in the mood for his over protective papa bear shit.

"You're *not* supposed to be in here," he said, shoving a finger in my chest.

"Who the fuck says?" I pushed him.

"She says," Angel pointed at Max. "That's who. Now get out before I throw you the fuck out."

"Angel, baby." Jay grabbed his arm. "Let's go. They *do* need to talk."

"No." Angel kissed her gently on the mouth. "You asked me to watch out for your best friend. That's what I'm doing. I'm sick of this shit." He glared at me. "We heard her. We were there. So back the fuck up."

"It's fine," Max reassured him. "I promise. He was just leaving. Weren't you?" she asked me.

Crossing my arms under my chest, I leaned against the dresser. "Make me."

She huffed, her cheeks reddening. "Everyone out. *Now.*" When we didn't move, she threw her hands up in the air. "Fine, I'll leave." And with that, Max stormed out of the room.

Angel came toward me, stepping toe to toe with me. "If something happens to my baby because of your shit with Max stressing out my fiancée, I'll fucking kill you."

CHAPTER EIGHT

Max

ONCE I LEFT the party, I headed to Josee's place. I needed out. A change. An actual home I could call my own. What the hell was I thinking when I planned the party? Did I expect Dale to fall to his knees and beg for my forgiveness? No but I wasn't expecting him to be a complete asshole about everything. But he had been right about one thing. I *should* have told him more about the baby myself and not make Coby feel forced into telling him. But I couldn't. The words froze on my tongue and the only thing that came out of me was pure hatred. I wanted to make Dale stew and think about the pain he had caused me. Two wrongs didn't make a right and shit but I didn't give a fuck at this point.

Before I knew it, I was standing on Josee's front step. Knocking twice, I waited.

When the door opened, it revealed a disheveled Josee. Her hair was a mess, her eyes glossed over.

"Did I interrupt something?" I asked, my cheeks heating.

She frowned. "What?" Understanding brightened her gaze. "No. I wish." She laughed. "I fell asleep on the couch after a couple glasses of wine. What are you doing here? I thought you had a party."

"I did," I muttered, glancing down at my feet. Kicking a stone, I cleared my throat, my cheeks heating even more. My stomach churned while time seemed to slow down. I took a deep breath and then another before I met my friend's gaze.

"Max?" she said softly. "What's going on?"

"Do you still have that house for sale?"

She raised an eyebrow. "I think this conversation needs to be held over a bottle of wine." She took a step back, sweeping her arm to the side. "Welcome to my humble abode."

I sighed, heading into the house.

"Make yourself at home," she said, heading to the kitchen.

I was about to walk into the living room when something soft brushed up against my feet. I jumped back, finding a black, fluffy cat rubbing its body against me. "Hi, kitty." I smiled, kneeling to pet it. The cat purred, the sound rumbling from deep within its body until it vibrated into my hands. I smiled. "You have the loudest purr ever." As if the cat could understand me, the purr grew louder.

Josee giggled. "That's Pig. His purr is like no other."

I laughed with her, the sound foreign to my ears. It had been long time since a laugh leaving my mouth was genuine. My eyes burned, my heart swelling that it took a cat's purr to make me feel better even if it was just for a couple of minutes. "Hello, Mr. Pig," I said, my voice thick. "It's nice to meet you."

Pig shoved his head into my hand.

"He's too cute." I picked him up, snuggling my face into the crook of his neck. His purr trembled into my soul, wrapping me in a blanket of peace. I rose to my full height and followed Jo to the couch with Pig in my arms.

"Strange. He's never like that with anyone." She shrugged. "He must like you."

"Or he feels my pain," I whispered.

"Here." She handed me a glass of wine, ignoring my comment. "Let's talk."

I was really starting to hate talking.

We sat on the couch in the living room, the cushion sinking beneath my weight. I let out a sigh, leaning my head back all the while running my fingers through Pig's long, black fur. "Is that your family?" I asked, pointing to the pictures lined up on the mantel above the fireplace.

"Yup," she took a sip of wine, curling her feet under her. "My parents and my two brothers."

"How are your parents doing after everything?" I asked, remembering how her oldest brother had died a couple years ago in a fishing accident.

"They're getting by." She narrowed her eyes at me. "Just because you're being nice and asking about my family doesn't mean I'll let you off. You *will* tell me what's going on."

I scoffed. "You sound like Dale."

"What do you mean?"

I placed the glass on the coffee table. Pig meowed at the movement but adjusted himself on my lap, kneading his claws into my skin. The pain was sharp but somehow it reminded me I was still alive, that I had so much to be thankful for even though I didn't feel like it at the moment. "You both know me well, it's scary. My girls ... my sisters know me but not like you two. You have an unbiased view." I shook myself. "I don't know. I'm rambling."

"No." She placed a hand on my shoulder. "Talk."

"Dale and I had a fight tonight. We tried talking but it only turned into us yelling at each other and ..."

"Sex?" she asked, raising an eyebrow.

"Not quite but I can't help but be attracted to him." My cheeks heated. "God, I hate him. I hate him so much, and I hate him even more because I can't control these feelings. I need out. I need away from it all and to start over."

"And you want to buy the house I have for sale?"

"Yes."

Josee had been trying to sell her old place for years. Ever since she became successful in the art industry, she moved and got something bigger but that tiny house still remained.

"Please," I pleaded. "You know I'm responsible."

"Girl." She laughed and placed her glass on the coffee table. "I know you are." Pinning up her mess of curls, she winked at me. "Besides, I know where you work."

I gave her a soft smile. "I know you were wanting to rent it out but I would like to buy it."

"Max, if you want to buy the house, it's yours. I only chose to rent it out at first because I couldn't get any buyers. I'll have my lawyer draw up the paperwork tomorrow but I trust you." Josee reached for her bag and pulled out her keys. After fiddling with it for a couple of seconds, she handed me a single key. "You can start moving in whenever you are ready."

My throat burned. "Really?" I asked, taking the key from her.

"Yes," she said, softly. "Of course. I know you've been through a lot, and I want to do anything I can to help."

"Thank you." I threw my arms around her, Pig protesting at the sudden movement and jumped off my lap. "Thank you so damn much."

She laughed. "You're welcome."

Releasing her, I slipped the key into my purse. "I'm going to have my own home."

"You are." She patted my hand. "But haven't you had your own home already?"

I shrugged. "It's not fair of me to say this because everyone has been wonderful to me after … after the baby …" I swallowed hard. "Anyway, I just need something to call my own."

"Does Jay know?"

"I'll tell her when I leave here." She would be pissed I didn't talk to her first, but eventually she would understand. Although, I wasn't sure how everyone else would take it knowing I would be alone.

"Where are you staying tonight?" Josee asked, pulling me from my thoughts.

"I'm not sure." I wrapped my fingers around the key, taking in the moment of reprieve I would finally have something to call my own.

"You're more than welcome to head on over to the house. It has some furniture in it but it's just been sitting there so it might smell a little musty."

"Okay." A heavy weight lifted from my shoulders. "Thank you, Josee. If there's anything I can do for you, please don't hesitate to ask me."

"Well …" She winked. "Those two new guys in Vice-One. They're fucking hot."

"Two new guys?" I frowned, trying to remember if I had met them or not. "Oh. Lian Wolfe and Henley Jinx?"

"Yeah," she sighed. "They're fucking hot."

"When did you see them?" I only had met them in passing but never spoke to either of them. They seemed nice enough. Angel trusted them which was all I cared about. He needed good guys on his team after two of them got medically discharged and a third, being on stress leave.

"I went to the clubhouse to find you. They were working with Angel on some construction stuff or something. They didn't notice me thank God, 'cause I was a hot mess." Her cheeks reddened, a nervous laugh escaping her full mouth.

"Whatever, Josee. You're beautiful. With your curly hair, freckles, and perfect skin, they would eat you up," I teased.

Her eyes widened. "That's what I'm afraid of."

I laughed, shaking my head. "So, both of them, huh?"

"Yeah." She winked. "Although they could be gay. They're always together."

"Have you ever thought they could just be best friends? Maybe they have a bromance going on." I reached for my wine, elated the conversation had become fun and no longer about me.

"Even if they are gay, maybe they'll take me for a spin just for one night." She waggled her eyebrows.

"You are too much." I grinned.

We spent the next hour or two chatting about nothing important. It was nice. No talk about the human trafficking business. Nothing was said about the motorcycle world. Nothing. We chatted about books, makeup, clothing, what we were watching on TV when both of us had time. It was perfect.

But I found myself drawn to my best friend. I hadn't been treating Jay well, taking my anger and frustration out on her when it wasn't her fault. None of this was her fault.

Josee had confessed later in the evening after a couple glasses of wine that she had a tiny crush on the two new recruits. I already knew that but after having some alcohol, she felt the need to tell me again.

After my third glass, I decided to call it a night and head to the place Josee had given me. My new home. A part of me no one could take. It was mine and mine alone and, for that, I would always be grateful to her.

CHAPTER NINE

Dale

I FELT HER *before I saw her. The tiny brunette fussing with her nails took the breath right from my lungs and breathed new life into my fucking soul.*

The impact from the explosion had forced us on our asses but after double checking with everyone, we were all fine and fucking dandy.

Angel had made his way to the other woman sitting on the picnic table. Her red hair was pulled back into a ponytail that had come loose around her shoulders after the building got hit. He said something to her. She scowled.

NUMB

I bit back a laugh knowing Angel had met his match. Most women fell all over themselves to get their bodies wrapped around him.

I glanced at the big ass hole in the building. You could see right through to the bar.

A bomb.

In the middle of the motherfucking town. No one checked to make sure we were all right. Why would they? This shithole of a place was run by the corrupt and forced into the ground by the evil we were trying to bring to its knees.

"My nails," the little one exclaimed.

The taller woman frowned at her friend.

She had said something but I couldn't make out her words when the small female glanced my way.

Who are you? I found myself wanting to know every single thing about her, but another part of me wanted to have her spread out beneath me, begging me to take it further. I craved her screams. These unexpected feelings soaring through me were unusual. I didn't like them. But then I did.

"Do you need the ambulance?" I found myself asking.

The little one smiled up at me. "Yes."

I took her hand, leading the way. "What's your name?"

"Maxine."

From then on, I knew I was done. She was standing in front of me, yet I couldn't reach her. Her words whispered across my skin. Her touch brushed along my bones. I became unraveled by her mere laugh.

"I love you."

I shot up in bed, my heart racing at the voice still whispering in my ear. Fuck. Rubbing the ache in my chest, I pushed and prodded until all I felt were my fingers and no longer the pain I deserved.

The dream scrambled through my mind. I had no idea if it was real or not. If it had been a memory or just a moment of hope. Pieces of what I had with Max came back every now and again but the only way to know if they were accurate would be to actually talk to her. Instead, like the asshole I was, I shoved her far away from my heart.

Suddenly, the alarm on my phone went off. I had an appointment with the local doctor in town meaning I wouldn't have to travel to the city but at that point, I would rather saw off my leg with a rusty spoon.

I didn't remember falling asleep. After Max left her own party on Saturday night, I had done the same not too long after. I didn't need to be around Angel, knowing my neck was on the line. I never had the intention of hurting anyone or stressing anyone the fuck out but his words hurt.

"If something happens to my baby because of your shit with Max stressing out my fiancée, I'll fucking kill you."

I would never do anything to hurt Jay or their baby. The issue Max and I had was far from being over but I would never take that out on a pregnant woman.

I enjoyed pushing Max, but I loved it even more when she pushed back. And fuck me, did it ever make me hard when she became all feisty.

Seeing as there was no time to rub one out, I pushed those thoughts aside and headed to the doctor's office.

"Mr. Michaels," the receptionist said as soon as I stepped foot into the small office building. She greeted me with a smile from the perch at her desk.

"Uh … hi." I mentally smacked myself. I had all sorts of training with etiquette and how to be a proper gentleman. The Navy didn't just raise sailors, they raised men. But at that point, all of my training went to shit.

The receptionist's smile grew. "The doctor will see you now." She giggled to herself. "I always wanted to say that." She rose from her chair, her bright green eyes taking me in as they slid down my body.

Way to keep it professional, lady.

She cleared her throat. "Dr. Santos is right this way." She led me down a long hall. Banging sounded, followed by grumbled sighs. "Excuse him. He's not normally like this."

"Yes, I am," came a deep reply.

She jumped, spinning around.

I looked up, noticing a large man standing in the doorway to another room.

"Dale Michaels?" he asked, nodding my way.

"Yes, sir," I said automatically. Somehow, I knew this man came from power. His demeanor was rough but dominant and one dark look from him put the receptionist in her place.

"You may go," he told her, waving a hand in front of him.

She nodded, racing back to her desk, and left me alone with only who I could assume was Dr. Santos.

"I'm sorry to keep you waiting," he said, stepping out into the hall. "And please excuse my abruptness. It's been a long morning already. This isn't my usual office."

"You came from the city," I stated, stepping into the small room.

"I did. Your doctor from the hospital called me directly." Dr. Santos followed me and shut the door behind him. "I know you probably don't want to be here. I've been assigned to your case because apparently I'm known for handling difficult" —the corners of his lips twitched— "situations."

I sat on the couch. "I don't know what the point of this meeting is. I don't remember shit. The shit I think I remember is just that … Shit. All of it is fucking shit. And if you want me to lay down while you write in your notepad with your fancy designer suit, you can kiss my white fucking ass."

Dr. Santos raised an eyebrow. "Are we done?"

I grunted, crossing my arms under my chest. "Depends."

"On what?"

"You hear to prescribe me pills?"

"Nope."

"You going to force me to talk?"

"Not if you don't want to." Dr. Santos sat on the couch beside me, leaning his arm against the back of it. "You don't have to talk. We can watch the baseball game."

"You like sports?" I asked, turning my body toward him.

"I'm from a shitty town in Mexico. All I had as a kid were sports. So yeah, I like them." His dark eyes pierced into mine.

"You remind me of someone I know." I rubbed the back of my neck, feeling the walls around me crumble just enough that I could get out my next words. "I fucked up, doc." I let out a slow breath. "I fucked up bad."

***

(Max)

I had finally finished unpacking. It only took me a couple of days but seeing as I had nothing else to do, I focused everything on getting my little home the way I wanted it.

Standing outside the studio, I leaned against the door frame. The room was perfect. Not too small where I felt cramped but also not too big where I felt I had to walk miles just to get a set of paints.

Although the room was complete, I still wasn't inspired. It was frustrating the hell out of me and I had no idea how to fix it. Josee had been patient, knowing I worked well under pressure, but she was paying me to do a job. If I didn't get something done and soon, it would reflect badly on her. I knew that. *She* knew that. I just didn't know what to do without forcing something even though it might have to come to that.

Taking my coffee out to the front deck of my home, I went to sit on the patio chair when a black truck pulled up the driveway.

No. He couldn't be here.

My heart started racing. My palms became clammy. But while I was trying to force the impending panic attack away, my body hummed for the man I hated.

When Dale stepped out of the large vehicle, I bit out a curse. I didn't need this right now and he was not helping with my creativity lull.

"What are you doing here?" I demanded, gripping the mug tight in my hands. "And how the hell do you know where I live?"

"We need to talk," he said, walking up the steps.

My stomach flipped. He always had a deep voice that made my insides stir but ever since his accident, his voice had become lower. Rougher. I could almost feel it sliding over my skin like his calloused hands. A shiver raced down my spine.

He raised an eyebrow, his lips pulling into that sexy smirk of his I wanted to slap off his face.

"We talked already." I cleared my throat. "Tell me how you found out where I live."

"People talk." He shrugged. "Our group of friends don't hold a lot of secrets."

"You're lying. They wouldn't tell you shit if I asked them not to."

He chuckled. "Woman, I can get any information I want from them. All I have to do is bat my baby blues. That's how I got you, isn't it?"

My cheeks heated, my nostrils flaring. "There's nothing more to say," I grumbled, heading for the door."

"Yes …" He loomed behind me, slamming the screen door shut. "There is," he breathed in my ear. "You're just pissed because you know I'm right. You can't get me out of your head. I invade your dreams. I come to you during those lonely nights when all you have are your hands." He groaned. "I'm right, aren't I?"

"You're an asshole," I breathed, stomping on his foot. "Now get the fuck out of my way."

His laugh hardened. "Oh, baby, you know I like it when you get feisty."

My body stiffened, my mind taking me back to a time when we were okay. When it was just us and nothing else mattered. "I'll show you fucking feisty." I shoved him back. "I'm done talking," I said, keeping my voice firm and opened the door.

"Well, I'm not," he said, following me inside the house.

"Dale," I cried, slamming the mug on the counter. "You can't be in here."

"Well, I am, so you better as fuck talk to me." Each step he took toward me caused me to take a step back. The closer he was, the less control I had and it was exactly what he wanted.

"What the hell do you want?" I placed my hands on my hips.

"I want you to tell me about her."

I faltered where I stood. Leaning against the patio doors, I crossed my arms under my chest. "There's nothing to say."

"Like hell there isn't, Max," he snarled, coming toward me. "I deserve to know—"

"You deserve to know?" I laughed. "Seriously, Dale. We already fought over this. I'm not telling you shit and you sure as hell don't deserve to know anything." I was being a bitch. I knew it. My grandmother would be disappointed in me but this man standing only a few feet away, broke me. He didn't even know how badly he had caused me to fall within myself. He forced me to drown in the sea of utter despair when I gave birth to our dead daughter.

My chest tightened, my breathing quickening as the evil of my nightmares threatened to take hold. "I can't do this." I went to walk away when a rough hand wrapped around my arm.

Dale pulled me back against him, brushing his nose into the crook of my neck. "You need to talk to me," he muttered, circling his arm around my waist. "I need you to tell me what happened."

My heart jumped at being this close to him. My knees shook, my head involuntarily leaning to the side to give him better access to my neck.

His mouth brushed over the soft skin just under my ear, a purr escaping his lips. "I need to know. Please."

That snapped me out of the daze. "It's not going to do anything," I said, my voice cracking. I pulled from his grip and took a couple steps away from him before I jumped in his arms and begged for him to do whatever he wanted to me. A part of me wondered if I should. Maybe it would clear my head, motivate me to paint and help us move on. I bit back a scoff. Who the hell was I kidding? That shit only happened in movies.

I slowly turned back around to face him and took a deep breath. "I saw you."

"What do you mean, you saw me?" He frowned.

"I watched you fuck other women after you laughed in my face when I confessed my feelings for you. I told you I was pregnant and you accused me of fucking someone else. When I threw those parties at the clubhouse, it was my hope that you would open up to me and tell me you had made a mistake, but instead I walked in on you. You would take women to the dark corners of the clubhouse. Bring them to the bathroom. Sometimes one woman, two, even three at one point."

"Shit," he said, rubbing the back of his neck. His shoulders dropped, but the guilt he felt was nothing compared to the pain and anguish he had caused me over the past couple of months.

"I saw you fucking them," I said, my voice small. "Your hands on their bodies like you touched me."

"I may not remember everything but I sure as hell know when I was with those women, it was *nothing* compared to what I had with you," he snapped.

"Well, you sure have a funny way of showing it." I waved a hand in front of my face, admitting defeat. "But it's done. I need to move on."

"No."

"Excuse me?" I raised an eyebrow. "What the hell do you mean *no?*"

"You are *not* moving on. Not from me. I refuse to allow it."

I laughed, shaking my head. "Are you fucking kidding me right now? Are you telling me you want a relationship with me? After all of this time, does Dale Michaels finally want to settle down?"

"Fuck," he growled. "I don't know. But I *do* know that I won't allow you to move on." He stepped toward me.

"You can't tell me what to do, Dale. It doesn't work that way." Before I could guess what would happen next, he had me in his arms and threw me on the couch. I pushed him, struggling beneath his rough hold. "Dale," I cried, trying to shove him off me. Although my mind didn't want it, my body heated with desire for him.

Dale didn't say anything. But he made sure to speak with his hands. They roamed up the sides of my body and back down. His fingers gripped my hips, pulling me further beneath him.

"Dale." Although I didn't want him to, I knew this wasn't right. Not for me. Not for either of us.

His mouth brushed over the shell of my ear. "I remember the first time you told me to stop. When I did, you confessed you didn't actually want me to. You wanted to fight me. Hottest fucking thing ever."

I shivered, remembering what he was referring to. I had been scared he would think I was a freak but the dominant man inside of him won out and he did what I had asked. The fact he remembered pierced me in the heart, but I couldn't let him know that. "I don't know what you're talking about," I said, no longer struggling beneath him.

He licked up the length of my neck. "Sure you don't. Just like when you told me you loved me. You didn't mean that, either, right?"

"Fuck you."

His teeth closed around my ear. "I'm trying."

I whimpered. "You … you …"

"What?" His hands massaged into the flesh of my rear.

There was little clothing between us with him in his sweatpants and me in shorts. A couple adjustments and I knew he could be inside me. I shook my head. No. I couldn't. Not after everything he had done to me. But I wanted him. I wanted him to take me away and allow me to just feel. No emotions. No tenderness. I wanted rough and fast. I wanted it so hard that one thrust would force us to break.

"I hate you," I said instead. "So damn much." God, I couldn't stop this. Hell, I didn't want to.

Dale sat back, pulling me with him. His lips trailed down the length of my jaw. "Say it again," he demanded, fisting my hair in his hands.

"I hate you," I repeated.

"Good," he growled and crashed his mouth to mine.

I gasped at the rough impact, opening instantly to him.

His tongue forced its way into my mouth, sliding along mine. The kiss became hard, desperate. It was like our souls were calling out to each other.

Dale tugged my head back, thrusting his tongue into my mouth.

A shiver trembled through my body. Memories of our time together, rushed back. Moments of passion, hours of ecstasy, all invaded my mind.

Digging my fingers into the hair at his nape, I tugged and pulled, deepening the kiss. Our tongues meshed, dancing. Both of us trying to take ownership over the other.

I could feel his body harden beneath mine, a part of him that had given me so much pleasure in such a short amount of time.

His hands traveled down my back and gripped my hips, pulling me hard against him.

A shot of electricity hit me straight in the center.

When our hips connected, we started moving. Clothing covered and breathless, I could still feel him everywhere. Not where I wanted him most but this would do. It had to. I didn't know if I could have sex with him again. As much as I wanted—

"Stop." He released my mouth with a wet smack, tugging my head back. "Stop fucking thinking. Feel me, kitten."

"Shut up," I snapped, shoving him.

"No." His eyes burned into mine. "You shut the fuck up." He grabbed my hips, undulating his beneath me. "You feel how fucking hard I am for you?"

"Good," I panted. "I want you so fucking hard you explode. I want you to beg *me*." These demands were not the norm for me. I didn't know what was happening but all my emotions were becoming jumbled and, for once in these shitty weeks, I just wanted to feel. Skin against skin. Breath mixing with breath. I wanted to hear our moans and screams. I wanted this man to ruin me and, in turn, I wanted to force him to his knees.

Dale threw me back onto the couch, covering my body with his. "I'll beg, Max. I'll fucking beg until you tell me to stop." His teeth grazed down the length of my jaw. "I'll beg until you give me permission to do whatever I want to you." Dale covered my mouth with his, the kiss slow and deep.

I moaned, taking all of him in, and wrapped my legs around his hips.

He pushed his hips into me at the same time I lifted mine.

We repeated our movements until I found I couldn't stop.

Dale controlled every inch of me, much like he had done in the past. But now it was different. So damn different I didn't know where he began and I ended.

I wanted to lose myself in him. Even though I hated him, I knew he could make me feel good. He could take away this pain and destroy me just the same. I had given him my heart and he crushed it in his hands.

Dale inched his hand under my tank top and cupped my breast. Of all the times I was thankful I was still in pajamas, this was one of those moments.

He released my mouth, pulled the fabric higher, and latched onto my nipple.

Arching beneath him, I pushed my breast harder into his mouth.

He sucked and pulled, nipping me until I cried out at the delicious pain. He repeated his movements with the other one.

"Fucking delicious." Fisting the fabric, he pulled it over my head.

NUMB

My breathing picked up at the dangerous heat in his eyes as they roamed down my naked torso.

I hadn't lost all the weight from the pregnancy. Knowing stretch marks scarred my skin, I moved to cover myself when he grabbed my hands.

"Don't you dare cover what our child did." Something switched behind his gaze as he stared at the marks. His jaw ticked, his chest rising and falling. Brushing the back of his knuckles over my lower abdomen, he met my gaze. "You're fucking perfect."

***

(Dale)

I didn't go to Max's house with the intention of kissing her, let alone having her writhing beneath me.

Once I left Dr. Santos' office, I felt stripped bare. Completely exposed for the world to see. He was a good guy. Not judging me in the least. He didn't push when I didn't talk and even threw on a ball game. I liked the guy but the session had me on the brink of losing it. I didn't share shit. Ever.

Without even knowing it, I arrived at Max's house before I knew what I was doing. I wanted to talk and sort some of our shit out. But her sass and feistiness shoved me over the edge until I couldn't control my actions.

When I saw the marks on her stomach, it drove me past the point of madness. No longer was I feeling guilty but outright enraged with wanting to show her how sorry I was. But the words refused to leave my mouth.

I wasn't lying when I told her she was perfect. When she almost covered her body, it pissed me the fuck off and I promised I would show her just how beautiful I thought she was.

Crushing my mouth to hers, I tasted her tongue, sucking it between my lips until she purred. She was so damn delicious, it took everything in me not to pull my pants down, move her shorts a little, and shove my cock deep inside her. But I wouldn't fuck her. Not yet. Not until she gave me permission. I had already done enough.

"Dale," she whispered against my lips. Her hands roamed down my back, sliding beneath my shirt. Her fingers dug into my muscles, her nails scratching at my skin. She wanted me. Her sweet heat washed over me, calming some of the rage I had felt since waking up from the coma. But it still wasn't enough. It would never be enough.

Somehow, I knew this moment would end before I intended it to so I savored it and took what I wanted until she pushed me away. Until then, I needed to see how far I could go before she stopped me.

Pushing my hips between her legs, I rubbed my pelvis against hers.

She moaned, spreading her legs wider.

Fuck me, this woman was going to give me the biggest blue balls in the history of sexual frustration. But I didn't care. I found I needed to make her feel good first. Something poked at my mind, hinting that I had been selfish before. A part of me wondered if she liked it because she never pushed me away.

Pulling her further beneath me, I leaned an arm on the cushion just above her head. It gave me the leverage I needed to circle my hips and push them into her.

She gasped into my mouth, cupping the back of my legs and pulled me tighter against her.

NUMB

My dick was hard—any harder and it would fucking pierce through my sweatpants.

She wanted me to beg. Well, little did she know, I had been begging since the first moment I met her.

Inching a hand beneath her shorts, I cupped her ass and rubbed myself over her sweet pussy.

Her breathing picked up, her hips following my movements. Releasing my mouth, her eyes glossed over with the darkest amount of lust I had ever seen. "Dale."

I read her body language and knew she was close to having a release. Taking that as my chance, I brushed my mouth over hers and stopped moving my hips.

She whimpered.

A small smirk spread on my face. Cupping her jaw, I turned her head and kissed up the length of her neck. "I'll make you come, sweet girl. I'll make you come so damn hard, you'll always remember me."

Her eyes squeezed shut, her mouth set in a grim line. She wanted to tell me off. She wanted to push me away but she couldn't. I knew it and took advantage. I was an asshole but I wouldn't hurt her. Not again. I would spend my last breath, groveling at her feet and kissing the ground she walked on before I ever destroyed her heart.

Hooking my fingers into the waistband of her shorts, I pulled the fabric low enough that I could get access to her pussy.

Her eyes remained shut but her breathing picked up.

"Don't worry, kitten," I whispered in her ear, tightening my hold on her jaw. "I'll take care of you."

Brushing the back of my knuckles over her bare mound, I pushed a finger between the soaked folds of her beautiful cunt. My dick almost exploded right then when she bucked against me.

Rubbing my finger over her swollen clit, I pushed and tugged until she cried out and was squirming beneath me.

But all I could do was watch her. A rosy glow hit her cheeks, her mouth parted on a silent cry, her hands dug into the back of my legs. I didn't stop. I couldn't.

I rubbed until she screamed. I rubbed until she begged me to stop. And then I rubbed harder and faster.

"Fuck," she cried out, shaking beneath me, and only then did I thrust two fingers inside of her. Her eyes popped open, her body arching beneath me.

I thrust until there was nothing left. Her pussy clenched around my fingers, sucking and pulling at me until I inserted a third finger.

She moaned, licking her lips. Her hands circled around my neck, bringing my head down to meet her lips.

Licking my way into her mouth, I gave her what she wanted, and when she came for the fourth time, only then did I stop.

****

(Max)

I needed his dick inside me. I wanted him to fuck me like he never fucked before. I wanted to break him and have him shatter me just the same. But instead, I did the only thing I knew how and pushed him away.

After Dale had me coming around his fingers several times, I shoved him off me. Much to my surprise, he let me.

He sat back on the couch, cupping the raging hard-on sporting between his legs.

My mouth watered at the sight but I shook my head. I couldn't have sex with him. Not right now, maybe not ever. As much as my body needed it, my mind finally won out.

"You should go," I muttered, pulling up my shorts and lowering my tank top. My fingers brushed over the stretch marks caused by our baby.

"Yeah. Fine." He rose to his full height, glancing down at me over his shoulder. "You can fight it all you want, kitten, but I will be balls deep inside of you again."

"Not if I say no," I threw back at him.

A wicked grin spread across his face. "Remember the conversation we had when we first started fucking? No? Well I do. But I won't repeat it." He leaned over me, his face mere inches from mine. "I'll just tell you what you told me." He kissed my cheek, his mouth trailing down the length of my jaw to my ear. "No is *not* a safe word."

CHAPTER TEN

Max

"NO IS NOT a safe word."
I had been surprised Dale even remembered that conversation. I wasn't into kink with the other men I had slept with, not that there had been many before Dale. One to be exact. One man before Dale. No wonder I had it bad for the guy. I had no idea what sort of sexual activities I was into but from the moment Dale looked at me, I knew there was something more. A darker side to him behind his joking exterior. I could see it without him showing me. I didn't know his past, his childhood, whether he had a family. I didn't even

know if he had kids. My heart skipped a beat. What if he had children already and didn't want more, that's why he reacted the day he did.

Being with Dale had made me question everything.

I realized quickly I liked it when he demanded things of me. I found a part of me needed it. Maybe that was why I had only been with one guy before him. Nothing could satisfy me.

I liked kink and, without making me feel ashamed, Dale embraced it. He had loved when I begged. When I pleaded for him to control me. I felt safe with him and once I let my walls down, only then did he push me away.

But no matter what Dale told me or did to me, I became lost when a part of me felt like everything made sense all at the same time.

After he made me come several times and I kicked him out, I was inspired. But I was also a damn idiot.

"Don't you dare cover what our child did."

His words taunted me because I had no idea what the hell they meant.

I went into my office and started painting. Knowing Dale was the reason for this new-found creativity, I embraced it.

After I finished my first painting, I called Josee and exclaimed how excited I was. Knowing she would come over, I hung up quickly before she could demand anymore answers. I needed to show her I was finally able to give her the work she needed me to do.

Stabbing the brush into the white and cream paint mixed with a little pink, I slid the brush over the blank canvas. I had no intention of designing something that could sell but after spending a couple hours with Dale, *he* was the reason I felt even remotely creative.

I was almost done with the second painting when the doorbell rang.

Rushing out to open the door, I saw Josee's questioning glance and pulled her inside. "Come, come, come. You have to see." I tugged at her arm and took the bottle of wine from her. Twisting off the cap, I took a long swig before thrusting it back in her arms.

"What the hell, Max?" she asked, a hint of amusement flashing in her gaze.

"Come." I tugged at her arm, dragging her to my home studio.

"You sounded different on the phone. What gives?" Josee followed me. It wasn't like I was giving her a choice really. *Could she walk any slower?*

"Jo," I whined. "Seriously."

She laughed. "Fine, fine." She picked up the pace.

Once we reached the back of the house, I pushed open the door and shoved her inside. "Look."

She glanced around the room, her gaze moving between the paintings and me. To the paintings, back to me. "You painted." She stepped further into the room, walking around each canvas. "You painted a lot."

"The two leaning against the wall are the newest and then the third I'm working on now. But they're new," I exclaimed, clapping my hands together. "They just poured from my fingers."

"How the hell did this happen? Are you high?" She came toward me and placed the back of her hand against my forehead. "Are you sick? You haven't painted this fast in months and you're on your third? When did you start?"

I swatted her hand away. "No, I'm not sick." I checked the time on the clock, letting out a slow breath. "I started painting three hours ago."

"Holy shit." Her eyes widened. "Even before all this …" —she waved a hand in front of her face— "stuff … you've never painted this fast."

"I've been inspired." I knew it would be weird seeing Dale again but I needed to thank him. Or maybe I would just show him. God, a couple orgasms later and I couldn't get him out from under my skin. But something struck me as odd. He never wanted anything in return.

"What happened to cause this?"

"Uh…" my cheeks heated. "It just came on suddenly."

"You're a horrible liar." Her grin widened. "Tell me. 'Cause whatever it was, needs to keep happening. Your gallery opening will have the best of the best there if you keep this up."

"Nothing happened. Nope. I was just inspired." I looked away and started organizing some paints on the table.

"It was Dale, wasn't it?"

My head whipped around. "How the hell could you know that?"

"For one, your shorts are on inside out and they're backwards," she said, pointing at my waist.

I looked down, my cheeks heating even more at the tag sticking out of the waist. "Oh … oops."

"So, did you fuck him?" she asked, sitting on the stool by the canvas.

I coughed, rubbing the back of my neck. "No. We just made out and I kicked him out after." My heart pained. Why the hell did I feel guilty? *Because it's not who you are.*

After everything he had done, I regretted telling him to leave my house. God, what was wrong with me?

Was I that addicted to him that I didn't care about my heart any longer? No. It was because I refused to put my heart in the game again. I wanted sex. Mind-blowing, life-altering sex. I didn't care what I had to do. I would fuck Dale again and show him exactly how it felt to be used.

****

(Dale)

I could still feel Max's body tightening around my fingers. It had been a couple hours since I had her coming undone beneath me, and it would be several more before I could shake this feeling of need from my mind. I scoffed, slamming my fist against the punching bag. I would *never* shake this feeling. I wasn't kidding myself. Max had always been my undoing. I was just too fucked up to see that. I was an asshole. First and foremost. But it drove me fucking mad I couldn't remember everything. I wasn't sure if it was a good thing or not. But I made a pact with myself that I would grovel and beg for her forgiveness.

Hopping from foot to foot, I danced with the heavy bag in front of me, slamming both of my fists into it until my arm muscles vibrated. My body hurt. It ached to the point of utter destruction. But the pain made me feel alive. For once in my life, I felt like I had a purpose. The Navy was my calling, but Max was my reason for surviving. I knew that now. Maybe I always had but my judgment was clouded by the other women, sex, and alcohol. It didn't make anything better that I didn't remember the other women. I got flashbacks now and again but the only person I came even remotely close to having a memory of was Max.

NUMB

After finishing my workout, I took a shower and headed over to the King's Harlots clubhouse. Working with Angel and the guys on renovating the club kept my hands busy and my mind focused. But it still wasn't enough. I hoped Max would be there. Not that she would talk to me in front of our friends. Shit. I was like a fucking schoolboy, needing to make sure she paid attention to me.

Once I reached the MC's building, I found my brothers huddled over a table lined with blueprints. The new recruits I had briefly met, Lian and Henley, noticed me first. They both nodded.

Angel's head popped up next. "Dale, just in time."

"Time for what?" *For you to threaten me again?*

His brows narrowed, his dark gaze focusing on me. His stare down became so intense, I had to look away.

"You get the shitty part of going up on the roof," Asher joked, clapping his large hand on my shoulder.

Thankful for the interruption from Angel thinking up ways he could beat my ass, I grinned at Asher. "You've jumped out of a damn plane but you can't go up on the roof?" I shook my head. "Pussy."

Asher grunted, punching me in the arm. "That shit is unstable."

"No, it's because you're a large fucker. The roof can't hold your weight." I climbed up the ladder. "Fatty."

"Fuck you." Asher laughed. "Just do as you're told for once in your life."

I rolled my eyes and climbed up the ladder leaning against the wall. We had been working on the club for the past couple of months. When multiple motorcycle clubs had been hit, this one was no exception. The girls had an even bigger target on their backs because they were women. They lived in a man's world, and as fucked up as it was, I almost wished the explosion would have put an end to their club. It wasn't right of me to think but I wanted Max safe. I wanted *all* of them safe. Too much shit had gone down in the short time we had known them.

"Hey, Dale," Coby said when he reached the top of the ladder. "You just hanging out or are you going to do some work?" He sat beside me, handed me a beer, and took a swig from his water bottle.

"Still not drinking?" I asked, nodding toward the bottle in his hand.

"No. Good thing Brogan isn't a drinker either." He stretched out his legs, lifting his face toward the heat of the warm sun.

"How's everything going?" As much as I hated talking about my own feelings, it never ceased to amaze me that I could talk to Coby about anything. It was like one look from him and all my feelings were sucked out of me. He should have been a psychologist.

Coby grunted.

"That good?"

"As each day passes, I love that woman more and more." He turned to me. "I will say this until the day I take my last breath, I do *not* deserve her. Not one fucking bit."

"What happened was *not* your fault, brother." I took a long gulp of the cool liquid, the carbonated bubbles tickling my nose. Fuck me, it tasted good.

"Maybe not but it doesn't mean I won't stop feeling guilty."

"True." I nodded. "I get it. I may not have what you have but—"

"You will."

My head snapped around. "What?"

"You will have what I have. Max loves you, and I know you love her."

My mouth opened and closed. Well, that was new. For once in my life, I had no idea what to say.

"Listen." Coby took a deep breath. "You both have been through a lot. Probably as much shit as Brogan and me. It may not be the same kind of shit but nonetheless, it's shit."

I chuckled.

His lips tugged at the corners but he kept his face impassive. "Love overrules all. Straight out. You don't have to admit you love her. She doesn't need that hearts and flowers shit. She needs *you*. Yes, you destroyed her heart but you have the rest of your lives to make up for it."

"How the *fuck* do I do that?"

"Take it one day at a time. Be there for her. Spend every moment you can with her. Show her you're not going anywhere. Have you talked? Have you actually had a conversation with her without it turning into a fight? Or something more?"

The back of my neck heated at our last fight turning into the hottest make out session I had ever experienced. "No," I muttered.

"Exactly. Don't push her, Dale. She may have been easy to control in the beginning but right now, she doesn't need your domination. She needs you to be her equal."

"We've always been fucking equal."

"No," he turned his body toward me. "Listen to me." Rubbing a hand through his short dark hair, he took a breath before looking at me.

And that was when I saw it. Pain. The agony hidden behind his eyes made my heart skip a beat. Even though he had told me everything, I still couldn't get over the guilt radiating off him. But I could also see it in Brogan. Whenever they were together, both of them were tentative around each other. I wasn't an emotional guy but fuck me, their issues hurt my fucking heart.

"I know what it's like to completely dominate someone," Coby continued. "Call it kink. BDSM. Whatever the fuck you want. The need to control only became stronger after Leah died but now, I don't need it as much. After what Brogan and I have been through, I realized it's give and take. Control Max in bed, but don't you dare start controlling her in her everyday life. Not unless she asks for it."

"Why not?" I asked, curiosity getting the best of me.

"Because right now she needs a friend. She has her sisters but it's different. Unless you're us. I can talk to you about anything." He frowned. "Which is odd as fuck."

I grunted, shaking my head. "Well … I never asked for your lectures."

"I'm not lecturing you," he snapped. "See? You don't listen." He poked a finger in the side of my head. "Max needs you to listen to her. Have you asked her how she felt?"

I slapped his hand away. "How can I when she won't even talk to me?"

"You're not dumb, brother."

"Are you telling me I should just not bother talking and wait for her to come to me first?"

"Ding, ding, motherfucker."

"You have some serious issues." I pulled back the rest of my beer.

"I do." Coby winked. "It's why my girl and I get along so well. We're both sick in the head."

I laughed. "Thank you for this and for not judging me." God, I felt like a girl.

"No thanks needed, Dale. Just get your head out of your ass and be there for Max. That's all she needs right now. The rest will fall into place. And stop acting like a woman."

I opened my mouth to give him a smart remark when the tiny hairs on my body stood on end. They vibrated and hinted, begging for that single touch from the woman who invaded my thoughts and dreams since the first moment I met her. It was all I needed. And that was when I heard her voice.

Max and her sisters stood around the trailer while the guys continued mulling over the blueprints. Brogan had laughed at one point and shoved them aside. The woman could draw up a building in a matter of minutes.

I glanced over at Coby.

His gaze was warm as he stared down at the woman who stole his heart just like he stole hers.

She caught his gaze, giving him a wide smile and a little wave.

Never would I have imagined that Coby would find someone who completed him in every single way imaginable.

I want that.

"You'll get it, brother," Coby whispered.

The back of my neck heated, not realizing I had spoken aloud. Clearing my throat, I went back to working on the roof. But not before I caught Max staring up at me.

***

(Max)

I could feel him watching me. Every nerve ending on my body came alive just at the mere thought of Dale. It was enough to drive a sane person mad.

After I had shown Josee my current work inspired by the man who tore out my heart, I headed to the club in need of a break. But my fingers were itching to get back to the blank canvas sitting on my easel.

"He's watching you," Brogan said, sidling up beside me.

"Yup. He sure is." Not like there was anything I could do about it.

"Have you both talked yet?" she asked, sticking her pencil behind her ear.

"If you mean by talk, did we yell and scream at each other and almost have sex? Then yes, we talked."

She sighed, her gaze drifting back up to the roof. "Sex is a way of communicating in some cases."

"You mean like with you and Coby?" I snapped my mouth shut at my outburst. "I'm sorry. That's none of my business."

"No." She waved it off. "Don't be sorry. It's hard to talk about. We have our moments but we're getting by." She pasted on a smile for reassurance. "Don't worry about us."

But I did. I wasn't there for her when she needed me most.

"Don't ..." She shook her head. "Don't look at me like that."

My eyes burned. "I'm sorry I wasn't there for you. When everything happened, I mean."

"It's not your fault. God" —she threw her arms around my middle— "I wasn't there for *you*," she cried, squeezing me.

I leaned down, pulling her in for a proper hug. "You're too damn short."

She laughed, sniffling a moment later. "We need to hang out more. Just the two of us. I feel like we haven't really gotten to know each other over the years."

"I would like that. I have another art showing coming up."

She pulled back, her smile widening. "We'll be there. All of us."

My back stiffened, my gaze shooting to the roof. When I saw that Dale was no longer working on top of the building, I frowned.

"Looking for me, kitten?"

I jumped at the smooth deep voice in my ear.

Dale chuckled, stepping in front of me. He leaned toward me, his mouth mere inches from mine. My heart fluttered. Just when I thought he was going to kiss me, he pushed a strand of hair behind my ear instead. That small touch sent a surge of heat racing through my body, forcing an ache between my legs.

I chewed my bottom lip, staring up into Dale's bright blue eyes.

"Well ..." Brogan cleared her throat. "I'll leave you be."

I took a step back, brushing a finger over my ear Dale just touched. "What do you want?"

His eyes twinkled. "To talk," he finally said.

My mouth fell open. That was *not* what I was expecting him to say. No smart remark. No dirty comment. No sexual innuendo. My stomach twisted. The disappointment sitting on my heart bothered me.

"Please," he added, his voice gentle.

I searched his face. For what, I wasn't sure. To laugh at me maybe. To tell me the joke was always on me. But instead, I decided to do what my grandmother would want. "Okay." I turned to walk away and stopped. "But not alone," I told him over my shoulder.

He raised an eyebrow. "And why not?" His voice dripped with a hint for something more. Something I had always wanted from him. Something he had given me in the beginning when it still wasn't enough.

"Because we fight and attack." I turned back around and walked to the picnic bench across the driveway. "At least if we're in the company of our friends, you can keep your hands to yourself."

"I'm all for a public display of affection, baby." He grabbed my hand, spinning me toward him. He leaned down to my ear, his hot breath brushing over my skin. "But I'll do what you ask and be a gentleman. For now."

Much to my surprise, he followed through on his promise and let me go.

"Dale," I said when he headed toward the picnic table.

"Let's talk," he grumbled, thumping down on the table hard and scrubbed his hands over his face.

"Fine." I sat beside him. "What's going on?"

"What are you talking about?" he asked, staring straight ahead.

"You're being cautious around me. I'm not fragile. I won't break." I knew I wouldn't because it already happened.

Dale sighed, letting out a soft curse. "I'm trying to be patient. I don't want to push you but fuck me, I love it when you push back."

My cheeks burned. "You were never like this in the beginning. You weren't controlling. Not in the way you are now."

"I want you to be my equal," he whispered.

My breath caught. "I don't know what that means."

"Neither do I." He turned his body toward me. "I need you to take me to her."

I jumped off the table. "I can't."

"Max."

"No." I spun on him. "You don't understand. I can't do it. I'm not strong enough."

"Like fuck you aren't." He took a step toward me but stopped when he caught movement behind me. "We're not done," he said, walking away.

I watched him go. I didn't stop him. I didn't run after him. I didn't demand answers and make him tell me he loved me. God, I was stupid.

"Max," Angel's booming voice came from behind me. "You good?"

"No." And that was the most honest thing I had admitted to in months.

CHAPTER ELEVEN

Dale

WHEN I SAW Angel approaching us, I hightailed it out of there as fast as I could. I didn't need his shit. I respected the hell out of him but when it came to Max, it was none of his fucking business.

I would make her mine again. No matter what our friends said. I would make them see we belonged together. That I needed her. That she was the only reason I woke up from the damn coma in the first place.

My walk turned into a jog until I was running at full speed. My lungs ached. My muscles jumped and twitched, protesting each movement but that only made me run faster and harder. If I could run myself into the ground, I would. I needed to get away. To run back in time where Max and I weren't fighting. I craved the day I could make her smile again. To see her look away shyly as I brushed a strand of hair behind her ear. And when she chewed her bottom lip, I would kiss her and take her breath like it belonged to me. I would fall at her feet, kissing the very ground she walked on before I ever let her go again.

Running faster, I poured every emotion into the pavement beneath my feet. It took months, but I finally admitted to myself that I had made a mistake. Even in the beginning, I never showed any interest I wanted a relationship with Max. That was one of the only things I could remember. I was confused, not being able to remember what was fact or fantasy. But I knew I had been scared. No one wanted me as a child, how could I fathom that a woman wanted me as a man? But it had been too late. How could we ever come back from it?

After a couple miles into my run, I slowed down to a full stop, breathing through the pain piercing my lungs. Fuck me, it felt good. So damn good to feel something other than this confusion. Not remembering everything was driving me insane.

I needed to see Dr. Santos.

Placing my hands on my knees, I bent over at the middle, taking deep breaths.

"You can't run away from your problems."

Squeezing my eyes shut, I took another breath before looking back at Coby standing behind me. I never heard him approach. The fucker was like a damn ninja.

"Maybe not but I'm determined to try," I muttered.

"She'll come around," was all he said.

I laughed. "I can't talk to her if I have Angel breathing down my neck. He's determined to keep us apart."

"That's not true and you know it." Coby took a step toward me. "He doesn't want you to hurt her again. You have to understand where he's coming from."

"How the hell can I, Coby?" I snapped, my fists clenching at my sides. "Max and I can't talk without fighting."

"And that's how some people get their points across but when you don't listen to what she has to say, that's why he steps in."

"How the fuck am I supposed to listen to her when she doesn't tell me shit?"

"Patience." Coby rubbed the back of his neck. "I don't like talking about what happened but I'm telling you this because clearly you aren't listening to me."

I winced. "Coby."

"No." He raised a hand, stopping me. "I love Brogan. She loves me. But sometimes talking doesn't do shit."

"What are you saying?" I asked, frowning.

"Sex, Dale. That's what I'm saying."

"You want me to fuck Max in order to get her to talk to me? Somehow, I don't think that would go over well." As much as I wanted to feel her body wrapped around mine, I wouldn't fuck her until she hinted first.

"I'm not saying …" Coby huffed, scrubbing a hand down his face. "What I'm trying to explain is that sex can be a way of communication."

I thought about that a moment.

"Sex can also be when you are most vulnerable," Coby continued. "And people who live the BDSM lifestyle need to communicate with each other. The Dom needs to know what his submissive likes. The sub needs to let their Dom know if they aren't comfortable in the situation and so on. They give and take. But sometimes, words aren't enough."

"Why, Coby, are you trying to tell me you're into bondage and sadism?" I asked, trying to lighten the mood.

Coby glanced my way. "That's for Brogan to know only."

"Touché."

"I'm just trying to tell you that sometimes words aren't always needed when speaking with your partner. Learn to listen to Max without hearing her voice."

I did know her. Didn't I?

But maybe Coby had a point. Although I didn't like holding back. This new-found urge to demand for her to listen to me almost pushed me over the edge. Every time we were near each other, I couldn't help but want to reach out and touch her. My body stirred, my cock growing at the mere thought of getting back inside her sweet body.

Fuck.

Clearing my throat, I started jogging in place and shook out my arms.

Coby chuckled. "Work it out, man. Before you lose your shit. You don't need to scare her away."

I didn't respond but something told me there was more to Max then she was letting on.

***

(Max)

Seven days. Seven. Damn. Days.

Dale had actually left me alone. He came to the club, helped the guys with fixing up the place and doing the renovations instructed by Brogan, but other than that, nothing. Nada. Zilch. I was losing my ever-loving mind. I needed his touch. His mouth on mine again. I needed to feel him growing beneath me as I took us both over that edge of powerful bliss.

I had no idea why Dale was being a gentleman. No. Not a gentleman. He outright *ignored* me.

Stabbing the paintbrush into the glob of purple paint, I slammed it against the canvas. The rough impact caused a little more paint to touch the canvas than I would have liked but it was an easy fix. Too bad my life didn't work the same way.

"Stupid men. Stupid, stupid men," I grumbled, hitting the canvas with the brush after each word.

"Are you going to call this painting the angry one?" Josee teased from behind me.

I swore under my breath, repeated my movements and continued stabbing the canvas.

She laughed. "Someone's sexually frustrated."

"You have no fucking idea," I muttered, my cheeks heating at my confession. It annoyed me how shy I was. I had only become sexually experienced because of Dale but talking about it was still embarrassing.

"Yeah." Josee pulled a stool up beside me. "I do."

I paused, glancing at her. "Really?"

She shrugged. "I'm not searching for it or anything but my hands can only do so much."

I laughed. "They're not cutting it anymore?"

"God no." She waved a hand in front of her face. "I don't want a relationship. But I wouldn't mind being used for a night."

"By Lian and Henley?" I waggled my eyebrows.

She threw her head back, a full belly laugh leaving her mouth. "I would cut off my left arm for that."

I couldn't handle one guy, let alone two. I also didn't think Dale could share. Not like he and I were together or anything. My heart picked up speed. I shouldn't worry about what he thought. He clearly didn't worry about my feelings in the beginning. My chest tightened to the point a vice-like grip squeezed my lungs. *Deep breaths, Max. Deep breaths.*

"Max." Josee touched my arm, her brows furrowing in the center. "Talk to me."

Talk. Everyone wanted to talk. Well, I just wanted sex. I didn't want to talk. I didn't want to say a damn thing. I wanted Dale to stop this hesitation of his and just fuck me already. "I'm fine," I whispered, breathing through the impending panic attack.

"What's going on?" she asked, giving my hand a gentle squeeze.

"Dale's been weird this week."

"Weird? Isn't he always?"

"No." I shook my head. "I mean, he hasn't paid any attention to me for the past week. He won't talk to me. As hard as it is for *me* to talk to him, I was getting used to our fights." I shrugged. "I know it doesn't make sense but it's the only time I feel connected to him. Which that doesn't make sense either since I'm ..."

"What?"

"I'm supposed to hate him."

"Oh, Max." Her lips pressed into a thin line. "Listen, I'm not the person to be giving relationship advice and I know you're hurting. But have you thought that maybe he wants something more?"

"After all of this time?" I paused. "Why would you think that?"

"I don't know but sometimes it can take a tragic accident for someone to realize the mistakes they made."

I thought a moment. "He hurt me."

"I know, honey." She smiled softly. "I really do. I'm sure you've been told this a thousand times already" —she rolled her eyes— "but be patient."

I bit back a scoff. If she only knew how patient I had really been. "I don't want to be patient anymore."

"I know." She patted my hand. "I should go and let you get back to abusing that canvas." She winked.

I smiled, zoning in on the painting before me.

She rose from the stool, gave my shoulder a light squeeze, and left the room but not before I heard her clear her throat. "Hey, Dale."

My heart jumped.

"You know who I am?"

"Oh, yes," she mumbled something more to him that I couldn't hear.

He laughed. "Well, it's nice to meet you too," came his smooth reply.

I smiled to myself, knowing she had threatened him in some way. I had made a promise with myself the next time I saw him, I would demand answers. Even though I had never given him them in return, I would command he give me something more.

Jo said her goodbyes as Dale walked into the room.

"Can we talk?" he asked, hovering near the door.

And the thought of demanding answers from him went out the window as I stared at him. I sighed, turning back around on the stool and continued painting. "Sure." I no longer had the strength to fight. If he didn't want anything to do with having a relationship with me, I wouldn't push him. I couldn't. For my own sanity.

"You're working on something new?" Dale asked, sitting on the stool beside me.

"Yeah," I answered, stroking the brush down the canvas. "I've been inspired." My cheeks heated remembering exactly how that inspiration came to be. "I have a showing coming up in a few months. Some famous artists are going to be there and Josee wants the best from me."

"I'll be there," he answered automatically.

I glanced at him. "Really?"

"Yes, kitten. Anything I can do to support you, I will." He smiled.

Who was this guy? Dale had always been sweet but something had changed since his coma.

"Why are you acting this way?" I asked, realizing as soon as the question left my mouth that it was probably more confusing then I intended.

His eyes narrowed. "What do you mean?"

I shook my head, a shaky laugh escaping my lips. "Why have you ignored me for the past week?"

He searched my face, the muscle behind his jaw twitching. "I would never ignore you."

I scoffed. "Could have fooled me, Dale. You haven't talked to me. You acknowledge me in passing but nothing more."

"I'm trying to be patient," he confessed.

"Patient?" It was my turn to be confused. "What do you mean?"

"You know what I mean, Max. I won't push you." His gaze fell to my mouth. "But I can only hold back for so long before …"

"Before what?" I asked, heat crawling up my back.

His eyes met mine. "Before I fuck you."

My breath hitched at the idea of having his powerful waist between my legs again. To feel him full and throbbing deep inside of me was something I had been yearning for since he woke up. "You can't hurt me again," I whispered.

"I won't hurt you."

"No, I'm saying you can't hurt me again because I won't let you."

"Max." He reached for my hand.

I couldn't. I didn't need him to touch me only for him to destroy me in the process. I rose to my feet. "I can't."

"Baby," he pleaded, linking his fingers in mine. "I'm … I'm sorry."

My breath caught in my throat. I stared down at him. It felt wrong but right at the same time. At this point, the power of control was being placed in my hands.

Dale brushed his fingers over my palm. He kissed my knuckles, letting his lips linger.

"Dale," I whispered, watching him.

His mouth moved to my wrist. His lips parted as he gave the soft skin there a gentle nip.

A surge of heat rushed through me. I couldn't do this but I wanted to. The argument in my head was settled.

I needed him.

Pulling my hand from his, I stepped between his legs and brushed my fingers down his cheek.

He only stared up at me, his gaze warming beneath my touch.

I realized then that he wasn't the man I had fallen in love with in the beginning. No. This man was shattered, broken by the mere gunshot that had almost taken his life.

I pushed my fingers through his dark blond hair, grazing them over the wound at the side of his head. He had been lucky. So damn lucky he came out alive with only a couple memories gone. Those could be replaced but *he* couldn't.

"I know I can't make up for what I've done," he finally said, breaking the intensity of the silence surrounding us. "I only wish I could remember so I can right the wrongs I've caused you. I will never forgive myself. I need you. Not to forgive me. I can wait for that for whenever you are ready." He cupped the backs of my bare legs, his thumbs brushing back and forth. His touch was soothing. His caress contradicted what was going on in him. His body was stiff, ridged, while his hands were soft. He was holding back.

"I need to hate you, but I can't." My fingers grazed down the length of his jaw. "I want to hate you. I've tried." My throat closed up, words lost on the tip of my tongue.

His eyes fluttered closed, his breath coming out in a whoosh. "I know. I don't expect anything less from you."

"Why?" I pulled from his grip when it only tightened around me. "You didn't want anything to do with me after I told you how I felt and that I was pregnant. Did the accident make you change your mind? Are you feeling guilty?"

"Of course I'm feeling fucking guilty, kitten." His body tensed. "I'm trying to remember. The doctor said I might never remember or that I can hit my head and everything will come rushing back. Who the fuck knows? But what I *do* know is even if you and I never end up together, I need to make up for what I've done."

My eyes burned at the desperation in his voice, the pleading behind his words that I would listen. But, how could I? My grandmother raised me to forgive but there was no way I could forget what he had done to me …

And our baby.

CHAPTER TWELVE

Dale

IF IT MEANT seeing Max smile again, I would cut off my arm and beat myself with it. I would let her hit me, claw at my skin, rip out my fucking soul just to hear her laugh.

I tried telling her how I felt, but when she stared at me with hesitation in her eyes and worry on her lips, I looked away. She didn't believe me. Hell, I couldn't blame her but it still hurt. It hurt worse than the bullet that almost killed me. It was a never-ending ache in my chest that traveled down to the pits of my soul. It was a constant reminder of how much I fucked up.

"You can't expect me to fall in love with you again just because you said you're sorry." Her voice was soft but filled with so much strength, it took my breath away. How this woman could think she was broken beyond repair was beyond me.

"I would never expect that of you." I wrapped my arms tighter around her waist, careful not to touch her beautiful ass for fear I would lose all control. "I'm only telling you how I feel," I confessed, leaning my head against her stomach. I inhaled, letting the scent of roses wash over me. I pulled her tighter, wishing with everything I was worth that I could dive inside her and stay there.

Brushing my nose back and forth, a soft purr escaped me.

"What if you get your memory back and you no longer feel this way, Dale?" she asked, running her fingers through the hair at my nape.

"I ..." Was that even possible? "All you can do is trust that I will still feel the same way as I do now."

"Trust you," she echoed. "You're asking me to trust you." She pushed my shoulders. "Let me go."

"Never." My head snapped up. "No matter how hard you fight, I'm not going anywhere. I will prove it to you."

She struggled against me. "Dale," she said on a sob. "I can't do this."

"You can." I brushed my nose along the cotton of her dress sitting against her abdomen and inhaled. The sweet scent of her washed over me. My body stirred, the darkness inside of me almost rearing its ugly head. My body wanted to fuck her while my mind wanted to talk.

"Dale, stop." She pushed harder, forcing me back. "We can't."

"We will."

She glared down at me.

The look was so dark and damaged; she couldn't hold my gaze because I had to look away. The pain and heartache I had caused her was there. It was so close, I could feel it.

"I think you should go," she finally said even though she was still in my arms.

"No." Coby told me not to push her but I couldn't stop myself.

"No?" She stopped struggling then. "After all you have done, you're sitting here and telling me no?"

"Damn straight." I had to force myself not to stand and get in her face. As much as I wanted to demand her reaction, I also didn't want to scare her away.

"What do you want from me?" she whispered.

I want to make you fall in love with me again. "Whatever you can give me."

"I don't know if there's anything left to give." She looked away, a lonely tear rolling down her cheek.

As soon as she broke eye contact, I rose to my feet and cupped her nape. Forcing her to look into my eyes, the next words leaving my mouth were the most honest thing I had ever said, "I'll take all of your pain ... all of the heartache I have caused you. I'll even take your hate. Just don't stop looking at me."

***

(Max)

He hurt you.

126

You love him.
You lost the baby.
He lost the baby too.

I was confused over my feelings for Dale. On one hand, I wanted to forgive him but on the other, I wanted to unleash them all and show him how I really felt.

"You hurt me," I told him.

"I know." He looked away.

"No." I pushed him. "Look me in the eyes, Dale. It's what you demand of me. I expect you to do the same."

He met my gaze then.

"You really hurt me. The doctors said many factors played into our baby dying but stress was a main one. I blame you." I shoved him. "I blame you for everything."

"I know," he repeated, swallowing hard.

I pushed him again. "I don't think you do."

His brows narrowed in the middle, his gaze turning to a darkness I had never seen before in him. But it didn't stop me. I couldn't control my actions any longer.

"You ripped out my soul," my voice cracked. "I loved you. I don't know why. You were an asshole but you still made me feel like the most beautiful woman in the world. I know you didn't want a relationship but I couldn't help falling for you. You did that, Dale. *You* made me fall for you."

"You are."

My breath hitched. "I am what?"

"The most beautiful woman in the world."

"*Shut up,*" I screamed, beating my fists against his chest. "Shut. Up. You don't get to tell me nice things while I break. You can't do that."

"I can and I will." But he didn't touch me. "You're beautiful. You're strong. You're the strongest fucking person I know."

"Stop," I yelled, slamming my fists against him.

"The only thing I want is you."

"No," I cried harder. "You don't mean that. You never meant that."

"I was stupid. I didn't know what I wanted but now I do."

"I can't do this with you." I gripped his hoodie, breathing in the scent of him. "I can't handle it."

Dale wrapped his arms around me, brushing his nose into the crook of my neck. He pulled me close, enveloping me in him. All I felt was Dale and it only made me cry even harder.

I struggled, fighting to break free. "Please stop."

"Sorry, kitten. It doesn't work that way." Fisting my hair, he tugged my head back before crashing his mouth to mine.

I gasped, sighing into his mouth. This was what I wanted. It was what I needed before but now, I was desperate for him.

Not giving me a chance to breathe, he thrust his tongue between my lips, tightening his hold on my hair.

I moaned, taking all of him in. This was what I was waiting for. Not the sweet man who ignored me. But the dominant one who controlled me with just a kiss. He had been holding back before but now, he pushed me against the wall and ground his lower body into mine. He reminded me that this was where I belonged and where I intended to stay.

Breaking apart the kiss, he stared down at me. "If I only kiss you and nothing more, I will still be the happiest man in the world."

Leaning my head against his chest, I took a deep breath and another. I wanted more. But the raging feelings sitting on my chest reminded me of the pain he caused me.

"I can't do this," I whispered. "I can't be in the same room as you without wanting your hands on me."

"I know," he said, his deep voice vibrating through his chest. "I've wanted you since I woke up."

"You had me, and you pushed me away." My hands moved of their own accord and pushed under the fabric of his hoodie. They grazed over his abs before reaching his chest. With my palm open, it splayed over his heart. The hard beating of the muscle pumped through my hand. "You broke me."

"I know I did, baby." He cupped my nape, running his fingers through my hair. "But I am here to fix what I fucked up."

I titled my head back, looking up at him. "Then kiss me."

CHAPTER THIRTEEN

Dale

MAX COULD TELL me to cut off my balls and I would. When she demanded for me to kiss her, I did. But I took it slow. Deep. Utterly consuming.

Brushing my lips along hers, I inhaled her sweet breath. Forcing her mouth apart with my tongue, I licked and stroked before diving into her sweet warmth.

A soft whimper escaped her throat. Her hands inched around my neck, pulling me closer.

I groaned, pushing my waist into hers, and pinned her against the wall.

"Dale," she whispered against my lips.

Releasing her mouth, I trailed kisses down the length of her jaw, licking and biting a path in its wake.

Max scratched her nails into my hair and tugged my head back before crushing her mouth to mine.

Pushing her harder against the wall, I grazed a hand under her dress up to her ass.

She tensed, breaking apart the kiss. "Dale," she pushed me. "I can't do this. You need to leave."

"Max." I palmed the erection sporting in my pants, trying to ease the painful hard-on.

"No," she screamed, spinning on me. "Leave. Get the fuck out of here. *Now.*"

Clenching my jaw, I leaned down to her ear. "As much as you deny it, you know you want me. And that pisses you off. Next time, I won't take no for an answer."

Her breath caught. "You can't make me do anything I don't want to do."

I smirked, cupping her jaw. "Ah, you see, baby ..." I kissed the corner of her mouth. "I *can* make you do whatever I want because I know you want it too."

"Fuck you," she bit out.

I chuckled, biting her bottom lip. "We keep trying that."

Max shoved me. "Get. Out."

In a quick move, I curled my hand around her nape and covered her mouth with mine. The kiss was desperate and filled with so much pain, it only made me kiss her harder and faster. She wouldn't let me fuck her. Well, I sure as hell would let her know that I wasn't done with her.

It took everything in me not to force her onto the couch and shove my dick inside of her. I understood she was upset but this back and forth shit between us was starting to piss me off. I got that I hurt her. I understood I would have to grovel for her forgiveness but teasing me was not the way to make that happen.

Breaking the kiss, I left Max's office filled with anger, a raging hard-on and a stupid grin on my face. She would come to me. I made sure that damn kiss would be the reason.

Coby told me to be patient but there was only so much patience I could muster before it all went to shit and I lost control.

"Dale. Wait."

****

(Max)

"Dale." I ran out of the room, stopping him before he left the gallery. "Wait."

He paused, turning back around to face me.

"I ..." My chest rose and fell. I had no idea what to say to him after all the hateful words had passed between us already. But I needed him. At that moment. At that time. I just needed to feel again. Him inside me. Moving. Hard and throbbing. Making me feel alive. I needed him to make me feel like a woman. Like a damn human being who wasn't distraught and hated life. I needed him to make me feel like I belonged. Even if it was only for a little bit.

I wanted him to feel the pain rushing through me.

"What, kitten?" He took a step toward me. "What do you want to say that you haven't said already?"

My hands clenched into fists at my sides. My body trembled, the need for him became strong until nothing else mattered. Not our feelings. Not the past. Present.

Or even the future. What I knew was that I needed him to be in the now with me.

Instead of talking like I knew we needed to, I ran toward him and jumped in his arms. Crashing my mouth to his, I forced my tongue between his lips.

A deep growl rumbled from his chest and vibrated right into my soul.

Pushing my fingers through his hair, I deepened the kiss.

Dale ran his hands beneath my dress, cupping my ass and pulled me against him. His erection pushed into my center, igniting that familiar burn I had for him since the very beginning.

I kissed him with everything in me. Like my life had depended on it. Like I needed his taste to survive. I didn't care about anything else. I didn't care about life or how shitty it had been to us and our friends. All I cared about in that moment was getting him inside of me and forcing me over that delicious edge. I wanted to use sex as an outlet for our pain and I knew the only way to get through it was to do it together.

Dale carried me to my office and slammed me up against the wall, kicking the door closed behind him.

My hands ran under his hoodie. Breaking apart the kiss for a mere second, I pulled the sweatshirt up and over his head. My fingers ran down the ladder of abs adorning his stomach. The muscles twitched beneath my touch.

Dale pulled the straps of my dress off my shoulders, brushing his mouth along the skin before sinking his teeth into the flesh.

The pain caused electricity to jolt right into my center.

Gripping the sides of my thong, he ripped it in half. Pushing the dress up my body, he pulled it over my head. He groaned, his scarred, tanned skin a contradiction to my pale form.

He licked his lips, peering down at my naked body. "So damn beautiful."

Circling my hands around his neck, I pulled his head down to meet the impact of my mouth. Running my fingers through his hair, I tugged his head back and fucked his mouth with my tongue.

He snarled, pushed my knee up to my chest, and thrust a finger hard inside of me.

I cried out, arching against him. "Dale," I whimpered against his mouth.

He broke the kiss, watching me.

I swallowed hard at the intense heat in his gaze.

Inserting a second finger, he thrust deep and stroked my clit with his thumb. "You're going to come for me."

I nodded even though it wasn't a question. Biting my bottom lip, I gripped his shoulders, moving my hips back and forth against his hand.

"That's it, Max. Ride my fingers. Show me what you're going to do to my cock." He leaned a hand against the wall beside me, towering over me. He pulled his fingers free from my body, brushing them from my core to the tight spot between my ass.

I gasped, tightening my legs around him.

In one full sweep, his fingers brushed back to my clit. "So fucking wet."

Much to my surprise, he brought his hand up to his mouth and sucked his fingers between his lips. He moaned, swallowing the taste of my body. "Do you want a taste of this sweetness, Max?"

A breath left me on a whoosh.

Dale thrust his fingers back into my lower body, once, twice, before bringing them up to my mouth. The acidic scent of my pleasure wafted into my nose. Brushing his finger over my bottom lip, he rubbed the juices from my body onto my mouth.

"Kiss me," I demanded, tilting my head.

His mouth covered mine, the evidence of my desire for him fusing between our joined lips.

"What do you want?" he asked, his deep voice rough and laced with promises of undying pleasure.

"More." I glanced down between us, watching him reach into his pants and pull out his straining cock.

"Not good enough." He leaned his forehead against mine. "Tell me what you want."

"Fuck me."

"Eyes on me, kitten," he demanded. "Watch me."

My gaze snapped back to his.

"I need you to look at me." His hold on my jaw tightened. "Understand?"

I nodded. The sound of a tinfoil package sent a shiver down my spine.

"I'm only going to ask this once." He licked down the length of my jaw to my ear. "Are you sure?"

"Yes," I breathed.

He leaned his head from side to side, the sound of a crack reverberating around the room. Keeping hold of my jaw, he grabbed under my knee with his free hand and thrust into me so damn hard, I screamed.

He paused, keeping his gaze on mine. He looked at me like he was peering into my soul until he found what dark kinky desires I had so he could use them for his own pleasure.

Dale's cock was thick and full, throbbing inside of me, but he didn't move. He was so damn still it made me twitchy.

I cried out in frustration and began moving my hips.

His smirk turned into a wicked grin as his hold on my jaw only tightened while I slid my body up and down his cock. He wanted me to show him how much I needed him. I thought I had been in control but really, he was the one controlling me the whole damn time.

My thigh muscles burned, my heels dug into his ass but it only made me move faster and harder. I gripped his hips, riding and taking from him what I wanted. What he had been desperate to give me these past couple of weeks. He felt good. Damn good. And when he still didn't move, I took it upon myself to give us both the pleasure we craved.

"That's it, baby," he kissed my mouth. "Ride my cock. Take from me what I can give you. Take what you need."

My movements grew fast, hard. *Rough.*

Our breathing picked up. His dick swelled. My pussy clenched down around him.

A tingle spread from my toes to my center until his name left my lips on a hard cry.

Only then did he move.

Dale dropped me on my feet, turned me around and thrust back inside of me so hard, another release shattered through me.

His rough calloused hands, cupped my thighs, spreading me open for him. His hot breath scorched the side of my face, his mouth moving gently over the soft spot just under my ear.

I kept my hands against the wall, pushing back against him and met him thrust for every violent thrust.

"I can feel your cunt dripping," he said, his rough voice sliding over my skin. "Your sweet juices are running down my balls, kitten. Is this what you wanted? All of this damn time?"

"Yes," I whimpered, slamming my ass back against his hips.

"Fuck, Max. You feel … damn good," he panted, his fingers digging hard enough, they were surely going to cause bruises. But I didn't care. I craved the feeling of his marks on my body.

"Harder, Dale," I begged. "I need it."

Hooking an arm around my middle, he lifted me and fisted my hair with his free hand. "Of course you need it," he snarled in my ear. "I'm the only man who can make you feel this way. As much as you hate me, you crave my cock deep inside you. Don't you?" He thrust harder.

I cried out. "Yes."

"Then come again." He pulled my head back and cupped my throat. "Come so damn hard I smell like you for days."

***

(Dale)

Max came. Hard. Violent. Her screams were so fucking loud, they forced an orgasm to rip out of my balls and shoot straight into the condom wrapped around my dick. Releasing her suddenly, I pulled off the condom and wrapped my hand around the straining muscle while I finished my release on the flesh of her ass.

Her eyes widened.

The release was hard. I bellowed out her name, letting out a snarl when she pushed back against me.

Righting my pants, I brushed a finger through the cum on the cheek of her rear and shoved it into her mouth.

She moaned, closing her lips around my finger.

"That's right, kitten." I kissed her neck. "Taste me."

She licked and sucked, lapping it up like an ice cream cone. "I've missed your taste."

I grinned and pushed her to her knees. Brushing my fingers down her cheek, I pinched her chin. "Then be a good girl and *suck*."

CHAPTER FOURTEEN

Max

MY BODY BURNED with desire for the man deep inside me. It had been hours since our moment at the gallery. Dale had come back to my place and as much as I knew we needed to talk, right then I just wanted to feel. I had shut off all my emotions and wrapped myself around him. Feeling. Needing. Craving.

"Max." Dale brushed his mouth over mine as he shuddered against me.

Running my hands down his sweat-soaked back, I placed a final kiss on his mouth before crawling out from beneath him. I got dressed, throwing on shorts and a tank top, and sat on the edge of the bed.

"I need a smoke," Dale muttered, rising from the bed.

"You don't smoke," I reminded him.

"I know. Still need one though." He came around to my side of the bed and pinched my chin. Tilting my head back to meet his mouth, he smacked a hard kiss on my lips. "Hmm … so damn delicious."

I shivered. My scent was all over him. My taste on his tongue. But it was only that. Sex. Nothing more. This wasn't what I wanted but it was what I needed at the same time.

"You should go," I told him, itching to get back to a new painting.

"You kicking me out of your bed, baby?" He brushed his mouth down the length of my jaw.

"Yes." I gently pushed him back and rose from the bed. "I need to paint."

He grunted, smacking me gently on the ass. "Fine."

My body heated, the slight tingle of pain spreading through me like fire. "Come back later?" I blurted, grabbing hold of his arm.

Dale did up his jeans, leaving the top button undone.

I swallowed hard at the treasure trail that dipped below his belt.

"I will come back until you push me away for good." He kissed my head, leaving the room as he threw his hoodie on over his head. "Oh, and Max?" he called from the hallway.

"Yeah?"

"This will be the only time you'll get a chance to kick me out of your bed." He peeked his head into the room, his gaze roaming down my scantily-clad body. "Remember who your pussy belongs to." And with that, he left the room.

I sighed, scrubbing my hands up and down and my face.

What the hell was I doing?

I was playing with my heart and I damn well knew it would be me that got hurt in the end.

***

(Dale)

It had been a month of nonstop sex.

Screams, passion, and the delicious begging I had come to crave from Max's lips. I knew she was using me but I was using her body to tell her how I feel. Both of us needed each other to feel something. Anything other than the pain we both dealt with on our own but could never share. I had no issues talking to Coby but when it came to the woman I was fucking—the words froze on my tongue.

We used each other to comfort the pain we felt, channeling it, and unleashing it through our bodies.

Max and I were both stubborn that talking about it only turned into fighting which turned into sex. I could still hear her screams and it had been hours since I left the warmth of her sheets. I had made good on my promise. She never kicked me out of her bed again.

We didn't talk but like Coby suggested, I made sure to show her how I felt through my body. Every word I thought, I unleashed them onto her skin with a kiss. A bite. A lick.

Every time we were done, she tried kicking me out; using the excuse she needed to paint. And then I would kiss her and the thought of painting left her when she kissed me back. It wasn't right. She needed to do her job and my dick was going to fall off but I also needed to make her feel good. It was the only thing I looked forward to doing anymore. I was medically discharged from the Navy. I worked for Angel's construction company as a side job. I wasn't good at anything else.

I fought. I killed. I fucked.

I was finally ready to admit how I loved Max then and loved her still. But I wouldn't tell her until I felt she was ready to hear it. I didn't want those three little words that impacted such a punch to hinder any progress I had made with her. Even if it was just sex.

My phone rang, jarring me from my thoughts. Grabbing it off the table, I hit speaker. "Yeah."

"Meeting at the club," Coby said and hung up.

My body vibrated knowing I would see Max in a couple of minutes. As much pain as I was in from the excessive amount of sex we had been having, my dick still grew.

I put on my running shoes, locked up my apartment, and headed to the club. It was only a couple of blocks away but the closer I got, the tenser I became. Every inch of me came alive over seeing Max. We spent the last month together, and I still couldn't get enough.

Once I arrived at the clubhouse, the hair at the back of my neck tingled. My muscles tensed. Scanning the area, I didn't see anything out of the ordinary. Hell, no one was around. The tingle shot down my arms and straight into the tips of my fingers. I needed to fight. And hard.

"Hey, brother."

I jumped, spinning around to find Coby standing at the doorway into the building.

"What's up?" he asked, taking a step toward me. The guy was good. He was scanning our surroundings. If I didn't know him well enough, I wouldn't have seen it. The slight flick of his eyes looking past me was fast, even *I* almost missed it.

"Nothing." I rubbed the back of my neck. "Something seems …"

"Off," he finished for me.

"Yeah." I followed him into the club, clenching and unclenching my fists, trying to ward off the impending rage traveling through me. "What's going on?" I asked when I saw Max standing by the bar. Every nerve ending came alive at the mere sight of her. She wore a sexy as fuck white dress I couldn't wait to dive beneath.

She glanced my way, her tongue peeking out to lick along her bottom lip.

My cock grew, remembering where that tongue had been earlier that morning.

She winked, turning around on the stool to go back to her conversation with Brogan.

Fuck. Me.

"You might want to take care of your issue before seeing Angel." Coby raised an eyebrow.

"What issue?"

He pointed at my waist.

I looked down, noticing the wood I was sporting in my pants. "Shit." I adjusted myself.

Coby chuckled, shaking his head, and clapped a hand on my shoulder. "I know how it is, brother."

I grunted.

"We're meeting in five," Angel said, walking by us without giving me a look.

"Angel," I said, following him.

He stopped. "Yeah."

"We good?"

His brows narrowed. "We are, but hurt her again and we'll revisit that question."

"I appreciate you watching out for her but what happens between Max and I is none of your fucking business."

"No?" He stepped into my face. "When her being upset effects my *pregnant* fiancée, you better damn well believe it is *my* business."

"I love you, and I respect you, *brother*" —my lips pulled back, baring my teeth— "but right now, I don't give a shit what you or anyone else thinks. I'm trying to do what I can for Max and make up for the wrong I've done without having you breathing down my neck. So, Angel? You can *fuck* right off." Instead of waiting for his answer, I turned around and headed back out to the main part of the club.

"Dale?" Max came up behind me, placing her hand gently on my arm. "You okay?"

Taking a breath and then another, I relaxed my body and pushed a strand of hair behind her ear.

She shivered, giving me a small smile.

My heart jumped. "I am now."

CHAPTER FIFTEEN

Max

I WAS USING him.

He knew it.

He was using me.

I knew it.

When the paintings started flowing out of me after Dale and I had sex the first time, I kept on seeing him.

I pushed out five paintings in one night before calling Josee.

She was happy.

I was exhausted.

NUMB

The gallery showing was coming up soon. I had asked Josee to push it back a couple of weeks so I could add more paintings to the set. She didn't complain once knowing some big named artists were coming from New York. Her focus all along had been to get my paintings into every major museum in the world.

My thoughts were forced back to the present when I saw Dale following Angel down the long hall leading to the spare rooms.

It wouldn't end well. I appreciated Angel's concern for my wellbeing thanks to Jay but this wasn't really any of his business.

We had all met up to talk about Tyler Bone getting kicked out of Dante's Kings, Jay's father's club. Tyler had been her ex, the vice-president of the MC and a douchebag.

I also needed to get filled in on everything I had missed over the past couple of months.

"Can I hold your hand?"

The deep smooth voice came from beside me.

Dale sat in the chair, running his hands down his jean-clad thighs before looking my way once again. "Max."

He wanted to hold my hand.

I hesitated. After all we had been doing together for the past month, holding hands should have been easy. But it felt like all my emotions were laid out before me. Like my heart had split open only to have Dale laugh at me again.

"Please," he said, keeping his hands folded in his lap.

Taking a deep breath, I reached a hand out to him.

He grabbed hold of it, kissed my knuckles, and linked his fingers between mine.

"Are you and Angel good?" I asked, cupping his hand. My hand was small compared to his but that touch alone made me feel safe. Like maybe my heart *could* heal.

"Everyone is worried I'll hurt you again," Dale grunted. "I would have kicked my ass long ago if I were him."

"I appreciate everyone looking out for me but it's no one's damn business."

He turned to me. "What are you saying, kitten?"

"I'm saying I can handle you." I sat up straighter. "Everyone just needs to chill the fuck out."

"You can only handle me because it's what I want." He pinched my chin, brushing his thumb over my bottom lip.

"What do you mean?"

His eyes twinkled with mischief. "It means" —he kissed my mouth, giving my bottom lip a gentle bite— "that if we were alone, I'd have you bent over this table. Maybe have your hands behind your back." He groaned. "Yup. Definitely behind your back."

"Dale," I breathed.

He grinned. "I know you crave that dominant side of me, kitten. Just like I crave your submission."

I looked away, my cheeks heating.

"Eyes on me," he snapped. "Or do I have to throw you over my lap and spank your ass for defying me?"

"Don't be an asshole," I said, glaring at him.

He hooked an arm around my shoulders, brushing his fingers down my cheek before gripping my jaw. "Remember who you belong to."

"Myself."

***

NUMB

(Dale)

Her word caught me off guard. Of course she belonged to herself. I wouldn't have it any other way but she needed to know that *I* also owned her. Even if it was just her body.

Max chewed her bottom lip, held our joined hands in her lap, but kept glancing back and forth around the room. Every now and again she would push a strand of loose hair behind her ear and munch on her lip like she was starving.

"What's wrong, baby?" I asked, giving her hand a light squeeze.

She let out a shaky breath, her cheeks turning a light shade of pink. "I don't want anyone losing their shit for us holding hands."

I frowned. "Why would they?"

"I know people … our friends … think I'm crazy for …"

"For this?" I asked, waving a hand between us.

She nodded slowly.

I sighed, rubbing the back of my neck. "Let's worry about making each other happy first before anyone else."

"Okay." She searched my face, pulling her hand free from my grasp.

An unexpected growl rumbled from my chest at the loss of her touch against mine.

Max's head whipped around, her eyebrow raising. "Don't push me."

Fuck. Leaning my arm on the back of her chair, I rubbed the scruff on my jaw. "Fine, but don't expect me to be nice about it."

"I wouldn't have it any other way," she whispered. Her voice had been soft, I wasn't sure if I even heard her correctly.

My body hummed. Grazing a finger down the side of her neck, I savored the sound of her breath catching. Her eyes fluttered closed, her mouth parting on a silent sigh.

If we didn't have a damn meeting, I would make good on my threat and bend her over right there.

Just as that thought slid through my mind, everyone started rolling into the room. I'd hoped we would finally get some answers. Max and I needed to be filled in on what the hell had been going on but I really wanted to take her home and fuck her until she couldn't breathe.

"I wish I could bring you all good news," Jay said, lowering her swollen body down into the seat at the head of the table. She let out a slow breath, her hands rubbing her pregnant stomach. "Tyler is causing shit," she added, placing her phone on the table. "Before we start, has anyone seen him or been in contact with him?"

A resounding *no* sounded around the room.

"Tell me now," Jay continued. "Because if I find out he's made contact, I won't be able to help you."

No one changed their answer.

"Fine." She let out a slow breath, placed a phone on the table, and pressed a button. "Okay, Daddy, go ahead."

"Thanks, nugget," Brian Gold's deep voice boomed from the small speaker. He cleared his throat. "The fucker is causing a rumble through the clubs. He's saying we kicked him out of the club without any reason at all. Most of you know we can't do that. Fuck.

Jay, this is not going to end well for him. Or for us. If he gets those fuckers on his side, it could be a full-on war. I know he's a fucking bastard but ..."

She shifted in her seat. "I know. Do you think he's in on this human trafficking shit?"

"Jay," her father paused. "Yeah. I do."

The air became thick. We had all been thinking the same thing. Just no one said it. Tyler Bone was a dick.

"All right." Jay let out a breath. "We need to get this shit dealt with before your grandbaby is born."

"You have my motherfucking word. As soon as that baby is born, you will have security so far up your ass, you won't be able to take a piss without someone watching," her father's voice boomed through the speaker of the phone.

Nods and grunts of agreement went around the room.

"I wouldn't expect any less, Daddy." Jay leaned back in her chair, glancing at Max.

Brian was right, though. We would all take care of the baby and Jay. Angel wouldn't have to worry about a damn thing.

Angel whispered something in her ear.

She smiled, patted his hand, and kissed him fully on the mouth.

He sighed, shaking his head.

The jealousy over what she used to have with Tyler had been imminent in the beginning but Angel fought for control over that. I was pissed at the guy but they were perfect for each other.

A shadow of darkness slid into the room as a cloud passed over the afternoon sun. It amped up the jealousy I had been feeling and sent my stomach into knots.

Scrubbing a hand up and down my face, I grabbed hold of Max's hand. I needed her strength.

Much to my surprise, she didn't pull away. Instead, she pushed her chair closer to mine and held my hand in her lap.

"I don't care what anyone says," she mumbled, turning to me. "I need this."

I wasn't exactly sure what that meant but before I could ask any more questions, a throat cleared.

I glanced up, catching everyone watching us.

"Are you with us?" Jay asked, looking between us both.

"Yes." Max shifted in her seat, a flush of red sliding up her neck. "Sorry."

"No worries, Maxine," Brian said from the phone. "Anyway, as I was saying, we were able to scrub off the tattoo and de-patch Tyler but after that, he lost his shit. It was odd as fuck. He's a dick but he was always calm. He knew it was coming. His reaction took us all by surprise and I'm man enough to admit, I let my guard down."

"What does he mean when he says they scrubbed off the tattoo?" Asher asked from the other end of the table.

"Exactly how it sounds," Meeka told him. "Not all clubs have the tattoos. We don't. But if someone is kicked out of a club who does have them, no matter if it's voluntary or not, the tattoo on their back gets scrubbed."

"By what?" Asher frowned.

"It's usually something sharp like a steel wool pad," Henley answered.

"How the fuck would you know?" I asked him, a cold shiver racing down my spine at the mere idea of someone scratching a tattoo off my skin.

"I don't think you want me to answer that question." Henley's gaze snapped to mine. "Do you?"

Lian elbowed him, giving him a small shake of his head.

And that only made Henley grin.

My eyes narrowed. Fucker was just as bad as Coby and Stone with his secrets.

"Um … okay, drama queens." Jay shook her head. "It's not that bad. If you're a bad boy or girl, yes, you get scrubbed but usually the tattoo gets inked over."

Meeka giggled which in turn earned a glare from Asher. He whispered something in her ear forcing her laughter to come to a raging halt. Her cheeks turned pink, a small smile forming on her lips.

I would bet my left nut he had told her some form of punishment would happen later over her teasing him. My body stirred at the mere idea of throwing Max over my lap and spanking her delicious ass.

As if she could hear my thoughts, Max glanced up at me, her cheeks reddening.

I smirked, placing my arm on the back of her chair, and brushed my thumb up and down the length of her neck.

She sighed, leaning into my touch.

Jay was talking, Brian's voice was coming from the speaker on the phone, but all I could concentrate on was Max not pushing away from me.

It was that small moment, that small touch in time where nothing else mattered. With my thumb against her neck, pressing and massaging, showing her what the feelings I had for her were. I loved her. I was so damn deep in love with her, it made my heart physically hurt and my chest tighten.

"Dale."

"Hmm?" I looked up, finding the whole room looking at me. "Sorry." I cleared my throat, a flush of heat traveling up the back of my neck. Fuck, this woman distracted me. She was my undoing. I didn't care about the organization or the shit Tyler had done. My main focus was getting Max to forgive me.

Coby's lips twitched.

Max smiled, her hair falling to the side. She pushed it behind her ear.

My blood stirred.

"What were you saying?" I asked, keeping my gaze on her hair. I licked my lips, my stomach twisting. What the hell? I was jealous over her hair. Fuck my life.

I shook myself and sat forward. "Sorry." I locked eyes with Angel. "Go ahead."

He grunted, shaking his head.

Jay looked between Max and me, her brows furrowing into a deep frown.

A tremor shot up the back of my spine. We locked eyes.

She raised her brows, challenging me.

I only stared back. Grabbing ahold of Max's hand, I brought it up to my mouth and kissed the back of her knuckles.

Jay glared.

Max gasped.

Angel swore.

And I grinned like a fucking idiot.

"Nugget? Jay? Are you still there?" Brian's deep voice boomed around the room.

"Yeah," she muttered, her gaze sliding from mine. "Continue."

"Everything all right?" he asked.

"Yes," she muttered, rubbing her swollen belly. "Go ahead."

Max shifted beside me, a small sigh leaving her mouth.

Don't worry, kitten. I'll make up for it. I'll make up for everything.

CHAPTER SIXTEEN

Max

DALE LET IT be known, publicly, that he and I were … in a relationship? Fucking? Were more than friends? Who the hell knew anymore what we were doing. But his little show forced a bitterness to come to light in my best friend. She was concerned he would hurt me again. Both of us knew if that happened, I would never be able to come back from it. I wasn't one to depend on a man or base my actions and feelings on them but I had fallen in love with Dale hard. And fast. So damn fast, my head spun and my body trembled with a need for him that shouldn't have been real.

I pulled away from Dale and crossed my arms under my chest. The battle between my body and my feelings for him turned into a full-on war.

I needed control.

I needed to put distance between us.

His eyes burned into the side of my head. But that didn't stop him. He placed his big hand on my thigh, giving it a firm squeeze.

"You're mine, kitten," he whispered in my ear, sliding his hand down my leg and under the hem of my dress.

I swallowed hard. While everyone was focused on what Brian had been saying, all I could think about was Dale's hand moving under my dress. But I didn't stop him, did I? I could have. I could have shoved him away and demand for him to leave me alone. It would have caused a scene. Angel would kick his ass. Coby would defend him. And I would cry like the fucking pussy I was. So, I let him continue. No matter how hard I tried not to, I gave in. Because his touch on my skin was the only thing that made me feel normal.

He moved his chair closer to mine and kicked his foot against the leg of mine. I was shoved forward, my lower body hidden beneath the table.

My heart sped up. I had no idea what he planned on doing but I could sense he didn't like that I pushed him away. I would be punished for it—and God help me—but it made my body burn for him.

With rough calloused fingers, he slid them up my thigh to the spot I needed him most. As much as I knew this shouldn't happen, not when we were discussing … Hell, I didn't even know what we were talking about anymore. My mind fizzled out at the feel of Dale owning me with just his hand. I shouldn't give in but I wanted to. I needed it.

Cupping his hand, I pushed it higher up my thigh.

"That's right, baby," he said low enough for only me to hear. "I got you now."

And he did. When his finger slid beneath the fabric of my panties, I leaned back in the chair and gave him my submission. All of me belonged to him whether I cared to admit it or not. I knew that now.

His fingers caressed.

My hips bucked. My heart raced. My skin became clammy.

No one in the room had any idea what was going on beneath the table.

As fast as the pleasure started, it soon turned into a dull roar. My body ached for this man sitting beside me.

Dale spoke when needed, answered questions when they were directed at him all the while fingering me and bringing me over that delicious edge.

I couldn't understand how he was in such control when I was ready to combust.

With one final flick of his finger, I coughed, the fast release rushing through me. I pushed his hand but that didn't stop him.

He smacked my hand away and grabbed my inner thigh.

Now that I could finally focus on the meeting itself, I smoothed down my dress as best I could with Dale's hand being in the way.

"Will Tyler come after you?" Jay asked, shifting her body in her seat.

Brian scoffed. "No. The guys won't leave me alone. I'm well protected, nugget."

"Have you heard anything about Charles or …" She glanced at Brogan. "Zane?"

"Charles is still a piece of shit and Zane … Fucking fucker has been off the radar since your girl raided his place and killed his sister." Brian covered the mouthpiece, his voice muffled as he spoke to someone in the background. "Listen," he said a moment later, "I have to go. But keep me posted. All of you. I want to know as soon as any of those bastards are in Brogan's chair." And with that, he hung up.

The air in the room became thick over Brian's words. We all knew Brogan had killed Tina Birtch. The reason as to why, besides the fact she was a sick bitch, hung over our heads. It became the elephant in the room until Jay ordered for us to leave and go on with our day.

"It doesn't make sense why Charles has kept himself hidden all of this time," I said to Dale as everyone filed out of the room.

Dale rose to his feet, looking down at me before grabbing my hand. "He's a bastard who likes fucking with our heads."

Maybe. "Dale?"

He leaned forward, his sapphire eyes piercing me straight in the heart. He cupped my nape, running his fingers through my hair and tugged my head back. "How does it feel?" he asked, kissing my chin.

All thoughts about Charles escaped my mind as Dale moved closer. "How … how does what feel?" I placed my hands against his chest, feeling the pulse of his heart beating hard against my palm.

"Knowing I made you come in front of our friends."

My cheeks heated. Shoving out of his grip, I stepped around him.

"Max," he called out for me.

"No." I left the room and spun on him, not caring in the least if anyone saw or heard. "I can't do this with you."

"That's funny because we haven't done anything yet." A wicked glint flashed in his gaze when he brushed his fingers beneath his nose and inhaled. "Mmmm ... I can still smell you."

I threw my hands up in the air, ignoring the flush of heat racing through my body. "You are so frustrating."

"Maybe." His face turned serious then, all teasing aside about how he made me feel. "But I know you enjoy it. You enjoy the unpredictability of it all. I push. You push back. You're just too damn scared to admit it."

I stared at him, my mouth agape when a laugh left my mouth. "I'm scared." I shook my head. "We're doing this now? All right." I could feel eyes on me. I had forgotten we weren't in fact alone. But the words tumbled from my mouth, not caring in the least who was around to hear them. "You're damn right I'm scared. I'm fucking terrified. I want you but I hate you and even then, I don't know if that's true."

"Max." His face softened but then something switched behind his warm gaze. It went from caring to deadly in a matter of seconds. "I'd be careful if I were you."

"What ..." A warm body stepped up behind me and I realized that Dale wasn't talking to me.

"What are you going to do about it?" Angel placed a hand on my shoulder, gently nudging me to the side.

But I stood my ground. This was between Dale and me. "Angel, it's fine. I can handle this."

"Can you?" he asked. "Because after all these months, I really don't think you can."

"What ..." I was taken aback. Angel never put his two cents in. Ever.

"Angel." Jay came up beside him, glancing my way quickly before looking back up at her fiancé. "Come. Let them sort it out. You *will* sort it out this time, won't you?" she asked me, her tone clipped.

My heart started pounding, my ribs feeling like they were closing in on themselves. "I'll deal with it," I muttered.

"Why the hell are you ganging up on her?" Dale grabbed my arm, pulling me back against him.

Angel rolled his eyes. "You only care because you're getting your dick wet again."

"Angel," Jay scolded, slapping his arm.

"It's the fucking truth," he snapped. "Listen, I'm done with these games. Either you two do something about your situation or leave each other the fuck alone."

"All of you need to mind your own business," I said, my voice firm. "How we handle our shit is between us. No one else."

"Max." Jay reached for me.

"No. I'm done, Jay. I love you but I need you guys to leave us the hell alone."

"You can't handle your shit," she cried. "Look at you two. You're strung the fuck out."

"You know what?" I shook my head. "Have you ever thought that maybe sex is an out? At least it helps us feel something other than the pain over our baby dying."

Jay snapped her mouth shut.

Exactly.

"Listen." Angel rubbed the back of his neck. "I know it's not our business but—"

"No, Angel." Dale moved me behind him. "Max is right. It's none of your business. You're not my Team Leader anymore, remember? That all went to shit when I got fucking shot. Which also happened under *your* care."

"Dale," I said gently, grabbing hold of his arm. "Let's go."

He pulled from my grasp, taking a step toward Angel.

"You don't think I feel fucking guilty over that?" Angel got in Dale's face, their noses mere inches apart. "You don't think we all do? Who the fuck was there when you woke up? Who dropped everything and told our boss to go fuck himself when told to stay on the mission? Me, Dale. It was all me. Not the other guys. Not your best friend. Not the woman you're in love with. *Me.*"

The rest of Vice-One circled around us.

"You didn't do shit for me," Dale threw back. "You were only there because you felt guilty. Coby had his own shit to deal with. And Max has nothing to do with this."

The fact he never denied being in love with me sat heavily on my heart. I couldn't deal with that now but my hands shook just the same. It also sent an unexpected flutter racing through my heart.

Jay moved to my side and grabbed my hand.

I looked up at her.

I'm sorry, she mouthed.

NUMB

I gripped her hand. There was no reason for her to be sorry. I had been the bad friend and now we were dealing with our … well, her fiancé and Dale.

Maybe Angel was right. Maybe we needed to go our separate ways.

***

(Dale)

Angel was so close to my face that I could see the gold specks in the brown of his eyes. His hot breath fanned over my face, the tension between us rising as each second past.

"What the fuck do you want from me? Of course I felt guilty. You all were under my care. And look at what the fuck has happened already." The veins in his neck popped, a red hue showing beneath his skin.

My muscles jumped. I was picking a fight with a fucking predator but I couldn't stop myself.

"You going to hit me?" I asked him, clenching my fists at my sides.

"You want me to."

It wasn't a question but I nodded anyway. I had been itching for a good fight since waking up.

"I'm not fighting you but I refuse to stand by and let you hurt her. Again."

"That's none of your business, *brother*, and you know that. Do you see me getting in your shit? Do you see any of us doing that? No. That's because it's not our fucking business." I went to walk around him and back to Max when Angel sidestepped in front of me. My blood hummed in my ears, the drive to fight was almost like sex. It was a euphoric high and as soon as the first punch was laid, the darkness was released. "Move," I demanded, my voice coming out deeper than I intended.

"Or else what, Dale? You going to run from your problems like you've done for the past couple of months? You can't always fuck your way out of your mess." Angel was egging me on now, and it was starting to really piss me off.

"Angel." Coby clapped a hand on both of our shoulders, separating us. "This shit needs to be dealt with at a later time. We have other stuff to worry about right now."

"No." I shrugged him off. "Keep going, Angel. Tell me how you really feel. Tell me how awful of a person I am for the shit I've done when I can't remember it. Tell me how using my girl is fucking wrong even when she uses me just the same. You can't tell me you and Jay have never fought and decided to fuck instead. Because you're so prim and fucking proper. So, tell me." I rubbed my chin. "Please. I'm all fucking ears."

Angel narrowed his eyes at me. Just when I thought he was going to hit me, he shoved past me, but he was careful not to miss shouldering me in the process. He grabbed Jay's hand, kissed her knuckles, and placed his hand on her swollen belly.

She smiled up at him but glanced my way. Her face paled.

Angel followed her gaze, the corners of his lips curling into a wicked snarl. "You want to fucking dance, brother?"

And that was when I charged for him.

CHAPTER SEVENTEEN

Max

WHAT HAPPENED NEXT was like it came right out of a movie. It was so fast, I couldn't tell what body part belonged to which man.

When Dale charged for Angel, although it took me by surprise, my heart broke for him at the same time. I had no idea he blamed Angel for getting shot.

"*Dale*," Jay screamed. "Get off my fucking fiancé."

Dale reared his arm and landed his fist straight into Angel's cheek.

Angel only grinned. The guy had a couple inches on Dale and he was probably twenty-five pounds heavier. He threw Dale off him. "You think you're fucking tough, don't you?" Angel shoved him onto his back, straddling his waist.

"Guys," Jay yelled at the rest of Vice-One. "Do something."

"It needed to happen," Coby said, circling the huddle on the floor.

"You have no idea what I've gone through, what we've all gone through after your accident. We almost lost you, asshole." Angel peered into Dale's eyes, wrapping his hands around his throat.

"You don't give a shit about me. You've been on my ass since the moment I woke up." Dale gripped Angel's wrists. "You don't fucking care."

Angel paused, his nostrils flaring. "I don't care," he repeated the words. "Fuck you, Dale." Angel pushed himself off Dale, rubbed the spot on his cheek Dale had hit, and turned to Jay.

She mumbled something to him, touching her fingers to the bruise forming on Angel's face.

"Dale." I rushed to him, helping him to his feet. "Let's go." I needed to get him out of there before things became worse.

Dale turned on me. "You don't care either, do you?"

My eyes widened. "What are you talking about?"

Both Coby and Asher took an arm and tried pulling Dale back but he stood firm, staring at me with those dark intense eyes of his.

"You don't care. I've apologized to you," Dale said, his words taking on a deadly tone. "I've done everything I can to make you forgive me."

"You apologized? Sure. Maybe. But words don't mean shit, Dale." I placed my hands on my hips, jutting my chin. "You have to show me. You can't expect me to forgive you instantly over what you've done. You have to give me time."

"How much fucking time do you need?" he boomed, coming toward me.

"Careful." Angel spun on him, placing a hand against Dale's chest, and forced him back. "I will lay you out right the fuck here if you so much as even think of getting in her face."

"Fuck off, brother." Dale glared at him.

"Get out," Angel demanded, shoving him back.

"Fuck you." Dale pushed him. "I'm not leaving without her."

"You are," Angel said, his voice flat. "And you will."

Dale grinned. "Make me."

****

(Dale)

I had officially lost my shit. I never wanted to hit Angel. I didn't even intend on going into this like I did but when his hand grazed over Jay's stomach, I snapped. I couldn't control it. This urge. *Max should have had a baby. She should have been stress free and able to carry our daughter to full term. I never should have shoved her away. I should have been there for her. Our baby should have survived. How the fuck was it fair that she didn't? How could a caring God let something like this happen? Max didn't deserve it, and I sure as hell didn't deserve her.*

All of these thoughts and questions only fueled the rage coursing through me.

"Dale."

I could hear Max's soft voice behind me but it did nothing to stop my fist from flying into Angel's face for the second time. The next thing I knew, I was flat on my back with the wind knocked out of me. My lungs constricted as I gasped for breath.

"You need to calm the fuck down before I do it for you," Angel warned, his voice calm and collected. He pushed himself off me and turned back to Jay. "Let's get the hell out of here. I don't want to have to knock my brother out."

Jay chewed her bottom lip, glancing between Angel and me. "You can't leave it like this."

"He's the shithead who won't see reason," Angel said, pointing down at me.

I jumped to my feet, punching him in the shoulder. "Let's end this then."

Angel glared at me, his gaze shooting daggers at me. "I'm too old for this shit." When he turned around, I grabbed his arm.

"*Dale*," he yelled, shoving out of my grip.

The rough move knocked Jay back, forcing her to land hard on her ass.

Gasps sounded around us.

Fuck.

"Watch who you're pushing, assholes," she snapped.

"Shit." Angel grabbed hold of her hands and pulled her to her feet. "Fuck." He cupped her stomach, turning his glare on me. "You need to get the fuck out of here," he said, his tone deadly.

I swallowed hard. For once in my life, I listened and headed out of the clubhouse.

Coby was hot on my tail, following me until I made it to the end of the parking lot. "That was cold, brother. Even for you."

"I didn't push her."

"Maybe not directly but you sure as fuck started it."

"It was an accident." I paced back and forth. "He's been on my ass ever since I woke up. I can't make things right with Max if he won't leave us alone."

"Then you need to deal with your shit alone and not here. Angel looks out for her because she's his fiancée's best friend. The mother of his baby who *you* just knocked over."

I looked away. I didn't need the reminder.

"What if something happens to their baby?" He slapped my shoulder. "Huh? Tell me. How the fuck will that make you feel?" Coby turned back around and headed inside the building before I could give him an answer.

Max stood outside the door.

Our gazes locked.

My heart stuttered.

What the hell did I just do?

CHAPTER EIGHTEEN

Max

HAVING AN IN-house nurse came in handy when accidents happened. Creena checked out Jay as best she could without having any equipment on hand and advised Angel to take her to the hospital just in case.

As they were leaving, I stopped Jay. "I'm sorry." I rung my hands together in front of me. "I have no idea what came over him." *But I definitely had a feeling.*

Jay hugged me, wrapping her arms around my shoulders. "It's not your fault. I just wish you two could be civil but ..."

"What?"

"Maybe you both need some time apart," she suggested when Angel came up to us.

"Angel," I whispered. "I'm sorry."

He grabbed Jay's hand, kissed her knuckles, and dropped their joined fingers between them. "I don't suggest bringing Dale around here for a while."

I nodded.

Before Jay could add anything, Angel wrapped his arm around her shoulders and led her outside.

My chest constricted over their words. Two people said we needed time apart. But would it really do any good?

"Max?" Meeka stood beside me. "You okay?"

"No," a sob escaped me. "Not at fucking all."

****

(Dale)

I hit Angel and lived to tell about it.

Bruises were already forming on my knuckles. I flexed and un-flexed my knuckles, the sharp pain jabbed me right in the gut. What was I doing? I fought my brother. A man who had been my mentor for most of my adult life. If it hadn't been for him taking a chance on me, I'd probably be dead somewhere or in fucking jail. And my way of thanking him was by hitting him instead.

Stretching my legs out in front of me before bringing them back up to my chest, I massaged the impending headache piercing through my skull.

I had been sitting outside Max's gallery for the past hour. Not exactly sure where else to go, I ended up there before I even knew what I was doing. I didn't want to go home. Even though I couldn't remember everything that had happened back at my apartment, I could smell the other women on my sheets. I washed them, threw fucking cologne on them, but it did shit all for the smell. So, I threw them in the trash and lit a match.

"Dale?"

My head snapped up.

Max stood a few feet away, keys in hand. "What are you doing here?"

"I didn't want to go home," I grumbled, slowly pushing to my feet. The protest in my muscles reminded me what I had done only a couple hours before.

"How's the hand?" she asked, stepping around me to unlock the door.

I shrugged. I deserved the pain. I embraced it. It made me feel alive.

Max let out a muttered curse. "All right, come with me."

I followed her into the building until we reached her office. She went right to a mini-fridge sitting in the corner of the room and pulled out a tray of ice. "Sit," she demanded, pointing to the stool beside the easel.

She wrapped some of the ice cubes in a cloth before kicking the door to the fridge closed and came toward me. "Give me your hand."

Every inch of me wanted to pull away from her. After accidentally shoving Jay, I didn't deserve her kindness.

Max grabbed my hand. Her small fingers wrapped around mine, holding the ice against the back of my knuckles. "What's this?" she asked, rubbing her thumb over the black soot on my wrist. "What did you do?"

"Coby told me about the women. I don't remember. I wish I could remember. So, I lit my sheets on fire," I told her, lifting my shoulders. "They didn't smell like you."

"Oh." She crinkled her nose. "You caused a lot of problems back at the club, Dale."

I grunted. "No fucking shit."

"Why?"

"I … Fuck … I saw Angel rub Jay's stomach and I lost it. I can't explain it but it forced this rage inside of me. It's not their fault. It's no one's fault but my own. But it's not fair. Not to you. *You* should be having a baby. *My* baby. But instead, I fucked up and took that away from you." All the words leaving my mouth stripped me bare until I was exposed and vulnerable. That was it. It was the truth. And I vomited my feelings all over her.

"That's not all of it, though," she whispered. "is it?"

I shook my head. "No."

"You want to talk. I'm listening. So, talk."

Scrubbing a hand up and down my face, I took a deep breath. And another. I blamed Angel. He should have protected me. He should have protected all of us.

"Dale?" Max placed a hand on my shoulder, her beautiful brown eyes staring back at me but they were void of emotion.

No trust.

No love.

Nothing.

What the *fuck* were we doing?

***

(Max)

"Why are you looking at me like that?" I asked, dropping my hand from his.

"Will you ever forgive me? Will you ever trust me again?" he asked, his voice rough.

"I … I want to. I'm confused and my feelings are jumbled. But I want to forgive you. I want to trust you." I sat on the stool across from him, gazing up at the canvas that held a hint of scenery. It was the cemetery where our daughter was buried. But no one would know unless they had actually visited the place.

"I'm trying to be patient," he muttered.

"Are you?" I asked, staring at the image in front of me. "Just because you're ready doesn't mean I am. You also just tried to beat the shit out of your brother and you pushed his fiancée."

"*That* was an accident. You know that." He rubbed the back of his neck. "And Angel is not my brother. Never was. Never will be."

"You don't mean that. I know the military code is a strong one. It doesn't matter if you're blood. You're still brothers and sisters. You're *family*." I gaped at him when he didn't respond. "Angel will come around. He'll—"

"I don't give a fuck," Dale snapped, shoving to his feet and knocked the stool over.

"What's going on with you?"

With each step he took, he was becoming unglued. The rage rolled off him in waves. I was like the prey being stalked by the hungry predator.

He started pacing back and forth, his eyes finding mine every couple of steps he took.

I didn't know what to say or even how to calm him down. Everything that had happened with Angel was uncalled for. And then with Jay? It was like some fucked up dream.

A chime sounded in the silence of the room. Dale stopped, checked his phone and put it back in his pocket before taking a step behind me. "The baby's fine."

A breath I didn't realize I was holding, left me on a whoosh. *Thank God.*

Dale pulled the empty stool behind me, pushing my hair off the back of my neck. "I have no idea what the fuck I'm doing. I know I shouldn't have fought Angel. It's not his fault. None of this is," he said, his voice husky. "But right now, I don't give a shit about anything else. I want you. That's it. And it's taking everything in me not to force you to your knees and show you exactly what I want."

I shivered at his words. "I don't know if we can make it through this," I confessed, chewing my bottom lip.

"I know." Dale picked a clean paintbrush off the rolling cart beside the table. "I don't care about that, either. I'm so fucking wound up, I just need to feel you." His mouth moved to my ear. "I need to control you."

I swallowed hard at the deep rumble of his voice. "What if I say no?" It wouldn't happen but I needed to know I had some semblance of power in our situation.

"Then I'll walk away. I'm done fighting." He kissed the soft spot under my ear. "For now."

"Take me away, Dale," I whispered, watching as the brush traveled down my bare arm, leaving a path of goose bumps behind it. The soft bristles sliding over my skin sent a shiver down my back.

Dale pushed the strap of my dress lower until I was able to get my arm free. Repeating his movements with the other strap, his mouth soon found my skin.

My breath caught, my heart hammering against my rib cage but all I could do was sit there. Mesmerized.

The fabric of my dress pooled at my middle, my nipples hardening to sharp peaks as the cool air kissed them.

With the brush in hand, Dale ran the soft bristles over the swollen nubs.

A shot of electricity hit me square in the center. I moaned, digging my fingers into the stool I was sitting on.

But he still didn't touch me. Only his mouth and the bristles of the paintbrush found my skin. It was intoxicating and highly erotic all at the same time.

Taking a brush in his other hand, he slid it down my spine, all the while focusing on my nipples with the other one.

The dual sensations ignited an unexpected pleasure so deep I couldn't help but beg for more. As much as I wanted him to touch me, this was what I needed at the moment. To be taken away. To go past the point of normal. To just *feel*. It was sensory overload, and I couldn't wait to combust in his arms.

For the first time in my life, I was the canvas, and Dale was the artist. My hands had caused many images to come to life just by the stroke of a brush and now he was doing the same to me.

He lightly tapped my hip, indicating for me to stand.

I did and, much to my surprise, he lowered my dress to my ankles until I was able to step out of the fabric.

A soft groan escaped him when he saw that I wasn't wearing any panties. After our moment at the clubhouse, I had taken them off. I wasn't sure if subconsciously I thought he would show up. Either way, all I focused on was making us both disappear.

"Sit," he commanded, his voice hoarse.

I kicked the fabric aside and sat back on the stool.

Dale pulled me back against him, wrapping a hand around my throat and continued brushing the bristles down my center.

His gaze remained on my face, watching me, waiting for me to fall apart in his arms.

The brush traveled from my jaw, down the side of my neck, over each nipple, and stopped just before reaching the spot between my legs.

Spreading my knees, I gripped my thighs, digging my nails into my own flesh.

His hot breath fanned my face, his heart beat thumping against my back. It picked up speed with each stroke of the brush.

"Dale," I whispered, needing his body inside mine. I forgot everything. All the shit we had been through.

The pain. The heartache.

The undying want for each other took hold, forcing me to succumb to the submission I was inclined to give him.

He pulled me further back against him until I was sitting on his lap.

Hooking my legs over his, I opened myself to him. "Please."

With the tip of the brush, he pushed it between my folds, grazing it ever-so-gently over my aching clit.

I arched against him at the unexpected sensation. The bristles, although soft, rubbed at the hard nub until

I cried out in frustration. They weren't hard enough. I needed his calloused fingers instead. His thick length. The scratchy feeling of his stubble. *Him.*

"What do you want from me, kitten?" he asked, tightening his hold on my throat, and rubbed the bristles harder against my swollen clit. He dipped the brush lower, grazing them over my core. He pushed and pushed until I couldn't take it anymore.

"All of you," I panted, rocking back and forth against him. His erection pressed into my lower back. Hard. Throbbing. So damn ready for me I couldn't help but tease him more. "Please. I can't take it."

"You want me inside you?" His mouth closed over my ear lobe, biting down until I whimpered. The unexpected shock of pain slammed right into my center.

"Yes. God, yes." My fingers dug into his knees.

"Hmm … beg me, Max. Tell me how much you need my dick in that sweet cunt of yours." He fisted my hair, pulled my head back and thrust the brush inside me.

My eyes popped open, a shockwave of euphoria slamming right into my center. "I'm begging, Dale," I cried out, pushing back against him. I rubbed my ass into his straining cock, riding the brush between my legs. "Oh, shit. Please."

"Tell me what the fuck you want," he demanded, pumping the brush in and out of me.

"Fuck me. Fuck me so damn hard I feel you for weeks." Spots danced in my vision. My heart picked up speed. I gasped for air. I needed him to fuck me but all I could focus on was getting the release I craved. The orgasm suddenly shattered through me, forcing his name to fall from my lips.

"That's it, baby." He gripped my throat, kissing my cheek. "How does it feel knowing you just got fucked by your brush?" he groaned. "My dick is hard for you."

I whimpered, rocking back and forth against him. "Please, Dale," I whispered. "I need to feel you."

Releasing me suddenly, he pushed me forward until I was bent over the stool. "You're going to feel me for the rest of your fucking life, kitten." Landing a hard swat on my ass, he ran his hand over the spot soon after.

I swallowed hard, gripping the stool in my hands. "Yes. Please."

Dale massaged and kneaded, spreading me open. "Your pussy is dripping for me."

My body vibrated, shaking in anticipation for what he would do next.

Suddenly, a sharp pain spread through the cheek of my ass.

I yelped, pushing back against him.

"You like that," he said, his voice rough as he bit me again.

When we first started sleeping together months ago, he had been dominant but nothing compared to this.

"Please, Dale."

"What do you want, baby?" he asked, brushing his fingers down my spine. "You want me to fuck you and take away this pain?"

"No." I smiled to myself. "I want you to fuck me and give me new pain."

"Woman," he groaned. "You're going to be the death of me."

I pushed back against him, rubbing my ass over the erection he was sporting in his sweat pants.

He fisted my hair, pulled me upright, and wrapped his other arm around my chest. "Say it."

I swallowed hard, licking my parched lips. "Fuck me. Hard."

With a quick move, he sheathed himself with a condom and thrust into me.

I gasped, arching against him.

"Ah, now, baby." He tightened his arm around me. "Trying to get away so soon?" His hips slammed into my ass, his cock fucking me rough.

"Oh, God." The pain from his size stretching me mixed with the pleasure forced incoherent sounds to leave my lips.

"You see, kitten." He kissed my neck. "There is no God when it comes to me fucking you."

I whimpered as his thrusts deepened.

He chuckled, licking his tongue up the side of my face before kissing my cheek. "The devil himself would turn away blushing."

"Please," I whispered.

"You want me to fuck this sweet cunt until there's nothing left?"

"Yes." I gripped his arm wrapped around me. "I need it."

"That's my girl." He kissed my cheek again before releasing me completely. "Lay on the couch."

I stood on shaky legs and headed to the couch at the far wall of my office when I was pushed face first onto it.

Dale covered my body with his, his cock sliding back into me. "Can you feel every inch of me?"

I panted, nodding, and spread my legs wider for him.

"You're so damn beautiful," he grunted, thrusting hard and deep. Pulling my hands behind my back, he held them tight and leaned back. "I'm going to fuck the shit out of you, kitten."

Dropping my left foot to the floor, I braced myself and gave him better access to my body.

"That's right." He brushed his other hand down my back before landing a hard swat on my ass. "You need this, don't you?"

"Yes." I swallowed hard. "Just like you do."

***

(Dale)

I did. She was right. I needed her so fucking hard, it was unnatural. I wanted to fuck her until my dick became raw. Until every muscle in my body was tight and throbbing.

When we started sleeping together again just over a month ago, it was never like this. This was different. Completely and utterly mind blowing. Dark and dangerous. Just what we both needed.

Holding her wrists tight in my hands, I lifted her from the couch and began thrusting hard and deep. My pelvis slammed against her ass, my cock prolonging the screams leaving her mouth. Her head thrashed from side to side but I wouldn't let up. I couldn't. No matter how hard I tried to give it to her gently, my body took over.

It was violent and toxic. Our bodies blending together as we both brought ourselves to the point of divine ecstasy. God, she felt good. So fucking good.

"Dale," she panted. "Please."

"What do you want, kitten?" I demanded. I needed to hear her say the words.

"Make me come. Make me come so damn hard."

Pushing her forward, I released her arms and wrapped my body around hers. I needed to feel her break and hold her until she came down from that euphoric high.

"Come for me, baby," I whispered in her ear. "Come all over my cock."

She whimpered, holding onto my arm wrapped around her shoulders. "You feel so good," she whispered.

I grinned, speeding up my hips.

"Dale," she moaned. "Harder."

Fuck, she was going to break my dick. Hammering into her with everything I had, I trailed tiny bites along her shoulder blades before sinking my teeth into her shoulder.

She screamed, shaking and trembling beneath me. My name left her lips on a guttural cry, the high-pitched sound piercing into my ears and hitting me straight in the balls.

My cock swelled.

"Fuck, kitten." I continued biting and licking, kissing and caressing until I jumped over that edge with her. I grunted, my cum pouring deep within her body.

Our releases crashed together, melting as one until we both submitted to the ultimate pleasure.

CHAPTER NINETEEN

Max

ON THE ONE hand, I needed to be alone.
On the other, I couldn't think about anything except for getting Dale back inside me every time I was with him. It was unhealthy. This obsession to fuck him every chance I had bordered on more than just a fling.

I was addicted to him. His touch. His taste. His breath on my skin. His grunts of pleasure whispering into my ears as we rode out that high together. It wasn't normal. We used sex as an out. It was a mask covering the subjects we didn't want to talk about. I still hadn't taken him to see our daughter. I also hadn't called my grandmother in a while because I knew she would be disappointed in me.

No longer was my heart in the game but my whole damn soul. I lived and breathed Dale Michaels in a way another human shouldn't. It was raw possession. Whenever I threw a party at the clubhouse and a woman went up to him, I appeared beside him before I even knew what I was doing. He never said anything because he did the same when a man started talking to me. And that would just turn into us fucking, demanding to hear from the other how much we owned each other.

"Max." Brogan came into the gym, frowning at the fact I was sitting on the floor. "You need to tell me what the hell is going on."

"What do you mean?" I asked, taking a sip from the water bottle.

She sat on the mat across from me. "You've lost weight. We hardly see you or Dale anymore. And do you recall backing out of your gallery showing?"

I winced, remembering Josee's reaction.

"Maxine fucking Stanton," she yelled into the phone. "You better be fucking dead. I can't believe you skipped out on your showing. Luckily for you, I used the excuse that there was an emergency in your family and you had to fly back to California to see your grandmother. You owe me. And no thanks to you, I still sold all of your paintings." Josee took a breath. "New York wants you in one of their prestigious galleries. You're fucking welcome."

The phone slammed in my ear making me jump.

"Who was that?" Dale asked, rolling toward me.

"Just a message from Josee," I said, breathing through the racing of my heart. She didn't get mad like that often. If she did, it was never directed at me. But this time, it was.

I had lied to Dale that night, telling him the showing was pushed back to another day when really, I just wanted to forget the world and have him fuck me senseless.

"I don't know what's going on with you two, but whatever it is, it's not healthy."

I met Brogan's gaze, remembering that she was sitting across from me. "I don't know what we're doing," I confessed. "I can't control it. I don't want to do anything else. I don't want to feel or think. I just want *him*."

"It doesn't work that way." She reached for my hand but hesitated, pulling back suddenly. "Trust me. I know what you're trying to do but sex isn't an out. Yes, it can help momentarily but when your heart's on the line—"

"My heart hasn't been in this since Dale woke up from the coma."

Brogan sighed. "Max, your heart has always been in this."

My eyes burned, my throat closing up. "I hate what Dale did but I can't stop myself. I need him. We'll talk. I know we will. I just don't know when. But right now, we need all of you to back the fuck off."

Brogan wrapped her arm around my shoulders. "It's about damn time."

"Excuse me?"

"I know Angel has been on Dale's case. Coby and I have sat back and watched. It's no one's business. We both understand that. If you use sex to channel your pain and take comfort in each other, as long as it's what you both agree on, that's all that counts."

"I want to trust him."

"You need time." She squeezed me tighter. "Both of you do."

"I don't know if I can give him my heart again when it's no longer beating." I rubbed the spot in the middle of my chest. "It feels like it's just a dead weight, sitting in my chest." I dropped my head in my hands. "God, I'm so stupid. How could I think I could fuck him and not have feelings for him at the same time?"

"No, you are not stupid, Max." Brogan squeezed my shoulder. "You're in love. Big difference."

A smart retort was on the tip of my tongue but after thinking it over, she was right. After what happened last time when I confessed my true feelings to Dale, I wasn't sure when I could repeat those words again. If ever.

****

(Dale)

My dick was going to fall off. Either that or it was going to become limp, never to be used again after the hard-fucking Max kept giving it.

I tried ignoring it but every time I moved, my muscles twitched, protesting and straining beneath my skin. We had been going at it hard for the past week. I didn't know what happened but Max came at me like a feral beast. I never complained while our use of the other turned into an outright possessive *need*.

Coby had called a little bit ago, telling me about a meeting with just the guys from Vice-One. I wasn't in the mood to see Angel but I knew it would have to happen eventually so I was a good little boy and made my way to the clubhouse.

I sent Max a quick text, letting her know where I was as I stepped foot into the building.

"Hey, Dale."

My head popped up just as I hit send on my phone.

Angel leaned against the bar, his arms crossed under his big chest.

"Hey," I said slowly, glancing around the room. "Where is everyone?"

A smug look passed over his face. "It's just you and me for now."

Fucking fucker. Coby set me up. "Great. You going to get in my face again?"

"That depends," Angel rubbed the scruff on his jaw. "You going to push my fiancée again?"

I winced. "Listen, man, I'm sorry."

"Her and the baby are fine." Angel's gaze darkened. "Do that again though and ..." A wicked grin spread across his face. "Let's just say that the shit this Organization does will be nothing compared to what I do to you."

I barked a laugh, shaking my head at the possibilities. "Truce?"

Angel narrowed his brows before letting out a sigh. "Yeah. Fucker." He closed the distance between us and clapped a hand on my nape. "I love you, man, but fuck, you're a stubborn shithead, you know that?"

I grunted. "I'm sleeping with a woman who hates me. So yeah, I know."

"Fuck, man." Angel sat on the stool, the metal creaking beneath the added weight.

"Is there really a meeting?" I asked, ignoring the pity in his dark eyes.

"Yeah, there is." Angel rubbed the back of his neck. "Coby's friend, Lucas, found Zane. Charles is still missing but right now, I'll take whatever the fuck I can get."

I sat beside him. "I'd love to skin that bastard alive."

"I'd love to see him in Brogan's chair." Angel leaned back against the bar top. "She's a scary little thing."

Under normal circumstances, I would have laughed but in all honesty, Angel was right. Brogan Tapp had more balls than most men. I had seen her work but nothing prepared us for what I knew she wanted to do to Zane. The other half of the duo who destroyed her boyfriend. Coby was strong but I knew he never came back from that night and it ruined whatever light he had left.

"Where is Zane?" I asked, excitement rippling through my body much like the orgasm did earlier that morning.

Angel pointed to the floor.

I frowned and then suddenly it dawned on me. "Wait. He's here?"

Angel nodded. "We picked him up. The bastard's in the basement as we speak."

"How?"

"I had Greyson grab him for us." Angel shrugged like it was no big deal and it was just an everyday occurrence for us.

Greyson Mercer, Brogan's step brother, was an evil bastard. The President of Hell's Harlem may have had everyone else fooled including his step sister but I saw that same darkness in him that I saw in Coby, if not more so. The fucker was a damn good actor. But I left it alone and kept that piece of information to myself.

"Where did Lucas find him?" I asked Angel.

"Of all places? At a bookstore." Angel shook his head. "He was waiting to be found. Probably lost his shit over his sister dying and wanted to go with her like some Romeo and Juliet thing."

"Odd as fuck, man. Odd. As. Fuck."

"Truth." Angel rose to his feet. "We're having this meeting without Jay. As much as she wanted to be here, I made her stay home. Stone and a couple of the guys from her father's club are watching her."

"I bet she loved that." I laughed.

"Not really but I don't give a fuck. Shit is going down soon. I can feel it in my bones. We need to end this once and for all before something else happens."

"Where's Asher and Meeka?" I asked, realizing I hadn't seen them in a couple of days.

"Home. Meeka isn't feeling well but with what they went through with Charles, I'd like to keep them as far from this shit as possible."

I nodded in agreement. They had gone undercover trying to bring Charles down. The only good thing that had come out of the situation was them finding each other after being best friends for years.

As if on cue, everyone filed into the club, but the only person I noticed was Max.

Her eyes were red, the skin just beneath them swollen and puffy. She had been crying, and I knew without a fucking doubt it had to do with me.

Scrubbing my hands up and down my face, I took a deep breath and walked up to her. "Max."

She jumped, spinning on her heel. "Dale." She placed her hand against her chest. "Hi."

"Hi," I said gently, pushing a strand of hair behind her ear.

Her eyes fluttered closed and when they reopened, my heart skipped a beat.

I could see it. A little hint that maybe in time, something good could come out of this fucked up situation. *Hope.* It was all I had at the moment.

We kept going back and forth. Maybe this would end. Maybe it wouldn't. But I was damn determined to make every moment with her count.

She cleared her throat, stepping away from me, and headed into the meeting room.

I followed her and sat beside her but I didn't touch her. Not this time. Instead, I crossed my arms under my chest and wondered what the fuck we were doing.

Our eyes met.

The dark shadow behind her gaze became more pronounced, the hint of hope no longer there. It was quickly replaced with a darkness I felt.

The bags under her eyes indicated she hadn't been sleeping. And where was I amidst all of this? Fucking her like a piece of a meat.

Shit.

***

(Max)

Whatever game we were playing, neither of us was going to win. But when he touched me and looked at me like I was all that mattered, a tiny bit of hope sat peacefully on my chest.

When Dale sat beside me and kept his hands to himself, a part of me wondered if it was over. I wasn't sure when. Maybe days. Weeks. Even years. Maybe we'd find each other again when we were old and gray.

A heavy weight lifted off my chest although the tightness remained. I loved him. I *still* loved him. I probably always would.

A relationship based solely on sex wasn't good for either of us but I found it healed us in a way.

"Can I hold your hand?" Dale asked, his voice rough.

I nodded.

He slid his fingers between mine, pulling me closer to his side. "We need to talk," he muttered, brushing his nose along the shell of my ear. "But right now, I'll talk holding your hand."

"I know we need to talk but I like the sound of that. This …" I held up our joined hands and kissed his knuckles. "I like this," I whispered, wiping away the lonely tear rolling down my cheek.

Dale kissed the side of my head, letting his lips linger before pulling away.

"They're in here," Brogan said from the doorway, giving us a small smile. She looked between us. "I interrupted something, didn't I?"

I swallowed hard, shaking my head.

"Look at me, kitten," Dale said gently, ignoring her.

I met his gaze.

"No matter what happens …" He brushed his fingers down my cheek. "I'm always here. You know that, right?"

A soft sob escaped me. I nodded quickly.

"Wait, the room is occupied," I heard Brogan say, shutting the door behind her.

"I ..." I swallowed excessively. I wasn't used to this side of Dale. I could handle asshole Dale but not sweet and caring Dale. It threw me off and fucked with my head. "I need you to be an asshole right now."

"Why?" He kissed my knuckles.

"Because." My breath hitched, watching his mouth brush over the soft skin. My gaze flicked back to his. "It makes it harder to admit my feelings for you."

He paused, his gaze flicking behind me just as Brogan let everyone in. He sat back, released my hand and pushed his chair away from me.

I stared at him. "That's how it's going to be?"

"What the fuck do you want from me, Max? You *want* me to be an asshole? You think I've *been* an asshole?" He leaned toward me, kissing the corner of my mouth. "You haven't seen anything yet."

CHAPTER TWENTY

Dale

AN HOUR AFTER the meeting, Coby and I headed down to the basement. Angel and Greyson stayed outside while Henley, Lian, and Grey's club stood watch around the building.

I left Max after placing a hard kiss on her mouth. She wanted me to be an asshole because it was easier for her. I rubbed the back of my neck, trying to ease some of the tension that had built up in the taught muscles.

"Focus, brother," Coby muttered.

"You're lucky I don't kill you now." Brogan leaned against the table, checking out her nails. "I'm getting bored. If you don't answer my questions, I might just do that."

Zane smirked, the split in his lip letting out a drop of blood at the movement. "I love it when you play dirty."

Coby stiffened beside me.

"You see" —Brogan paced back and forth in front of him, ignoring his comment— "I could just unleash my boyfriend on you. You do remember him, right?" Brogan grabbed Zane's jaw, digging her fingers into his cheeks and turned his head toward Coby. "That's the man your sister tried to destroy. But little did she know, our love is stronger than she ever was."

Coby grinned.

"Your girl is something else, my man," I mumbled.

"Fucking right she is." Coby's eyes darkened as they zeroed in on the woman who had taken over his whole world.

"My sister was a little bitch," Zane spat. "If she would have let me loose on him, he wouldn't be standing—"

Brogan's fist flew across Zane's face. "Oh," she gasped. "I'm sorry. My hand slipped."

"Fuck you, whore," he spat at her feet. "I could rip you apart."

Brogan threw her head back and laughed. "You're fucking funny. Coby, my love, could you give me a hand, please?"

"Of course, baby." Coby pushed off the wall and headed behind Zane. "I suggest you tell us where Charles is if you want to survive a couple more hours tonight."

"Fuck you," Zane yelled. "I haven't done shit. It was all Tina, Charles and—" He snapped his mouth shut.

"And?" Brogan raised an eyebrow. "Is there someone else?"

"No." Zane shook his head.

"You said Tina, Charles and ..." Brogan looked at us. "Who the fuck is he talking about?"

"Shit." I texted Angel.

Me: Emergency.

As soon as I put my phone away, Angel was down the stairs. "What?"

"There's someone else," Coby said, clapping his hands onto Zane's shoulders. "And our friend here was just about to tell us who."

"You don't know what you're talking about. There is no one else." Zane shook against his restraints.

"Brogan," Angel barked. "Work your magic because I have a woman to get home to."

"With pleasure." She grinned, grabbed a rusty butter knife off the table, and turned to Zane. "One last chance, baby boy. That's the term your sister used, isn't it?"

"My sister was a sick fucking freak," Zane growled. "She got off on that shit more than I did."

"But you didn't stop her," Brogan screamed, slamming the knife into his knee.

Zane shouted. "Fucking bitch."

"Brogan," Coby said, his voice firm and shook his head.

She took a deep breath.

He cursed, shaking in the metal chair.

"Give me my knife," she grumbled, pulling the knife free from Zane's knee. "You don't deserve to have it in your body." She went to the table, gripping the edge.

"Coby." I stepped up beside him, nodding my head toward Brogan. "I got this."

He gave my shoulder a light squeeze before heading to his girlfriend.

"You see, Zane." I stepped behind him, leaning down to the bastard's ear. "Those two are too involved in this. But me? I wasn't there. I have no emotion in this. I can kill you and be done with it and not even look back. And you know what? I'm not going to. I want to see you suffer." I wrapped my fingers around his throat, tugging his head back. "I want to see you writhing in pain, begging for your life like Coby begged for his. You didn't do anything when Tina fucked him, did you?" I lowered my voice so only he could hear. "You enjoyed it, didn't you? Were you jealous?" I asked, cupping the knee Brogan had stabbed.

Zane jumped. "Fuck."

"Were you jealous?" I asked, repeating my question slowly. "Tell me."

"Yes," Zane yelled.

Coby and Brogan turned around at Zane's outburst.

"Tell him you're sorry," I demanded. "Tell them both."

"Fuck you. I'm not saying shi—"

Digging my finger into the wound, I pushed until Zane screamed.

"Fine," he bellowed.

"Not good enough." I held out my hand. "Brogan."

She grinned, handing me a knife.

"Say it," I stabbed his other knee, towering over him. "Tell them how fucking sorry you are."

"I'm sorry," he cried. "Shit, stop." He struggled against the chair.

"Good boy." I kissed his head. "Now tell us who the other person is."

"I don't know. I swear to fuck I don't know. Tina dealt with him. Not me. She was fucking him too."

Yeah, because that last piece of information was important. "You're lying."

"No," he swore. "I'm not. Look me in the eyes. I'm not lying."

Brogan leaned over him, her nose mere inches from his. "If I find out you haven't been honest, I will kill everyone you've ever loved."

"Too late," Zane growled. "You already did that."

Brogan grinned. "I guess my job is done then." She rose to her full height, met my gaze, and nodded once.

In a quick move, my hand slid across his neck.

Blood spurted from the slice in his throat.

Zane gasped for air, his head falling back.

I hooked an arm around him. "That's for hurting my friends and for taking those girls." His death had been too fast but we needed to move on and clean up quick.

I watched as the life left Zane's eyes.

Angel stood across the room from me. Our eyes met. He nodded. I nodded back. I avenged Coby and Brogan. It wasn't enough. Knowing what they went through, it would never be enough. But Zane wasn't even the biggest problem.

"What do we do about this unknown fucker?" I asked, wiping my hands on the cloth Brogan handed me.

"I'll talk to Lucas. See if anyone else has been spotted with Zane and Tina that we never noticed." Coby hooked an arm around Brogan's shoulders. "But first, we need a moment."

"Take all the time you guys need." Angel cupped his shoulder. "You did good. All of you."

Brogan shivered. "Not good enough. I want that other person. The leader. Tina and Zane were too big of pussies. This new guy we never knew about is good. But he's not good enough. He'll slip up. They always do."

She had a point.

"True." Angel stopped just outside the main entrance to the club. "I don't want any of you alone tonight. Dale, I know you and Max—"

"She won't be alone," I told him.

"Good." He scrubbed a hand down his face. "I'm going home to Jay. We'll debrief in the morning."

CHAPTER TWENTY-ONE

Max

ONCE EVERYONE CAME up from the basement, I headed outside. Angel went home to Jay. Coby and Brogan went to her room at the back of the building. And Dale was nowhere to be found.

My phone dinged.

Creena: How's it going there?

Me: Busy.

Creena: Good.

Me: You spending the night there?

Knowing she was staying with Asher and Meeka for the moment, I wasn't expecting to get the next text.

Creena: No. ;)

I wanted to laugh. Knowing it was the right reaction but the sound never left my mouth.

I sighed, put my phone away and was about to walk home when I heard deep voices coming from around the building.

Dale caught my gaze but stood off to the side, talking to Greyson, Lian, Henley, and other guys I didn't recognize.

When I started walking down the parking lot, Dale caught up with me.

"You shouldn't be alone," he said. "But …"

I stopped, standing in front of him. I opened my mouth to speak when I caught something in his gaze. It had been the same darkness I had seen in Coby. Every time there was a mission or a fight, he went right to Brogan. It happened with Angel and Asher as well. Sex was a stress reliever. "What happened?"

Dale's body was stiff, tense. With his hands clenched at his sides, he took several breaths before giving me a small smile. "I need a drink."

"That's all you need?" I asked, staring up at him.

He took a step toward me, pushing a strand of hair behind my ear. That touch had become so familiar, I craved it.

"I'll take whatever you give me, kitten."

"I don't know what's going on," I told him, "but I really don't want to be alone either … come home with me." It was a dangerous suggestion. Knowing we had been taking our individual pain out on each other for the past several weeks, there was no doubt he would end up in my bed by the morning.

"I'll sleep on the couch."

A knot formed in the center of my chest but all I could do was nod.

We walked back to my place in silence. It was unnerving, the unanswered questions flowing around us.

"What happened tonight?" I asked, needing the sound of our voices to drown out the demons of my mind.

"Zane got what he deserved," Dale muttered, brushing a hand through his hair.

"Because of you," I said, noting the darkness surfacing. It billowed around us, both suffocating and intoxicating at the same.

"Yeah." He met my gaze. "Because of me."

"Are you okay?"

Dale stared straight ahead, his jaw clenching. "Yeah. I'm fine, kitten."

"How about you and Angel? Are you two good?"

"We are. Avenging our brother and his girlfriend kind of helped."

I inched my fingers around his forearm, holding him. It wasn't much but I had hoped that small touch would let him know although we had our issues, I wanted him happy. Taking a life, no matter if it was deserved or not, was difficult. I had seen death and destruction. Living a MC life, it was a given. "I'm glad that's over. I hope Coby and Brogan can move on now."

"I hope so too but I think that will take a long time."

"And therapy," I added, my heart aching for them.

A couple more minutes in silence and we were standing outside my small house.

"Are you coming?" I asked Dale, walking up the porch.

"I wish," he whispered.

My cheeks heated.

"I can't go to bed yet. I'll sleep on the couch. I'm fine with that. But …"

I turned to him. "What?"

He shook himself. "Nothing."

But I knew that look. It was the same look Coby gave Brogan after she had someone in her chair. Dale needed to have sex and as much as I wanted to give that to him, with the revelations that came to light today, he would have to wait. I needed to be in some sort of control. Even if it was just for a little bit. A couple minutes. Hours. Days.

Brogan had been right. I *had* lost weight. All the baby weight disappeared in a matter of weeks. I was too focused on Dale instead of taking care of myself. And sadly, he had been the same way.

"Do you have any beer?" he asked, clearing his throat.

"In the fridge." I kicked off my shoes and headed to the couch, pulling the blanket from the back onto my lap. "Can you grab—" A bottle came into my view. "Thank you." I twisted off the cap and pulled back half the bottle before letting out a low moan.

Dale chuckled. "I love a woman who enjoys beer."

My eyes widened over his choice of wording.

"I mean …" Dale blushed. "Fuck."

"It's fine." I took another swig. *Holy hell.* "I know what you meant."

"It's been a long ass night." He drank from his own bottle, his gaze flicking back to mine every so often.

"Don't worry about it, Dale." I shrugged. "No big deal." Crossing my legs in front of me, I leaned my head against the back of the couch.

"I didn't know you had brothers," he said, nodding toward the pictures on the mantel above the fireplace.

It was an easy conversation. One I could appreciate at the moment. "Yeah. Five of them." I finished my beer, placed the bottle on the table, and sat back. With my hands in my lap, I turned toward him. "How about you? Any siblings?" I asked, remembering that I didn't know anything about his family.

"No," he mumbled. "Just me. Like Angel, I was thrown into the system at a young age. I bounced from foster home to foster home and enlisted in the Navy when I turned eighteen and ..." He smiled. "You know the rest."

"My brothers are older. I miss them but we've never been close. I was an oopsie. My dad was a douche and left when my mother was pregnant with me. She died of cancer when I was a kid."

"Shit, kitten, I'm sorry." He reached for me but pulled his hand back before he could link our fingers.

I shrugged, ignoring the sense of loss from him not touching me. "I was young. My brothers were affected more by it."

"And you lived with your grandmother?"

"Yes." My chest tightened. "When she goes, it will hurt but ..." I laughed. "But she's the strongest woman

I know. I think she'll even tell death off when it comes down to it."

He smiled, drinking the rest of his beer.

We sat in silence for a couple more minutes before Dale said the dreaded words I didn't want to hear.

"We need to talk but—"

"Right now, I need you to be an asshole," I said quickly, the confession fumbling from my lips. I met his gaze briefly before looking down at my hands. "I can't handle anything else."

"You fell in love with me when I was nice, a good guy as you call it, and you fell in love with me when I was an asshole." He pushed a strand of hair behind my ear. "We keep going back and forth. This isn't healthy for either of us."

But I didn't want to know what could come next out of this. I didn't want to know what tomorrow would bring or even what the next hour would consist of. Right now, I just wanted to feel. No fighting. No angry words. "I just want this. Every time we talk, it hurts. I need a night off. I don't want to feel pain. I don't want to hate you. I just want …"

"What, Max?" He grabbed my hand, kissing my inner wrist. "What do you want?"

My breath hitched. I chewed my bottom lip. "I just want to *feel*."

***

(Dale)

Max was mere inches from me.

She was close but still thousands of miles away just the same. I could feel her before I touched her. Her breath on my skin. Her hands on my body. But we still didn't touch. We didn't talk. We only stared. I would do everything in my fucking power to have her come back to me. No matter how long it took, she would be mine again.

"Dale," my name left her lips like a breathless kiss.

"Max," I growled, pushing my thumb into the pulse point on her wrist. Her heart sped up the harder I pushed. Her mouth parted, her pink tongue peeking out to lick along her bottom lip.

My body vibrated, the remnants from the kill hours before still grated on my nerves. I didn't enjoy taking a life, and I knew it would affect me mentally in the long run but at that moment, I just wanted to fuck away the tragedy. Sex after a mission had always been my thing. It was for all of us. We either drank, fucked, or fought. Not always in that order. And right now, my goal was to get back inside Max.

The longer we sat there, the more I wanted to drive my body into hers.

"I'm ..." Max's breath hitched. "I should go to bed."

"You should." I released her wrist, trailing my fingers up her bare arm.

"It's been a long night," she added, a rosy glow hitting her cheeks.

"It has." I leaned toward her, my mouth inches from hers. A little further and I would be kissing her but I knew as soon as our lips touched, all bets were off. The obsession I had over this woman would turn into a full-on need to dominate and to own.

"Blankets are in the closet," she whispered. "Whatever you need, Dale."

I need you.

She stood from the couch, giving her body a shake. "Well, goodnight."

***

(Max)

I wasn't sure if Dale felt it but something had switched since we left the clubhouse. I couldn't explain it. I couldn't even fathom what it was that I needed but this driving force to demand for him to do whatever he wanted to me, was on the tip of my tongue. I didn't care if this was unhealthy. I didn't care if this was it and after, we both went our separate ways, right now I just wanted to feel him moving inside me. I wanted him to completely own me. In every way possible.

For the past hour, I had been pacing. Back. Forth. Back. Forth. The question of if I should head back downstairs or just sleep it off banged around in my head.

Insomnia was a bitch and tonight she was making me her unwilling slave. Forcing me to submit to the madness of the thoughts racing through my mind, I headed downstairs. I needed to know if Dale felt it too.

I blamed my lack of sleep on the nightmares invading my dreams when really, it was because of Dale being in the same house as me. It was a stupid decision on my part. I should have just stayed with Angel and Jay like they suggested. But the masochistic side of me wanted Dale close.

The closer I got to him, the more intense the need for him became. My body vibrated. The bones beneath my skin trembled. The desire I had for the man unfurled deep within my soul. I needed us to fuck whatever this was out of our systems. I needed him to

205

destroy me and put me back together because sleeping alone wasn't doing shit.

As soon as my feet landed on the main floor, I glanced around the living room and didn't see him anywhere. Maybe he left. *No, he wouldn't. Not when Angel demanded that none of us be alone.*

When I was about to enter the kitchen, Dale came out.

Topless.

His grey sweatpants hung low on his hips, showcasing that dark trail leading to the treasure beneath. His hard, chiseled chest was nothing like I had seen before. He was big. Much larger than I remembered. His abs twitched, hinting for me to lick them. And when he took a sip from the water bottle in hand, his bicep bulged.

Dale was a fucking God.

He raised an eyebrow, a knowing smirk splaying on his beautiful face. He knew I was checking him out but I didn't care. The plea for him to take me was on my lips but even then, I couldn't get it out.

Every nerve ending in my body came alive at the sight before me. I wanted to fight. I wanted to run and for him to chase me. I wanted rough and fast and then slow and passionate.

Dale's bright blue eyes darkened with lust. He threw the water bottle on the couch and leaned his head from side to side. The tendons in his thick neck cracked. With a slow sweep of his tongue, he licked his lips, taking a step toward me.

I stepped back, my heart hammering against my rib cage. Not sure how this would go, I wanted to turn around and run back up the stairs to my bedroom in hopes that he would chase me.

The sheer look of hunger from him made me nervous yet excited. It made me realize that no matter how hard we tried denying it, whatever we had was far from being over.

When he took another step toward me, a wicked grin spread on his handsome face.

I turned, running up the stairs when I was tackled from behind. I landed with an oomph, the excitement I felt seconds before growing at a billowing speed.

No words left Dale's mouth as his hands roamed up and down my body. His pelvis pushed into my ass. His erection grew the more he rubbed himself against me.

I bit back a moan, dug my fingers into the carpet on the stairs, and shoved out of his grip. Crawling up the stairs, I attempted to go as fast as I could on all fours when my ankles were pulled out from under me.

A gasp escaped me, my feet kicking out and landing against his stomach.

Dale grunted.

I rushed up the stairs but when I reached the top of the landing, Dale was on me.

He wrapped a hand around my throat and tugged my head back. "Fight me."

Oh, I planned on it. I kicked and shoved, prying out of his grip but he was too strong for me.

His fingers dug into my flesh. His hands tore at my clothes. It was violent but delicious, everything we had needed.

Dale licked his tongue up the length of my neck and ripped my panties in half. With two fingers, he thrust them inside of me. "Your pussy's soaked for me," he snarled in my ear, hooking an arm around my chest. "You like running from me."

Yes, I screamed in my head but no sound left my lips. All I could do was breathe as he took control. When he took from me what he wanted, I gave in completely. It was the only way I knew how to submit. The only thing I wanted as he pushed himself against me.

My breathing picked up. I panted. I moaned. I gasped for the air I hadn't breathed since meeting him for the first time months before.

"Tell me you need me," he demanded on a hard growl, pushing his hand roughly between my legs. "Tell me."

"I need you," I whimpered, rocking against him. "I need you so damn bad."

He kissed my temple, inserting a third finger. "Nice and deep, baby. Take me. Fuck my fingers, kitten."

I cried out, shaking in his arms. "Dale, please."

"What do you need?"

"You," I sobbed, moving my hips in tune with his hand.

Dale moved behind me, spreading my legs, and kissed my tailbone. He inhaled, brushing his nose along the length of my spine. Massaging his fingers into my ass cheek, he sunk his teeth into the flesh.

I whimpered, shaking beneath him. When a tinfoil package ripped behind me, I tensed, "No," I said. "No condom."

Dale stiffened behind me.

"Please." I looked at him over my shoulder. "I need to feel you." I craved every inch. Every hard vein and throbbing surface as he took complete control.

In a smooth move, Dale entered me.

I swallowed hard, biting my bottom lip to keep from crying out at the unexpected but intense pleasure.

He felt so damn good it took the air right from my lungs.

Dale kissed my cheek, squeezing my throat, and began to thrust hard and deep.

With each move, my breath quickened. Our bodies were fused together, moving as one.

He whispered over and over how good it made him feel but all I could focus on was him thrusting hard inside of me.

"Dale," I sobbed, digging my fingers into the carpet. The pleasure turned into a roar of undying need. The possession for this man became dark as I started moving back against him.

"That's it, kitten. Fuck my cock," he groaned, landing a hard swat against my ass. "Shit," he snarled, digging his fingers into the cheeks of my rear. "*Harder.*"

"Oh, God." I met him thrust for every pounding thrust. My body shook, the onslaught of ecstasy forcing spots to dance in my vision.

He didn't say anything as his hips sped up. With each rough thrust, he opened me completely. He took all the pain I had felt for months and unleashed that ultimate pleasure inside of me.

"Dale," I repeated on a hard moan.

His hot breath scorched the side of my face. His mouth moved along my skin. His hand moved to my shoulder, squeezing it tight. "You want to feel me," he eventually said, his hips slamming hard against my rear.

I whimpered, pushing back against him. "Yes."

"Why?"

"Because I'm … I'm addicted," I confessed. Not exactly sure what kind of answer he was looking for, I pushed against him every time he slammed his hips into mine.

Dale reached a hand in front of me, spreading my legs wider and dug his fingers into my thigh. "You feel damn good, kitten," he breathed against my neck.

Leaning my head back against his shoulder, I gave him everything he expected of me. My body. My soul. My feelings. My fucking heart.

"Please," I begged. "Fuck, Dale. Make me come," I screamed, my words turning into a plea for his control.

Dale grabbed my wrists, holding them tight behind my back, and drove himself even harder inside of me. "Feel my cock, baby. Feel me destroy this hot body."

"Yes," I cried out, pushing back against him until he growled.

"Fuck, Max." His fingers dug into my hip. His hot breath washing over me until all I felt was this man making me feel every damn inch of him.

"Come for me," I told him, pulling my hands free from his grasp, and cupped his heavy sac between my legs.

He jumped, pushing me against the stairs. "Fuck. Stop teasing me," he snarled in my ear and brushed a thumb over the tight area between my ass cheeks.

I jumped, a hot shiver racing down my spine.

"Remember the first time I took you here?" he groaned, rubbing the puckered area.

"Yes," I breathed, pushing back against him.

"You were so damn tight." He licked up the side of my face. "Your body makes me fucking hard." Suddenly, he released me, falling free from my body.

"What are you doing?" I asked, shivering at the loss of his cock inside me.

In a quick move, he had me over his shoulder.

I gasped. "Dale, put me down."

Landing a hard swat against my ass, he rubbed the spot soon after, repeating it until I writhed against him.

Once we reached my bedroom, he threw me on the bed and flipped me onto my stomach. "I'm taking you everywhere. Every inch. Every damn part of your body. I want you so sore tomorrow, every time you move you think of me. You're going to forget every man that's fucked this hot little body."

"One," I whispered, arching beneath him.

"One what?"

"I've only been with one man before you."

"Look at me," he said, his voice rough.

I met his gaze.

"You will forget him." Dale landed a hard swat on my ass. "You will forget everything about him. Every inch of him that was inside of you." Dale thrust slowly back into my body. "Feel that?"

I nodded, chewing my bottom lip.

"That's me taking control."

"Oh, God," I whimpered, fisting the sheets in my hands.

Dale ran the back of his hand down my spine, his fingers inching between the cheeks of my ass before pumping into my pussy nice and slow. It was pure torture the way he controlled my body. Every touch forced me to arch like a cat.

Pulling me to all fours, Dale knelt behind me. "Are you ready for me, kitten?"

I swallowed hard, nodding.

"Good." He kissed my cheek. "'Cause I'm about to make you fucking purr."

CHAPTER TWENTY-TWO

Dale

THE WAY SHE arched her back drove me absolutely insane. Max was responsive to my touch. So much so that if I didn't control myself, I'd be coming on her back before I even got a chance to fuck her tight little ass.

Running my thumb against the puckered opening, I pushed and prodded until she moaned. Lubricating her with the juices from her pussy, I inserted a finger, thrusting slow and deep.

Her head whipped around, her eyes burning into mine. "More."

"Patience, baby. I'll remind you how much you enjoyed my cock in your ass."

She licked her lips, pushing back against my finger.

Taking that as my cue, I released her and lined my cock up with the tight area. Running my hand up her spine, I gripped the back of her neck and pushed her face first into the mattress at the same time I thrust into her.

She cried out, shaking and trembling against me.

Holding her down, I pulled out slowly and drove back into her tight body in one smooth move. Her body convulsed, the sweet juices from her pussy running down my balls.

Fuck me, she was tight. I wanted her to break. I wanted to own her completely and force her to submit until we both got the pleasure we craved. This woman was nothing like I had ever experienced. She was more. Much more, but I knew I would have to let her go. Those thoughts forced my body to react until I took her harder.

"Dale, please," she begged, meeting me thrust for thrust. "I need to come."

"Oh, you will, baby." I made sure of it.

***

(Max)

The next morning, my body stirred. I rolled over onto my stomach, stretching my arms out beneath my pillow. My muscles twitched, protesting against the movement but I felt so damn good. Better than I had felt in months. Although the nagging feeling last night was it for us, I wouldn't allow myself to think about it.

213

I still hadn't taken Dale to the cemetery. I still never told him about his daughter. I didn't tell him anything. Trust was beginning to brew but a part of me wasn't sure if it was enough.

My throat burned, becoming raw with the emotion that this would be goodbye. I knew we would have to see each other. There was no way Angel would let me be alone while this Organization was around but once it was done, I was leaving. I couldn't handle being in the same city as Dale and not be allowed to touch him.

Dale used me for hours last night. Not letting up until I begged him to let me sleep when really I wanted to keep going until there was nothing left. I held onto him until I broke.

"No matter what happens, I will always be there. I'm only a phone call or a text away."

His words were sweet while his body remained rough. It contradicted his actions and messed with my head. I begged him to shut up. To just talk to me through his body but he didn't listen.

"I'm sorry. For everything."

My screams of pleasure turned into cries of agony. *"Please stop talking."*

But he didn't.

"No one will ever own my heart again, kitten," he had said between kisses.

The powerful passion sliding between us turned into soft and gentle touches from Dale.

With his arm draped over my middle, I pushed into his side. I had never craved sex like I did with him. I wanted it constantly and I knew he would never complain but sex was our out. We needed to talk but instead, we fucked. While we talked last night when he was deep inside me, it wasn't enough.

I kissed his cheek. *You are my first love, Dale.* I took a deep breath. *My only love. I love you. I will always love you.*

Brushing my thumb over his full bottom lip, I replaced it with my mouth. Tears blurred my vision. I prayed we could get through this and find a way back to each other.

Inching my fingers beneath the sheet covering his body, I pushed it off his shoulder and found my mouth touching his skin before my mind could catch up. My body burned for him. But I wanted slow. Not fast and hard like last night.

Dale shifted against me, brushing his nose into the crook of my neck and inhaled deep.

"Make love to me," I said, my voice cracking.

He moved me beneath him and knelt between my spread legs.

Reaching between us, I wrapped my hand around his cock. We didn't talk. Instead, I spoke to him through my body.

He grunted, thrusting his hips in tune with the strokes of my hand.

Dale pushed my knee up to my chest and thrust into me so damn hard my breath left me on a whoosh. My nerve endings tingled, every part of me coming alive just at the mere thrust of his length.

He kissed my neck, raining nips and bites along my skin.

I whimpered, taking all of him in, and let him be in full control.

Dale grabbed my hand, linking our fingers while his hips picked up speed. His groans and grunts of pleasure were music to my ears as I forced him to submit to that desire he craved.

Wrapping a hand around my throat, he forced my head back to meet the rough impact of his mouth. His tongue slid between my lips, matching the deep thrusts of his thick length. The dual sensations erupted into an explosion. His name fell from my lips on a scream.

He kissed me harder, not letting up, and only when he jumped over that edge with me did he slow down.

I sighed, shivering at the loss of his cock no longer being inside me.

Dale winked, kissed me softly on the mouth, and knelt between my legs.

Much to my surprise, his mouth was on me, his tongue inside me to the point I felt him everywhere.

I cried out, grabbing his hair, and lifted my hips toward his mouth.

He growled, the deep sound rumbling from his chest straight into my soul.

"*Fuck.*" He released me with a wet smack, licking his lips. "You taste good."

I panted, shocked that he would go down on me after coming inside of me seconds before.

Flipping me onto my stomach, he pulled me to all fours and ate at me like he was a starved man.

His mouth moved. My hips bucked. He groaned. I screamed. I didn't last long as his delicious mouth forced me to submit again and again.

****

(Dale)

Tasting myself on her was not something I ever thought I'd enjoy but it definitely wouldn't be something I would forget any time soon. Knowing a part of me was in a part of her, I couldn't help but have a little taste.

Max's wide-eyed stare as I ate at her until she came hard around my tongue forced me to lap at her center even harder.

"Dale?" she said an hour later as she got dressed.

"What, kitten?" I asked, pulling on my jeans.

"Why did you do that?"

"Do what?" I asked even though I already knew what she wanted to know.

"You know what I'm asking," she said, chewing her bottom lip.

I laughed. "For someone who begged me to fuck her ass last night, you sure are shy."

She huffed, her cheeks reddening even more. "Just answer my question."

"I don't know what your question is, kitten," I teased and sauntered toward her.

"Most guys would have thought that was gross. Going down on me after … you know."

Cupping her ass, I pulled her against me and brushed my nose into the crook of her neck. The scent of roses and sex wafted into my nostrils, sending a sense of calm washing over me.

"Tasting myself on you was one of the hottest things I've ever experienced." Pinching her chin, I tilted her head back. "I enjoy eating every inch of you, kitten. You should get used to it."

She shivered. "We never had sex like this. Not before your accident."

My back stiffened. "I don't remember so I can't comment."

"You said you remember every moment with me."

"I thought I did but I also thought you and I were fine and that we were a happy fucking family." I pulled away and did up the fly on my jeans before tugging a shirt down over my head.

"See, this is why I don't like talking to you." She shook her head and went to walk out of the room when I stopped her. "Dale." She sighed, leaning against me. "We need to talk about what you said. I own your heart but we keep pushing each other away."

"*You* keep pushing me away," I corrected. "I'm trying to have patience," I muttered, wrapping my arm around her waist.

"Is this over?"

"It never began." I hugged her against me, kissing the side of her head.

She turned in my arms, wrapping herself around my waist. "I—"

At that point, my cell phone rang, stopping Max from saying whatever was on her mind.

"Yeah," I grumbled.

"We're meeting at the club," Angel said.

"What's wrong?" I brushed my hand down Max's cheek, not wanting to leave this moment.

"Tell you when you get here," he said, hanging up.

"What's going on?" Max asked, finishing getting dressed.

"We're all meeting up at the club," I said, kissing her head.

"Okay."

I stared after her, watching her grab her purse and roughly put on lip gloss. She threw the purse on the bed and smoothed down her dress like she was trying to rub out invisible wrinkles.

"What's going on?" I asked her, not able to take the silence any longer.

"I'm fine."

She was anything but. "Talk to me."

She grabbed her purse and walked out of the bedroom.

I had no idea what the hell just happened. The intoxicating and delicious time we had together was going to end. I just didn't know when.

***

(Max)

"Max, baby, talk to me." Dale came up behind me, wrapping his arm around my bicep. "Talk to me."

"What do you want me to say, Dale? That I don't want us to leave my house because every time we do, it's like something happens where we start fighting again? Or that I want last night to happen over and over until we're so deep in each other we can't find our way out? That … that … I don't want this to be over but I know something needs to change?"

He rubbed the back of his neck. "I don't want this to be over any more than you do." He cupped my face, placing a soft kiss on my mouth. "Sit with me."

"We need to go," I mumbled against his lips.

He grabbed hold of my hand, leading me to the couch. "They can wait."

"Dale, it's fine. We'll go to the meeting and—"

"Ignore each other?"

"I think it's been a couple days since we've ignored each other." I smiled softly.

"Yeah." He patted the spot beside him. "Sit."

I did as I was told and joined him on the couch. "Ignoring each other was working. But I don't want to ignore you anymore."

"And I don't want to ignore you. It's not gonna happen, kitten. I'm done. This old shit between us …" He shook his head. "We'll be friends. Something."

"You think we can be in the same room and just be friends? What if I find someone else?" I touched his arm. "What if you find someone? I can't handle seeing another woman on your arm. Do you think you can handle seeing me with another man?"

He looked away, the muscle beneath his jaw working hard. "Fuck." He dropped his head in his hands. "I'll end up in fucking jail if I see you with another man."

I sat back. "Exactly."

"Where do we go from here then?" he asked, his big body stiff.

I leaned my head against his shoulder. "We need time. Or that's what I've been told anyway."

Dale swore under his breath. Pulling me onto his lap, he held me tight against him.

We sat like that for a while.

We needed time, but I wished it would hurry the fuck up.

CHAPTER TWENTY-THREE

Max

DALE TOUCHED ME. He held my hand and looked at me like I was the most important woman in the world. Knowing this could be all be over soon only made me hold onto him that much tighter.

Every so often, he would kiss my knuckles or the side of my head and whisper how sorry he was. How he wasn't the man I deserved. And every time those words left his mouth, my heart shattered into a million pieces. So many damn pieces, I had no idea how they could ever be put back together again.

Our friends didn't say anything but I could see the questioning glances, the unknown stares—if we would both explode on each other again. Little did they know that I was tired and that we were both done.

After telling everyone that we dealt with everything on our own terms, they backed off. I had never meant to tell them outright how Dale and I were sleeping together but when they wouldn't leave us alone, it was the only way.

"Max, do you have a second?" Jay asked, coming toward us. Her gaze zeroed in on Dale. "Are you going to push me again?"

"Listen." Dale let out a slow breath. "I'm sorry."

Her shoulders slumped. "I know." She looked behind her.

Angel caught her gaze.

"You're lucky, though. I've never seen Angel that mad and trust me, I've pissed him off many times but ..." She swallowed hard. "Just ... no matter what happens between you two, don't lose that friendship with your brothers. I don't want you and Angel fighting again."

"Fuck, neither do I. Your boyfriend's punches hurt like a bitch," Dale grunted, rubbing his jaw. "I *am* sorry, though."

"I know." Jay turned to me. "Think we can be civil?"

"Yeah." I squeezed Dale's hand, giving him a small smile.

Dale kissed my knuckles and made his way to Angel and the guys, leaving me alone with Jay.

"How is everything?" Jay asked, searching my face.

"We're dealing. We talk when we can." I looked back at Dale, my heart jumping in my chest with the love I had for him. "We're not fighting as often anymore," I added with a small smile.

"I'm sorry," she whispered.

"Don't." I shook my head.

She huffed, breathing slow and even. She rubbed her belly and winced in the meantime. "This baby needs to come out of me," she muttered, letting out a slow breath.

"You're due in a week. It could definitely be sooner," I told her, handing her a bottle of water.

She took the water from me and glared at it. "Once the doctors give me permission, I am getting fucking wasted until Angel has to peel me off the floor."

I laughed, ignoring the twinge of pain stabbing me in the chest. I would give up alcohol for life just to be able to hold my baby one last time. To have her stare up at me with love and adoration. To just be able to tell her again how much I loved her. My chest tightened, the air in my lungs shortening the longer I tried to breathe. I couldn't get the thoughts out of my head. What could I have done differently? Did I take the pregnancy for granted? Was I being punished for all the wrong I had done in my life?

"Max?" Jay touched my shoulder.

I jumped back as if her touch had burnt me. I couldn't …

God, I couldn't breathe.

"Max," her eyes widened. "Breathe."

"I'm … I'm …" I gasped for breath, the panic attack hitting me full force. "I can't …" I rubbed the ache between my breasts.

Out of nowhere, I saw Dale come running toward me. He moved me to one of the booths, knelt at my feet and cupped my hands. "Breathe, kitten."

Squeezing my eyes shut, I covered his hands with mine but my heartbeat was so damn loud, I couldn't control it. I couldn't control the feelings rushing through me.

"Max," Dale's voice was firm. "Breathe."

I didn't want to. I wanted God to take me away and let me be with my baby. Tears rolled down my cheeks. Seeing Jay's swollen belly and the fact she was about to have the baby any time now, triggered the panic attack. It shouldn't be like this. I couldn't lose myself every time I was near her.

Voices sounded around us but all I could focus on was Dale's smooth and calming voice.

I needed him to show me that I was strong. That I could get through this. That no matter what, I could find happiness again.

Throwing myself in his arms, I cried against his chest.

"Shit." Dale hugged me, holding me tight. "It will be okay. It will all fucking be okay," he said, his voice thick.

Sobs forced me immobile. I had been doing well and then everything hit me all at once. Jay's pregnancy. My feelings for Dale. The agonizing fear that he could leave me. Even though I knew it was possible, I didn't know how I would react to it. We needed time apart. I got that. I understood. But I still wasn't strong enough. I knew without a doubt that I wouldn't be able to pull back from that if he hurt me again.

"Don't hurt me," I whispered.

"What?"

I looked up at him through my tear soaked lashes. "Don't hurt me. Please. Not again. I'm not strong enough."

Dale searched my face, his jaw clenching. "It won't be me hurting you this time."

Cupping his cheek, I brushed my thumb over his bottom lip and replaced it with my mouth. My feelings wouldn't leave my mouth but I tried with everything in me to show him how I felt through that kiss.

"You are strong enough, kitten," he said, kissing my nose and then my forehead. "You are the strongest person I know."

I wished I could feel the same way.

Pushing out of his grip, I helped him to his feet. "I need to take a walk." I went to head outside when Jay stopped me.

"I'm sorry."

"Don't." I gave her a hug. "I love you. I just need a moment."

She nodded, her eyes glazing over. "I love you too."

Once I reached outside, I was tempted to hop on my bike and just drive.

"What do you want from me?" Dale asked, coming up from behind me.

"I want you," I told him, sitting on the picnic table.

"Really? Because somehow I don't think that's completely true." He came toward me and stepped between my legs.

My breath hitched, my fingers reaching out to grip his shirt.

"I *do* want you," I told him, curling the fabric in my hands. "Why don't you believe me?"

"It's hard to believe you when you constantly second guess me. I know you don't trust me. Not completely. I get it and I understand. But you keep pulling me in and pushing me away. Why, Max? It's fucking with my head." He pinched my chin, forcing me to look up at him. "I'm too old for these games."

"I ... I'm sorry." I swallowed hard. "You broke me."

"I don't remember. Not everything. I remember feelings. I remember that I hurt you. It's like snippets here and there but it's frustrating as fuck." He pulled away, pacing back and forth, and rubbed the back of his neck. "The doctors can't do shit for my memory but if I could get it back, even if it meant being reminded of everything I did to you, at least ..."

"What?" I asked, peering up at him through unshed tears.

"I could apologize for every wrong I caused you." He came toward me again and grabbed my hands. "I could spend the rest of my life, showing you exactly how sorry I am."

"I want to believe you."

"Then why the fuck don't you?" he shouted, the cords in his neck straining.

"Don't yell at me." I shoved to my feet, pushing him back. "We were doing good and now this. The only time we don't fight is when we're fucking."

"Max, we were never doing good. Don't fucking kid yourself. This?" He waved a hand between us. "It's damn toxic. If you can't see that, then we're both more fucked up then we thought."

"I don't know what to say or do anymore." That flight or fight response was nagging at me. Everything in me was telling me to run. To get out of there. To move on. But I couldn't. There was no way I could move on from this with Dale. Even we didn't end up together in the end, he would always be a part of me.

"Be with me," he said. "That's all I ask right now."

"Sex isn't going to solve anything," I muttered.

We stood there in silence. Time wore on and it felt like hours since we spoke to each other. This man standing in front of me forced these feelings to brew inside of me. He controlled my actions and my thoughts. It scared me how much I needed him.

"Please, baby." He brushed a hand down my cheek before pinching my chin. Tilting my head back, he placed a soft peck on my lips. "I need you."

I turned away, pulling out of his grasp. "I can't continue fighting with you."

"Where are you going?"

"Home," I said, heading in the direction of my house.

"Like hell you are." He grabbed my arm, spinning me around. "I'm not letting you walk out on me. Not again."

"Me?" I shoved him. "*I* walked out on *you*? All right. You want to talk?" I pushed him again. "Let's fucking talk. Let's talk about how I go to sleep at night and get woken up by nightmares because I fear you won't be with me in the morning. Or how about the fact that our daughter haunts me. I dream of her giggling. And it's not her being cute. It terrifies me. It's like my dreams are one big fucking horror movie. And this? Whatever we're doing? You're right. It is damn toxic but it feels fucking good all at the same time. So, if we're not going to move forward, then what the hell are we doing?"

His breath hitched. "Max."

"I'm tired and I don't want to fight with you anymore." I shoved from his grip and stomped down the driveway when I was suddenly picked up and thrown over Dale's shoulders. "Put me down. What the hell are you doing?" I demanded, beating my fists against his back.

"You keep trying to run away, kitten. Well, fuck that shit." He dropped me when we reached a dark alley. "You are going to stand here and listen to what I have to say."

"You can't force me, Dale." I pushed him.

"*Shut up,*" he boomed. "Just shut up."

I was taken aback, my mouth snapping shut at his outburst.

"I don't remember everything and it's driving me fucking mad. I'm sorry for what I've done. I'll never forgive myself and I'll regret it for the rest of my life that I wasn't there when you needed me most. I pushed you away because I was fucking scared. I know that now. All right? There. That's the truth. Take it or leave it. And you are right as well. This does feel good even though it will probably end up killing us. But I'm tired too. I don't care anymore about what is right and what is wrong. I just don't care." When he turned to walk away, I placed a hand on his arm. He glanced down at it.

"I …" I let out a slow breath, realizing it was time. "I want to take you to see her."

Dale searched my face, swallowing hard. "Now?"

"Yes." I nodded. "I think it's needed."

He grabbed my hand, leading me back down the sidewalk to the club. Just as we approached the building, Coby came outside. The silent man only looked at us before handing Dale his keys.

"How did he know you needed his keys?" I asked Dale as he guided me to Coby's SUV.

Dale looked over his shoulder. "He knows me well. Probably better than anyone besides you."

"Oh." I slid into the large vehicle and did up the seat belt. I looked up, noticing Dale still standing in the door way. "What?"

His finger skimmed lightly down my cheek. "You're beautiful."

My breath caught at the unexpected compliment. "Thank you," I said, the back of my neck heating.

He nodded once and shut the door before making his way around to the driver's side. When he joined me, he gripped the steering wheel tight in his hands. "Tell me where she is."

I blew out a slow breath, finding the courage I knew I didn't have but faked it just the same, and gave him the directions to the cemetery. "It's a family run business. They take care of it themselves too. The grounds are beautiful and peaceful. Quiet. I figured it was perfect."

Dale grabbed my hand, linked our fingers, and kissed my knuckles. But he didn't say anything else. Sometimes I wished I knew what he was thinking. Was he always this dominant? Did losing his memory make him that way? It was a conversation we should have had months ago but I got so wrapped up in the guy, I couldn't even breathe when I was around him.

Once we reached the cemetery, Dale pulled the vehicle into park. He stared out the window, his gaze roaming over the grounds with stones of all various sizes. "It shouldn't have been this way." His words were quiet, I wasn't sure I heard him correctly.

Before I had a chance to ask what he was talking about, he left the vehicle and came around to my side. Opening the door, he helped me out and as soon as my feet landed on the ground, he pulled me into his arms.

My throat closed, my chest aching at the permanent knot that had taken place in it months before.

His hands roamed down my back, holding me tight against his warm, hard body before he pulled away.

I swallowed hard at the mere look of utter pain and agony twisting on his handsome face.

"Show me," he demanded, his voice thick with emotion.

I grabbed his hand, leading him down a path in the middle of the yard. We didn't say anything as the solemn surroundings took over our thoughts. All of these people, someone's loved one, they were now at peace but every time I went there, it still broke my heart.

When we reached the back of the yard, I stopped in front of a small grave plot with *Baby Stanton Michaels* etched into it. "I didn't want to name her without you. As much as I was mad, I didn't feel that it was right. So … I gave her both our names."

Dale's breath hitched. He looked between the stone and me, back and forth until he did the unexpected and fell to his knees.

CHAPTER TWENTY-FOUR

Dale

IN MY WHOLE career in the military as a Navy SEAL, with all the training I had, nothing could prepare me for this moment. I had seen the ruthlessness of humanity. Desperation calling out to people where they would do anything to save themselves. Women getting raped. Children gutted like pigs. Men taking their own wrath out on each other trying to prove who was bigger and better. But nothing, none of those horrors was even remotely close to seeing the ground my daughter was buried beneath.

I wrapped my arms around Max, kneeling at her feet, and held her close. I squeezed her so hard, I half expected her to complain I was hurting her. But when a soft sob escaped her and she brushed a hand over my head, I held her tighter.

We needed time apart. I got that. But neither of us were brave enough to admit it. I only hoped that with distance, we could find our way back to each other.

What bothered me the most through this whole thing was how Max took it upon herself to deal with this situation on her own. She didn't call on her sisters for help. She didn't ask for guidance. She chose to be alone, and I didn't understand why. And I probably never would.

"Dale," she whispered, brushing her fingers through the hair at my nape. When I didn't respond, she lowered to her knees in front me. "Talk to me."

I couldn't look at her for fear I would start blubbering like a baby. I wasn't one to get emotional. Knowing what I had seen in my career, it made even the warmest of hearts turn cold. But losing a child could force even the evilest of monsters into a sobbing mess.

"Why did you do this on your own?" I asked, my voice coming out thick, even I didn't recognize it.

Her shoulders slumped. Picking at a piece of grass, she shrugged. "I didn't think it was fair having everyone else help me bury her when you couldn't be with us. I know I've said that I wanted to do everything on my own but the truth is … I was waiting for you." She met my gaze. "I just didn't want her lying in an ice box somewhere. So, I had her buried. I'm sorry I didn't wait for you so we could do it together but I couldn't stand knowing she wasn't at rest."

"Don't apologize." I cupped her cheek, brushing my thumb under her eye, and wiped away the lonely tear that had fallen. If only I could wipe away her pain just the same. "I'm here now."

"You are." She placed her hand on my knee.

That small touch sent strength soaring through my body. "I'm in love with you," I blurted.

Her mouth fell open.

Before she could say anything, I stopped her. "I don't expect you to say anything. I've been an asshole. I don't remember everything but I can feel the regret and see the pain I've caused you. I'm sorry for everything I have put you through. I was scared. It's not an excuse. I get that." I paused. "I never knew what love was until I met you, but even then, I pushed you away. I don't have a reason why and I'm not going to make up some shit excuse but I do love you. I know we'll probably go our separate ways. Maybe that will be forever, maybe it won't. But I needed you to know before that happened. So ..." I cleared my throat. "Yeah."

She smiled softly, tears now flowing down her cheeks. She wiped them away and turned in my arms, leaning against me. "My grandma told me you loved me. She hasn't even met you and she knew."

"You talk to your grandma about me?" I asked, kissing her head.

"I do." She sighed. "I want to tell you I feel the same but—"

"No." I pushed her forward and turned her back around to face me. "I want you to say the words when you mean them. You've said them before and I fucked up. I'm a patient man when it comes to you, kitten. I will wait until my very last breath to hear you say them and if you never say them again? I'll still keep loving you. No matter what."

"No matter what?" she asked, her eyes searching my face.

My blood boiled beneath my skin. "No matter what," I repeated, not liking the taste of those words on my lips. There was no way I could handle seeing her with another man but in all fairness, she saw me with other women. If I could kick my own ass, I would.

"Thank you for not pushing me." She held my hands between us, running her thumb over my palm.

"Never. Not when it comes to this. I know your limits." I brought our joined hands up to my lips and kissed her knuckles before placing a soft peck on her lips.

She returned the kiss, her salty tears coating my tongue. When she pulled away, she looked down at the grave. "I have a picture of her."

My heart hammered against my ribs. "You do?"

She nodded and reached into her purse. "For whatever reason, she doesn't look pale in the photo. She just looks like she's sleeping." She handed me the image. "That's your daughter, Dale."

My throat closed, my eyes burning with unshed tears. The image staring up at me was the most breathtaking thing I had ever seen. Max was holding our daughter, her lips pressed to our baby's forehead.

Squeezing my eyes shut, I let the tears fall.

***

(Max)

Seeing Dale break down in front of me was not something I ever wanted to see again. He cried as he stared at a picture of our daughter. He swore and cursed under his breath that it wasn't fair. He was right. It wasn't. But being with him now made me realize that this situation only made us stronger in the end. I would never wish this sort of pain on anyone. It brought agony to a whole new level. I would never get over losing her but with time, I could get through it. If Dale and I at least remained friends, it would be all I could ever ask for.

Crawling onto Dale's lap, I hugged myself around him and held him while we both shed our own tears of grief.

"I'm fucking sorry," he repeated over and over in the crook of my neck. "I will never forgive myself for what I've done to you. I should have been there. I shouldn't have put that stress on either of you."

His words hurt because they were true. Maybe our daughter would have been alive if I hadn't been stressed but that wasn't something I wanted to mull over. It would only drive us both crazy.

"I don't deserve you." His arms wrapped around me, holding me until I couldn't breathe but I didn't care. "I don't deserve either of you."

"Shhh. What's done is done." My heart felt lighter. "You're here now. You're here for us both." I leaned back, cupped his cheeks, and kissed him fully on the mouth. He loved me but I couldn't say those words back. Even though he knew. He had to. No one else mattered since I had met him months ago. From the first moment he had kissed me, no one else existed in my world.

I loved Dale.

But I didn't tell him.

CHAPTER TWENTY-FIVE

Max

IT HAD BEEN several hours since we left the clubhouse. Several more since we left the graveyard. After both of our breakdowns, we sat in silence until the sun set and the air became cool.

We were both mentally exhausted that we went right to bed when we got back to my place. Dale hesitated at first.

"No matter what happens, I need you in my life. So, we can at least start by being friends," I told him, grabbing his hand and led him upstairs to my room.

"I can't be friends with you and not touch you," he confessed, crawling into bed beside me. *"But if it makes you happy, I'll try."*

He had kept his sweatpants on out of respect for me even though I told him he didn't have to. It had been the first time since meeting him that he kept his hands to himself.

I didn't sleep. I couldn't for fear I would wake up to find the spot beside me empty.

Sometime during the night, Dale stirred beside me.

He bolted upright.

"Dale." My heart jumped. "What's wrong?"

He shook his head, dropping it in his hands.

I gently touched his shoulder, a sheen of sweat coating his skin. His body trembled.

"You're shaking." I cupped his cheek, turning his head toward me. "What's wrong?"

His eyes were bright. "I remember."

****

(Dale)

Getting your memory back was like your light being out and suddenly, someone plugged you in. All the memories came rushing back at once.

Every hateful word.

All the pain.

Every single woman.

All of them and, fuck me, there had been a lot. Why? Why the hell would I do that to Max?

I remembered laughing at her when she confessed her feelings for me. I could see the look of pain morphing on her face like it had just happened the day before.

"I love you," Max *confessed, her eyes warm. "I've been in love—"*

A laugh escaped me.

Her mouth snapped shut, her chin trembling.

Instead of being gentle about it, I kicked her out of my bed. *Fuck.*

"Dale?" Max said, her soft voice coming from beside me.

My mind was jumbled with memories. All of them so damn painful, I couldn't look at her. I didn't *deserve* to look at her.

"Hey." She kissed my shoulder. "Look at me."

"No." I shot out of the bed, pacing back and forth. "I can't. Fuck. I don't deserve you. I never have." I never would.

Her head flinched back slightly. "What's going on?"

"I remember." I stopped in front of her. "Everything."

"Oh." She looked down at her hands in her lap. "Everything?"

"Yes."

"The women?" she asked, her voice small.

"Yes." I remembered the whores because they definitely weren't ladies. They were a piece of meat to satisfy the itch I had because I was too stupid enough to realize that only Max could curb this craving.

"So, what now?" Max looked at me that time.

"I have no fucking idea. I can only imagine my doctors would want to know but even then, it's not important." I dropped to my knees in front of her and grabbed hold of her hands, covering them in soft kisses. I didn't know what to say. I didn't know what to do.

"Do you still love me?" Max asked, her voice cracking.

"It would be easier if I could say no." I pulled her onto my lap and wrapped my arms around her small body. "Because then it wouldn't be this hard to say goodbye."

***

(Max)

"This is it, isn't it?" I looked up at him through unshed tears, my heart hammering against my ribs. The blood rushed to my head, and if I was standing, I would have fallen over.

Dale swallowed hard.

"Everyone thinks we need time apart. I don't want to prove them right. I don't want … I don't want any of this to be right." A sob escaped me. "Why can't we be wrong and just enjoy it?"

"Because we don't talk." He cupped my cheek. "I don't want you to end up hating me more than you already do."

"I …" I placed my hand on top of his. "I don't hate you. My grandmother raised me better. I don't think I've ever hated you."

"This would be easier if you did." He leaned his forehead against mine. "But we can't be together if you don't trust me."

"I'm trying. I swear to God I'm trying."

"Hey." He pinched my chin, tilting my head back to meet his gaze. "I understand. I know you'd rather me be an asshole but right now I don't have the energy." His shoulders slumped. "I will spend the rest of my life loving you."

Tears flowed down my cheeks. *I love you.*

But no matter how hard I tried, those three little words never left my mouth.

NUMB

"You don't have to say it back." He kissed my forehead. "You don't even have to say it again."

As his words washed over me, mixing with the gentle caress of his fingers against my skin, the tears fell harder.

"I will love you now. Tomorrow. Next week. For the rest of my damn life. I'll love you from afar if I have to. Just don't forget me."

I threw my arms around his neck, holding him tight against me. "Never," I hiccupped on a sob. "I could never forget you." I kissed him hard, pouring everything I felt into that touch. All the pain, the heartache, the damn agony threatening to destroy us both, I unleashed it all into that kiss.

Dale fisted my hair in his hands, his hold on me tight for only a second before he loosened his touch.

"No," I said against his mouth. "Don't hold back. Give me all of you," I said between my tears.

He grabbed hold of my hair, holding my head in place, and deepened the kiss. He kissed me until I could feel him all the way down to my toes. His tongue pushed along mine, prodding and kneading, begging me to give him everything I was.

Reaching between us, I cupped him over his pants.

He jumped, a low growl leaving the back of his throat.

I wrapped my hand around him, tugging and pulling until he grew so damn hard it took my own breath away.

Every time his tongue swept against mine, a hot shiver trembled down my body.

Our mouths were fused while I pleased his lower body to the point of no return. I needed him to snap and take control. I wanted him to fuck away all the pain we had both endured. I wanted him to say goodbye to me through the powerful thrusts of his body.

"Max," he whispered against my mouth.

"Please, Dale." I took several breaths, my heart racing. "I need you. One last time."

"This won't be the last time." He hooked his fingers in the waistband of my shorts and pulled them down my legs. "No matter how long it takes." He lifted me onto my knees. "We will find each other again." He pulled out his straining cock and lowered me onto him.

We both let out a sigh at being connected once again.

"Forever, baby." He linked our fingers, leaning his forehead against mine. "I'll wait for you forever."

***

(Dale)

It was late into the night, and I couldn't sleep. Max's touch was imbedded on my skin. Her moans of pleasure would forever be engrained inside my skull.

She shifted beside me, hooking my arm over her middle. She sniffed, a soft whimper leaving her.

We had said goodbye using our bodies but she wouldn't let me leave. I wasn't exactly sure why. I knew I would see her again but we hadn't talked about what would happen when we did. If this was the final straw and all that shit.

I loved her, and when I finally told her those three powerful words, all the weight from the past several months lifted off my shoulders.

She didn't trust me completely yet but she also didn't want me to leave. It fucked with my head but it wasn't her fault. I couldn't blame her, although I tried.

I kissed her shoulder, squeezing her against me. I should leave before she woke up. It would be easier on both of us.

Placing a soft peck on the side of her head, I let her go and slid out of the bed. After getting dressed, I looked down at her sleeping form. My heart thumped. My chest tightened. This was it. This was goodbye. Not see you tomorrow or the next day. But fucking *goodbye*.

I made my way to the door, but before I could leave the room, I heard her shift in the bed.

"Dale," she whispered.

Her soft voice stopped me in my tracks but I didn't turn around. I couldn't for fear I would end up back in bed with her and we would be right where we started.

We couldn't move on if we didn't talk.

"I love you, Max. I will always love you," I croaked, opening the door.

"Dale," she cried, a sob escaping her.

I closed the door behind me but not before I heard those three words I had craved since I told her how I felt. I took a breath, letting them slide over my skin.

"I love you too."

And with that, I left Max's house.

CHAPTER TWENTY-SIX

Max

DEPRESSION SETTLED IN the moment Dale left my bedroom only a couple hours before. It felt like my heart was being ripped out of my chest all over again and this time it was because we had issues talking. I could sense the pain tearing through him but we both knew it was for the best. As much as I didn't want to admit it, we needed time apart but I also needed him with me just the same.

Going back and forth the way we had been for the past couple of weeks wasn't healthy. Maybe time away from each other would do us some good.

Unable to sleep any longer, I made my way to my gallery and decided to get some painting done. Josee had set up another showing for me. I couldn't be more grateful to her and her faith in me. I didn't deserve it, but I appreciated it just the same.

After the last time and not showing up, I was surprised she still wanted to work with me. But it was in her nature to be nice and helpful where needed. Much like Jay. God, I was a sucky friend.

After an hour, I was finally able to get a painting done but it only broke my heart. I painted before I thought about it. The strokes of the brush gliding along the page like they had a mind of their very own. When I was done, an image of hands holding each other stared back at me. They belonged to Dale and me. I only knew because my heart told me so. I had memorized every inch of Dale. Every vein. Every breath. Every beat of his heart. I knew every curve, every hard agonizingly delicious muscle. The ripple of his body shaking beneath mine as I forced him to submit to the pleasure he allowed me to give him.

With the painting done and my heart still hanging in my chest by the thread of my despair, I went in search of coffee. It had been so long since I made it for myself, I almost forgot where everything was. Dale had been the one to prepare it for me in the morning, waking me up by the fresh scent of the beans.

A lump formed in my throat. I swallowed hard, giving my body a full shake. I could do this. I could be strong. But my hands itched to call him. They reached for the phone on their own accord and just as I was about to press his number, I hung up.

How long was I supposed to wait until I reached out to him? It had only been a couple hours, and already I missed him like I missed my next breath.

I didn't know how. I didn't know when. But I promised myself I would be happy again. With or without Dale, I would move on from this.

***

(Dale)

"Tell me why you left her."

As soon as those words left Dr. Santos' mouth, a headache started piercing my brain. I pinched the bridge of my nose, taking deep cleansing breaths before meeting the doctor's gaze.

"I already told you why," I muttered.

"No." He pointed his pen in my direction. "You told me *when*. You never told me *why*."

I huffed, shifting my body weight on the leather couch. "Our relationship wasn't healthy. We both knew that. You can only base so much of it on sex before it destroys you." I grunted. I was starting to sound like Coby.

"You love her."

"Of course I fucking love her," I snapped. "Who wouldn't? She's perfect. She's … she's everything I'm not. But after remembering what I've done …" I shook my head, the guilt eating away at my heart. "She deserves better."

"She loves you."

I rolled my eyes. "Thanks for pointing out the obvious. They pay you for this shit?" I shook my head. "Listen, there's nothing more to say about this." I went to rise from the couch when Dr. Santos' next words stopped me.

"If you love her, no matter the shit you have both been through, you need to work through this or else it will end up making you both more miserable than you already are." He raised an eyebrow.

I slumped back onto the couch. "And how the hell am I supposed to do that? I know she still loves me. She hasn't told me because she doesn't trust me. Not completely anyway."

"Do you want her to trust you again?"

"Yes. *Fuck.*" I rubbed the back of my neck. "I will spend the rest of my life making it up to her but … it's been a month. I haven't seen her."

"Dale, it's only been two weeks."

"That's a fucking lifetime."

Dr. Santos let out a slow breath. "Listen, I'm going to tell you this off the record and based on my own personal experience. No matter how much you've hurt her, you're trying everything you can to make it up to her. All I can tell you is that time is the true healer in all this shit. Be there for her when you can. Do whatever it takes but don't push her."

"You sound like my best friend," I grumbled.

Dr. Santos' eyes twinkled in the dim lighting of his office. "Time, Dale. Give that to her."

But I didn't want to. I wanted her now.

I would spend the rest of my life regretting what I did. I just prayed Max could eventually forgive me. Or everything we had worked toward would have been for nothing.

CHAPTER TWENTY-SEVEN

Max

DALE: I MISS you. I shouldn't be texting you. Hell, I shouldn't even be thinking about you. But I am. Every second that passes, I miss you more.

My eyes roamed over every word, every single text. I read Dale's messages over and over but I couldn't bring myself to respond for fear that I would beg he come back to me.

Dale: I know you're reading my texts. You can't go without checking your phone. That's one of the many things I love about you.

NUMB

I laughed, wiping the tears from under my eyes.

Dale: Just tell me you're okay, baby. Please. That's all I need to know.

I couldn't tell him because it wouldn't be true. Every time our friends asked me if I was okay, I lied. Every time I laughed, it was all a damn lie.

Me: I can't.

My thumb hovered over the *send* button.

Dale: Tell me.

I took a breath and pressed *send*.

At that point, my phone rang. Dale's handsome face showed up on the screen. *Shit.*

"I can't do this," I said, answering the phone.

"I need to know you're okay," came his smooth reply.

"Are *you* okay?" I asked, challenging him.

"Fuck no. I won't be okay until I have you in my arms again."

Dropping my head in my hands, I let the tears fall. They rolled down my cheeks like tiny reminders of the pain and heartache I had endured over the past couple of months. "I need you," I whispered.

"What the hell are we doing?" he demanded, his voice raising. "Why aren't we together?"

"Because it hurts too much," I sobbed, my voice cracking.

"Max …" He took a breath. "Fuck this."

"Dale?" I pulled the phone away from my ear, realizing he had hung up. Was he coming over?

A couple minutes later, a knock sounded on the door.

My head popped up, my heart jumping in my throat.

The knock sounded again.

Finding that courage from deep within, I pulled to my feet and headed to the door. "Dale, I—" My eyes widened when I saw who stood in front of me. It wasn't Dale. It wasn't the man who had invaded my dreams all of these weeks. It wasn't the man I was in love with.

Tyler Bone smirked, rubbing the dark scruff on his jaw, and pushed me back into my house. He towered over me, keeping his hand wrapped around my arm.

"What are you doing here?" I demanded, attempting to shove out of his grip, but his hold only tightened. It had been months since I saw the guy. After everything that had happened with the baby, I shut myself in, only hearing about Tyler and his shit in passing. Besides causing problems for Dante's Kings, he left us alone.

Tyler didn't say anything, only pushing me further into the house. I didn't know what he wanted or needed, but his silence drove my nerves on edge. He had always scared me but now I was absolutely terrified of him.

"What do you want?" I asked again. "Where's Stone?" I knew he was supposed to be watching the house after Angel said he didn't want any of us to be alone.

Tyler didn't respond. He only licked his lips, his dark gaze roaming down the length of my body.

I shivered, glancing away. My stomach churned, bile rising in my throat.

"Tell him you don't want to see him," Tyler said, his deep voice scraping over my skin.

"What—" A knock sounded on the door.

"Tell him," Tyler commanded, pushing me to the door. "Tell him you're fine but you can't see him."

The knock sounded again.

"Baby, I know you're in there." *Dale.*

"No, just let me go," I pleaded, shoving against Tyler. "Please."

His hand gripped my jaw, digging his fingers into my cheeks. "Tell. Him."

"Fuck you," I said through clenched teeth.

A wicked grin spread across his face. He released me, slamming his fist against my cheek before fisting my hair. "Tell him."

My head rang, spots dancing in my vision. "I'm fine," I said, repeating his words.

"Louder," Tyler pushed me against the door. "Say it."

"Dale, I can't see you. Go away." My throat burned, my eyes brimming over with unshed tears.

"What the fuck, Max? Let me in," Dale demanded, rattling the doorknob. "Let me the fuck in."

"I'll call you later but I need to be alone right now," I told Dale, keeping my eyes on Tyler.

"You can't get rid of me that easily, kitten."

"*Leave,*" I screamed. "Get the hell out of here. I don't want to see you."

Tyler waited a beat before throwing me over his shoulder.

"Put me down, you bastard," I yelled, beating my fists against his back.

He ignored me and carried me up the stairs.

My heart beat faster with each step he took. Each move he made only made me hate him more. I struggled against him, thrashing my body in his arms but he was too strong for me. He wouldn't let me go— he carried me up the stairs to my impending nightmare.

Tyler charged forward, kicking open each door down the hallway until he found my bedroom. Only then did he pause.

"Please," I pleaded. "I don't know what you want. I haven't done anything."

He pushed his way into the room and threw me on the bed.

My stomach twisted at the thought of what was about to happen. "Tyler, we can talk about this."

He stared down at me from the foot of the bed. "You think talking will end this?" His voice was rough, nothing like I had ever heard from him before. "You think talking will stop all of this?"

"What happened? Why are you doing this?" I never liked the guy or what he had done to Jay, but I always made sure to steer clear of him. I thought it was the smartest thing to do, but apparently, I was wrong.

"Jenny's with *him*," he said, his morphing with rage.

I heard the slight slur to his words.

"What does that have to do with me?" I asked, slowly inching my way up the bed. If I could only reach my nightstand, I could grab the pistol Jay made me keep in it.

"Nothing but I can't do shit when it comes to them so you're my last resort." He started pacing back and forth. "She's having his baby. Do you know how many times I've tried fucking a baby into her? But she had none of it. She demanded we use condoms." Tyler laughed, the sound reverberating right into my soul.

"You don't have to do this." I wished I was Brogan and had her strength. "I can help you."

Tyler grabbed my ankles and flipped me onto my stomach. "Damn right you're going to help me." His hot breath scorched the side of my face. "You're going to help me feel good."

I swallowed past the bile. The scent of stale beer wafted into my nose. I pushed and kicked, but I wasn't strong enough.

Tyler bound my legs, wrapping something around my ankles. He pulled the restraint taught, the rope scratching into my skin. "I was kicked out of Dante's King's. They *will* regret it. Brian loves you like his own daughter." He chuckled. "I'll just use you as leverage."

"Please, Tyler, I swear I know nothing. I haven't been around." I pushed up on my arms, kicked my legs out as hard as I could when I fell off the bed.

"Fuck." Tyler wrapped his arms around my waist, throwing me back on the bed.

I screamed and thrashed beneath him.

Suddenly, a fist landed against the side of my head.

I whimpered, my vision fading in and out.

"I will hurt you, Max. I don't want to." He laughed, licking up the side of my face. "Actually, I'd love to make you scream out in pain." He groaned, pulling my arms behind me, and tugged my head back as far as it could go.

I swallowed hard, my eyes watering from the added force of my neck being stretched. "Please."

"Shut the fuck up. You can't try and talk me out of this. I'll make them pay. I'll make them all fucking pay."

Because Brian finally got the balls to kick this sick fuck out of his club, I would now pay for it. Life was funny, in a way. You do something right only for it to backfire on you. But no matter what Tyler did to me, nothing would be as hard as dealing with the loss of my baby.

***

(Dale)

She didn't want to see me.

Something was wrong.

"You need to calm down," Stone told me, leaning against my truck.

"Are you sure you didn't see anything?" I asked him.

"I haven't seen anything or anyone since Lian and Henley finished their rounds. I've been here since you left during the night." Stone frowned. "Are you questioning my abilities?"

"If something happens to Max, then you bet your fucking ass I am."

"Call her." Stone handed me his phone. "Now."

I did as he said.

"Hello?" came Max's soft voice.

A breath left me on a whoosh. "Are you okay?"

"Yes. I just need a moment. I'll call you later." Her voice was monotone. "I promise."

My heart jumped, my stomach twisting. "Okay." I hung up.

"Satisfied?" Stone asked when I handed him the phone.

"Nope," I answered. "Not one fucking bit."

NUMB

***
(Max)

My ears rang, blood seeped into my mouth but all I could focus on was the numbing pain that had swallowed me whole. I didn't know where the agony began and I ended. Every inch of me hurt. I could feel Tyler everywhere. Inside of my head. On my skin. He was in my thoughts, and I knew that was what he wanted.

When Dale had called, Tyler made me answer and tell him everything was fine. That I was okay. It took everything in me not to scream for his help but Tyler was drunk and psychotic. I never underestimated his twisted ways knowing what he had done to Jay for years.

Tyler fucked with my head, only making me think he would take things further than what he had but he never did.

There was a rule in our MC world. The fear of God was put into each and every member of every single bike club. You rape one of ours and death would be too easy. It went for both men and women. Although it never happened, sometimes someone like Tyler slipped through the cracks and got a piece before anyone could stop them.

I wasn't sure if Tyler had left or stayed to watch me squirm.

Footsteps sounded from the hallway.

"How does it feel knowing you're submitting to a man other than the one you love?"

Squeezing my eyes shut, I pretended to still be passed out but, of course, Tyler was too smart.

Grabbing a fistful of my hair, he straddled my hips and yanked my head back further. "I asked you a question."

I cried out, the sting of my hair being ripped out mixed with the abrasiveness of his clothes rubbing along the cuts on my skin.

"He's going to think of me every time he touches you." Tyler licked his tongue up the side of my cheek. "It's funny, though. Did you know that I wanted both you and Jenny? At the same time?" He groaned, rubbing himself into the flesh of my rear. "Both of you at the same time would have been fucking hot. But you were too innocent for me. I wanted someone who would fight back and fuck me, did Jay ever fight."

I grimaced at the thought of my best friend having to fend Tyler off her. I didn't know the details of their history. It wasn't my business but I knew Tyler had caused a lot of problems for both her and Angel.

"Please." I swallowed hard. "Let me go." I struggled against the binds wrapped around my ankles and wrists. I was fucked. There was nothing I could do to get out of this. I wasn't strong like Brogan. I knew enough self-defense to get by but, clearly, it meant shit in my current situation. "Tyler."

"No." He sunk his teeth into my shoulder until tears welled in my eyes.

I whimpered, trembling beneath him.

"I'm making my point, little girl." He shoved my head face first into the pillow. "They will remember not to fuck with me. Just wait until they find out everything." He chuckled.

"You don't need to do this," I said, even though he already had.

"Don't worry, Max." He kissed my cheek. "As much as I'd love to force myself inside this sweet as fuck pussy, I don't feel like dying anytime soon."

A breath left me on a whoosh. A part of me feared that Tyler would ignore the rules. Although this wasn't any better. It would be Jay's father's responsibility to see that Tyler got his.

We had it harder because we were women but Tyler wasn't stupid, he knew this would start a war. Even torturing me and playing games with my head wouldn't end well for him. All because he got kicked out of the club. There had to be more to it. None of this made sense. Why me? Why after all this time?

A laugh escaped me. It got to the point where I no longer cared about anything except for Dale. He was my strength. The reason my heart was still beating. He forced this new-found power inside of me. Without him or our baby, I didn't give a shit.

"They'll kill you anyways," I laughed even harder.

"You think so, do you? I've left marks on you that are permanent. Dale will see me every time he looks between your legs. How do you think he'll feel knowing another man was close to enjoying what he has?"

"You haven't fucked me," I grit out.

"But he doesn't know that."

My eyes widened. "What are you going to do?" There was no way I could get out of this. I was strapped down to the bed. *My* bed. Something I had shared many happy memories with Dale on. But now I was tied up, my legs spread out like a fucking star and I was naked. Tyler had cut my clothes off me, leaving them in shreds on the nightstand. They were where I could see them, knowing he put them there to taunt me and remind me that he was in control.

"You are a hot little thing. No wonder Dale likes controlling you."

"You don't know shit," I ground out, attempting to struggle against my restraints. Knowing Tyler wouldn't rape me, the fear that had slid into my body slowly left me. Although he could still kill me, I wouldn't put it past him that he would do whatever he wanted to me until there was almost nothing left. My mind racked for answers.

"I bet you two play; you submit and he controls every inch of you, doesn't he?"

I refused to give him the satisfaction of answering his questions.

Tyler chuckled, straddling my hips. "How about we invite someone in on our little fun?" When a phone came into view, Tyler pressed a button. "Pay attention, Max." He kissed my temple. "Let's see who's come to visit."

Suddenly, a video appeared on the phone. My eyes widened.

Dale stared back at me with duct tape wrapped around his head. He struggled against whatever binds held him in place. Bruises marked his face, his voice muffled by the gag over his mouth.

"What the fuck?" I screamed, struggling beneath Tyler. "Let him go."

"Now why would I do that, Maxine?" Tyler moved off my hips and knelt between my legs. "Because of Vice-One, we haven't been able to have a proper sale. They keep raiding our bunkers and killing off my men."

"You ..." I bit out a sob. "You're in on this."

"Ding ding ding," Tyler petted a hand over my head.

"Why?" I whispered.

"That's always the question, isn't it? Why? You see, I need to be in control. All of you took that away from me when you saved Violet."

My heart jumped. "What the hell does Jay's sister have anything to do with this?"

"Come on, Max. You're not stupid."

"Violet never said anything about you." I shook my head. "No. This isn't right."

"Of course she wouldn't say anything because she had no idea I was in on it."

Jay's twin had been missing for years. After only being saved a couple of months ago, she was now in hiding, going through therapy and healing on her own. The only person she would let visit her was Jay, and even that was few and far between.

"What do you want?"

"You, Max. I can't have Violet. I can't have Jay." Tyler fisted my hair. "There's no one here to protect you now."

I kept my gaze on the video, feeling all the strength I had, being forced from my body.

"All of you have been looking in the wrong place," Tyler continued. "You thought Charles was the front runner, the King shit of this organization when really, he's only a pawn. His brother messed with Coby and Brogan only as a distraction. And Zane?" Tyler laughed, a cold sadistic sound leaving his mouth. "The shit he and his sister did to Coby is nothing compared to what I'm going to do to you."

CHAPTER TWENTY-EIGHT

Dale

MAX STARED BACK at me from the small screen. Charles waved the phone in front of my face, taunting and laughing at me.

I had been stupid, letting my emotions get the best of me and found myself knocked over the head only to wake up in this damn room.

After telling Stone to go home, I did a tour of the grounds around Max's house but couldn't find anything out of the ordinary. Everything in me wanted to break down her door and check on her but after what I had already put her through, I didn't want to take the chance that it could push her away for good. Stupid me. I should have listened to my gut. I should have broken down that damn door. I should have done a shit ton of stuff. But I didn't. And I would pay for my mistakes.

I struggled against my restraints, the ropes holding me captive. Tyler was on top of Max from what I could tell and I swore to myself that I would gut him like a fucking pig. I would rip off every inch of him that touched her. I would skin him alive and bask in the sounds of his screams until he begged for me to kill him.

Charles chuckled. "I don't think he believes your threat," he told Tyler.

Tyler sneered, his hand wrapping around Max's throat.

She kept her gaze locked with mine. "You don't scare me," she said but the waver in her voice proved her wrong.

The last thing I remembered was standing outside Max's house. I was jumped from behind and I stood no fucking chance against the men who attacked me. It was how Charles rolled. He didn't play fair. He was a pussy, only hitting his target when they were least expecting it.

"Mmm ..." Tyler cupped Max's mouth. "Your girlfriend's nice and tight."

My pulse elevated, my vision clouding over. I yelled behind the gag, my body shaking and protesting against the ropes wrapped around my wrists and ankles.

Max shoved her head from behind his mouth. "Dale," she cried. "He's not—"

"Shut the fuck up," he yelled and the screen went black.

"Well, that was fun," Charles sneered.

No. Tyler wouldn't. He was a dick but there was no way ... He had known those girls forever ... Who the fuck was I kidding? He was an abusive asshole. Jay was living proof of it. Fuck. I needed to get out. But I was stuck. There was no way I could escape. Even with all my years of training, I couldn't get out of this mess. Max's life depended on me figuring out what the hell I could do to break free but I had nothing. And then a thought came to me. I started rocking back and forth, the chair creaking under my weight.

"Whoa." Charles snapped his fingers. "Keep him still. I don't need him getting free before it's time."

Whatever the hell that meant. I struggled and shook, protested and pleaded with whatever higher power that was listening to let me go. *Help me. Save Max. Fuck my life. Fuck all that I was worth. I couldn't go on if something happened to her.* Pulling all the fear and pain from within, I allowed it to wash over me, giving me the strength I needed.

Charles eyes widened. "Do something," he yelled to his band of merry bastards.

They grabbed and pulled at me, beat me, and tried to break me down but it didn't work. It only made me rock even harder. The fuckers weren't the brightest. Lock a man up when his woman's life was on the line was like locking up a rabid animal. I channeled that beast, letting it unleash all the power onto to these sick fucks.

The chair broke, coming free from the ground. Ripping off the tape wrapped around my head, a wicked grin spread on my face.

Adrenaline rushed through me before I charged for Charles. All his men couldn't keep me away. Not when Max was involved.

NUMB

Charles yelled, putting his hands up to protect his face but there was no point. I didn't want his face. I wanted his fucking soul.

***

(Max)

The look of utter shock on Dale's face over Tyler's words ripped at my heart. The bastard made him think he was raping me when he hadn't even touched that part of my body. Although I was naked and completely bare for him, Tyler only touched my inner thighs. The searing pain from when his cigarette burnt me still screamed with agony. The marks would be there forever. Dale would see them every time he looked at me, if we even got to that point again.

Tyler's life was over. As soon as I got out of this shit, I would end him. If it wouldn't be me, it would be one of us. No man, no matter who he was, made it out alive when fucking with another's woman. Vice-One had respect from every MC we had dealt with. Tyler would get ripped apart as soon as he was caught.

"You won't get away with this," I told him.

"Maybe not." Tyler ran a finger over the searing flesh between my legs. "But my marks will be with you until the day you die. I will be in your nightmares."

"Just get it over with then," I ground out, wincing at the pain in my thighs.

"Nah." He inhaled his cigarette, blowing the smoke in my face. "I'm not into rape. I just like making my women squeal like a fucking pig."

"You're a bastard," I whimpered.

"Yup." He kissed my cheek, moving off me. "I am. It's funny, though. We catch girls and boys but I've never actually kept one for myself. Maybe I should keep you."

"You wouldn't dare." I mentally slapped myself. Of course he would. The things he had done to Jay already were enough to prove he was fucked in the head. "Just let me go. You got what you wanted. You made Dale believe you raped me."

"I did ..." his voice trailed off.

I looked over my shoulder. "Please, Tyler. You don't need to do this. I won't tell anyone."

"But Dale knows." He rubbed his jaw before pressing a button on his phone. "Yeah," he said a moment later. "Tell him it's done," he said, flipping his phone closed before turning to me.

"What's done?" I demanded, fear taking up permanent residence deep in my soul. I squirmed against the restraints. "Tyler, what the hell is done?"

He strolled toward me, unbuckling his belt and pulled it from the loops with a snap.

I shook and fought against my bounds but they were too tight. The ropes restraining me bit into my skin, scratching and ripping apart the tender flesh. "No. Please. God."

"Is that what you said to Dale? Did you beg him? Did you tell him to stop even though you didn't want him to? You're a filthy little whore, aren't you? You submissive slut."

The first bite of the leather against my flesh pulled a gasp from my chest. Tears burned my eyes, a sob locked in my throat.

"That's it. Moan for me, bitch. You like pain. I've heard that too about you."

I shook my head. He was lying. There was no way he could know anything about me.

A sharp sting enveloped my skin once again.

"Moan for me," Tyler boomed, whipping me with his belt.

I bit my tongue to keep from crying out. I refused to give him any part of me. I liked it rough but I could feel my skin splitting with each impact of his belt. A sheen of sweat coated my skin. Ice cold fingers of fear gripped my spine. This was how it would be. I would never see Dale again. He would die thinking I was raped. Maybe Tyler would eventually go that far but for now, he only raped my soul.

The belt whacked over my skin, stabbing me in the heart.

My vision faded in and out, spots dancing in front of my eyes. Darkness threatened to take over but I fought against it. I couldn't let him win. I had been weak for long enough, I refused to let another man bring me to the brink of destruction.

"You're a tough little thing, aren't you?" Tyler sneered, running his hands down the fresh welts marring my ass and thighs.

I bit back a whimper at the sharp pain.

"But you're not tough enough." His fingers dug into the cheek of my rear, ripping into a cut caused by his belt.

I cried out, tears welling in my eyes. "Just be done with it," I pleaded, ashamed at myself for giving in.

Tyler chuckled, releasing me. "If I was a betting man" —he slid his fingers down the length of my spine— "I would bet Dale is losing his shit right about now. I can't imagine Charles will be alive for much longer."

"Just let—" Suddenly, my head was pulled back, strands of hair ripping free from my head.

"Shut the fuck up," Tyler growled. "I should just fuck you and be done with it. Give Dale something to really bitch about."

"Try it and see what happens, asshole."

My eyes widened at the unexpected voice coming from the doorway. "Jay, what are you doing here?"

"Well, now this could be fun." Tyler jumped off the bed. "Do you like what you see, Jenny? Care to join us?"

"I knew you were a sick fuck," she said, ignoring me. "But I thought you were too good for this. Clearly, I was wrong." Jay pulled a pistol from her back pocket and aimed it at her ex.

My heart hammered against my ribcage. There was no way I could let her shoot her ex. He had caused too much damage to her already. This would break her.

"Jay, help me." I shook against the restraints.

She met my gaze, came toward me, but kept the gun aimed at him.

"What are you going to do, Jenny?" He glanced down at her swollen belly. "I could get a lot of money for someone as pregnant as you."

"Jay," I pleaded. "Please."

She quickly untied me. "Shit, Max," she said, concern dripping from her voice.

"Give me the gun." I slid off the bed but when my feet hit the floor, they gave out beneath me.

Tyler chuckled. "Don't be a pussy. You liked my belt against your skin."

Throwing on shorts and a tank top, I bit back a hiss when the fabric touched my skin and snatched the gun from Jay.

"What the fuck?" she cried, reaching for it.

"You need to leave." I pushed her back.

"Like hell." She reached for the gun but I pulled it behind my back.

"No," I said, my voice firm. "This isn't your fight." Careful not to hurt her, I gave her one final shove and slammed the door shut, closing me in with Tyler. Clicking the lock into place, I ignored the banging on the door and turned to Tyler.

His grin only widened. Leaning against the wall, he crossed his arms under his chest.

"Tell me why," I demanded, my hands shaking. The searing pain rushing through my body forced me to waver on my feet.

Tyler shrugged. "I was bored."

I shook my head. "You won't get away with this."

"Oh, baby." He took a step toward me. "I already have."

"This is for attacking me." I cocked the gun and pulled the trigger. The blast rang out, the sound piercing my ears.

The bullet hit Tyler's knee cap, shattering the bone.

He screamed out, falling to the floor. "*You fucking bitch.*"

I took a step closer, the release from shooting him giving me the strength I needed all along. I didn't want to kill him but I wanted him to suffer. I wanted him to beg for his life like the girls and boys had that his organization had taken. "This is for all of those girls and boys that you and those sick bastards stole." I shot him in his other knee.

"*You fucking whore*," he screamed. "I'll get you for this."

"Words words. All I hear is blah blah blah."

The banging on the door continued, Jay's demands for me to let her in washing over me. But I couldn't. I needed to avenge her. Her sister. Everyone.

I wasn't sure where this new-found strength was coming from but after all the shit I had been through, I embraced it. "And this is for my best friend." I aimed the gun at his crotch and pulled the trigger one final time before I collapsed to the floor.

CHAPTER TWENTY-NINE

Dale

MY HANDS GRIPPED Charles' throat. After I had stolen his gun, I shot the two bastards who worked with him. Watching them fall to the ground in a bundled heap forced me to give into that darkness I had tried to ignore.

I squeezed Charles' neck. I took him by surprise, breaking out of my binds and knocking the chair over. An insurmountable rush of adrenaline soared through me.

Charles gasped, choking for the air I stole from him.

"Death would be too easy for you," I growled, the rage from everything that had happened over the past couple of months, finally taking full control. "Was it one of your men who shot me?"

Charles grinned. "The Organization will always be here. You can't end us."

I forced his head back. "Tell me what Tyler has to do with this."

Charles choked, his eyes bugging out of his head. His hands gripped my arms, his nails scratching into my skin. His fingers ripped the flesh from my bones causing a slice of agony to sear right through me but the pain piercing through my veins only made me squeeze harder.

"He's the boss," Charles croaked out.

The new revelation all made sense now.

Charles kicked his legs out from beneath me but I was stronger. That driving force to end him for all the shit he had done influenced my actions.

"Kill me," he begged, his voice strained by the restricted airflow into his lungs.

I grinned, leaning down to his ear. "I'm sorry. What was that?"

"Kill me, you bastard," he begged.

I loosened my hold on his neck. "Nah. Maybe I should let my friend loose on you. I hear Brogan killed Tina. But if it were me, I would have shaved off her skin and fed it to her."

"You're a sick fuck. Tina was a bitch whore who got what she deserved."

I stared down at him, briefly surprised by his words. "Jealous?"

Charles chuckled. "Not one fucking bit. Her and Zane have caused enough shit for this organization."

"Had." My grin grew. "I enjoyed watching Zane's life leave his eyes."

"He's dead." Charles paled. "You killed him."

"Ding ding, motherfucker." I slapped his cheek before gripping his jaw. "I should have made him suffer too."

Charles laughed. "The bastard was a pussy. The real threat was Tina and Tyler. Those two together could destroy the fucking world."

My heart jumped in my throat. "They were together."

"You bet your fucking ass they were." Charles laughed even harder. "Tina was a sick fuck, sleeping with her brother and Tyler. But I wasn't paid to care. We all ignored it."

Shit. That was new information none of us knew about. It all made sense now.

"You didn't know. Fuck, this is good. You should probably kill me before Tyler breaks your girlfriend."

A tremor of brutal rage soared through me. I yelled out, tightening my hold on Charles' neck and squeezed.

He never stood a chance.

When his neck popped, I squeezed even harder. A bone protruded from his throat, blood spattering my hands. This was too slow. I pulled the switch from my boot, flipped it open and jammed it into the side of his neck.

Blood sputtered from his mouth, his eyes rolling into the back of his head.

I leaned down to his ear. "Your boys should have checked everywhere for weapons," I told him, pushing the blade deeper into the artery.

But it wasn't enough. I enjoyed feeling the life leave his body. A body that had caused damage for many innocent victims. This was for them. This was for every girl, every boy, every single person he hurt. This was for taking Asher and Meeka months ago. For working with people that caused my best friend to fuck someone else to keep his girl safe.

I squeezed Charles' neck until there was nothing left. Until he was no longer writhing and squirming beneath me. I stabbed and then squeezed some more. And only then did I feel at peace. One down. Who the fuck knew how many to go. But Tyler would die at my fingertips for different reasons.

I rose from Charles' body and made my way back to Max's house.

With each step I took, the fury surrounded me. It enveloped my skin and gave me the strength I needed to avenge her.

When I left the room Charles held me in, I realized we were back at the same house he had held Asher and Meeka captive. He wasn't the brightest motherfucker.

I patted my pockets, letting out a curse that Charles had taken my phone. He was smart about that at least. I hated fighting a pussy. If you were going to hit me, at least own it.

I charged further down the hall, keeping my head low and the pistol high. Two large fuckers came into view as I rounded a corner and shots rang out before they even stood a chance. My heart stuttered, a flush of heat washing over my skin. I lived for this. Watching the two men fall to the floor in a bundled heap of dying limbs sent a course of euphoria through my soul. If it were anyone else, I may have felt some sort of guilt but when it came to anyone that had to do with taking these girls and boys, they deserved everything they got.

Rummaging through the pockets of the fallen men, I grinned when I came across a burner phone and quickly called Coby.

"Yeah," came his barked reply.

"Coby." I breathed a relief at the sound of my best friend's voice.

"Dale? Where the hell are you and what number are you calling from?"

"I need your help," I said, leaving the confines of the large house.

"Tell me."

I explained everything and demanded for someone, any of them, head over to Max's house and save her before Tyler ripped through her.

"Jay's already there."

"What?" My eyes widened. "No, he'll hurt her too." I would never forgive myself if something happened to her and her baby.

"Fuck." Coby let out another string of curses. "I'm calling Angel now on Brogan's phone. Tyler has lost his shit."

"I'm going to kill him," I warned Coby.

"Not if ... what ... what the hell are you talking about, little one?" he asked Brogan.

"Jay said Max kicked her out. I'm heading there now," I heard Brogan say in the background.

"What the fuck is going on?" I demanded. "Someone pick me the fuck up and get me the hell out of here."

"I'm on my way." Coby hung up.

"*Fuck*," I yelled. If something more happened to Max because of Tyler, I would skin him alive. I would kill everyone he was close to and make him watch. I would end the very existence he didn't deserve to have.

CHAPTER THIRTY

Dale

"WHERE THE FUCK is she?" I shouted, slamming my fist into the wall of Max's bedroom.
"Dale, geeze, calm the hell down." Angel came toward me. "I'm trying to get ahold of Jay but you need to chill the fuck out."

"Shit." I swung my fist for the wall again when Coby stood in front of me. Pulling my hand back suddenly so I wouldn't hit him, it wasn't fast enough and my fist connected with his hand.

His eyes darkened, his jaw clenching. "Let it out but don't you dare hurt yourself over this shit. Max wouldn't want that."

"Where is she?" I demanded, shaking out my arms and started pacing back and forth. There was a shit ton of blood on the floor of her room and that only made me lose it. I didn't know what had happened but if I found out it was Max's blood on the floor, I would end Tyler before his life even began.

After Coby picked me up from Charles' compound, Brogan's stepbrother's club showed up. They cleaned up the mess, not even asking questions about what had happened.

"She's at the hospital," Angel finally said, pulling me from my thoughts.

"Take me there." I barged out of the room.

"Come with me." Coby grabbed my shoulders, spinning me around to meet his face. "But first, you need to calm down."

"Coby." I shoved from his grip but his hold on my shoulders only tightened.

"Listen to me." Coby clapped a hand on the side of my neck. "Dale."

"What?"

"Don't blame her. For whatever happened, do not let her think you're upset with her over this. I know you two went your separate ways but she needs you right now."

A breath left me on a whoosh. "I would never blame her."

"Dale," Coby barked, shaking me. "Promise me."

"Fuck, man, of course. None of this shit is her fault. I don't give a fuck that she doesn't want to be with me. I won't leave her side until I know she's healed. I love her."

Coby's face softened. "It's about fucking time you said those words. Now let's get you to your woman. But first" —he pointed at me— "you need to change."

***

(Max)

My hands were curled into fists on my lap. I picked at my robe, wishing I could pick apart every inch of Tyler that had touched me. Shooting him did nothing to please me. It only made me feel like a horrible human being. Although he deserved everything he got, I wasn't like my sisters or Vice-One. I couldn't hurt someone and move on like nothing had happened.

After the doctor and nurses finished checking me out to make sure I was okay, an older policeman entered the hospital room.

I laughed, shaking my head at the irony of it all.

"What's so funny, Miss Stanton?" he asked, his eyes burning into the side of my head.

"I just think it's funny they send a man to check on a woman who was abused. By a man." My gaze snapped to his. "Makes complete sense if you ask me."

He raised an eyebrow. "We don't have many female officers in these here parts."

"Of course not." I jumped off the bed, my muscles protesting at the movement but I breathed through the onslaught of pain. "Listen, how about we save you the paperwork? Tyler attacked me. I defended myself. And I'm fine."

"Tyler's in surgery," the officer said.

"And I hope he dies on the fucking table." As soon as those words left my mouth, a loud voice came from the hallway.

"Where the *fuck* is she?"

Dale.

My heart stuttered, my knees buckling beneath me.

"Let's get you back up on the bed." The officer gently grabbed my arm and helped me onto the bed.

After everything that had happened, I forgot I would have to face Dale and … Jay. I swallowed hard.

"Max." Dale barged into the room, his wide eyes landing on me. "Kitten."

A dark bruise was forming on his cheek while his bottom lip had a split in it. I wanted to ask what happened and how he escaped Charles but, instead, I held my arms out and waited.

He pushed past the officer and barreled into me, wrapping his body around mine.

This was what I was made for. My thumping heart silenced in my ears. The love I had for this man gave me the sense of calm I needed since Tyler had attacked me. He tried everything in his power to break me. Maybe he succeeded. Either way, this man holding me would put all those broken pieces back together.

Dale brushed his nose into the crook of my neck and inhaled. His big body became relaxed while the rest of him held strong. He leaned back and cupped my cheeks. His eyes moved back and forth over my face.

"I'm fine," I said, placing my palms over his hands. "I promise."

His jaw twitched. "Tell me you'll put him away," he said to the officer but kept his gaze locked with mine.

"We *will* put him away," the officer answered, a hint of amusement lacing his words.

I turned to him. "Good. Because if you don't …"

"You'll take matters into your own hands?" the officer asked, raising an eyebrow.

"She won't have to." Dale cupped my nape, that small touch pouring strength into my soul.

"It seems" —the officer checked his notepad— "your girl here left quite an impression. The fucker will probably be pissing into a bag for the rest of his life."

"Excuse me?" Dale turned me to face him. "What did you do, kitten?"

"I channeled my inner Brogan." I shrugged. "It was no big deal." But it was. My body was shaking, my heart pounded in my ears. I could feel the impending panic attack trying to hit me square in the chest. I wasn't like my sisters. I couldn't kill and move on. I couldn't even maim. I realized then that I had only joined the club for something to do and so people would stop looking at me like a weak member of the opposite sex.

"Yeah." Dale kissed my forehead. "It's a huge fucking deal. Especially when you're sitting here trying to control a panic attack."

I frowned. "How did you know?"

"Years of experience, baby. And my brothers won't admit it, but we've all had one."

"I'll leave you two be but I just have one question," the officer said, clearing his throat. "Why did Tyler do it?"

"To fuck with my head," I told him. The officer didn't need to know anymore.

"No other reason?" the officer flipped through his notes. "There has to be another reason as to why—"

"There isn't. When it comes to a man like Tyler, he doesn't need a reason. He's sick and twisted." I shivered. "He was trying to get to my sister through me."

"All right." The officer pointed his pen in my direction. "Don't leave town," he muttered, leaving the room.

"You really cut off Tyler's dick?" Dale asked, sitting on the bed beside me.

"No." I scrubbed a hand down my face. "I shot it. And both of his knees."

Dale whistled. "That's my girl."

"After Jay showed up and got me free, I couldn't stop myself. I did it for the shit he had done to her. And the others. And … for what he did to me."

"He …" Dale swallowed hard. "He raped you."

"At first I thought he did. I hurt everywhere." I grabbed Dale's hand, holding it in my lap. "But he didn't. I tried telling you but he shut off the video. He only wanted you to think he did. But he left marks on me. He burned and whipped me, Dale. I need to prepare you for what you could see."

Dale held my hands firm in his. "As long as you're okay, that's all I care about."

"He's forever etched into my skin," I whispered, fresh tears welling in my eyes.

Dale pinched my chin, forcing me to meet his gaze. "No matter what he did or what marks he left on your body, none of it is your fault. Do you understand me?"

"I should have fought harder."

"No," Dale snapped. "You listen to me and you listen good."

I went to look away when his grip on my jaw tightened.

"Look at me," Dale demanded. Only when I met his gaze did he continue. "None of this is your fault. You didn't ask for him to attack you. You did what you could to survive. You shot him, Max. Not a lot of people would have the balls to do even that."

"I want him to die," I confessed, my cheeks heating at my outburst.

"You're not the only one," Dale kissed my forehead. "You feel guilty for thinking that."

"Yes," I let out a slow breath. "I'm not like all of you. I'm in this club for show." I shrugged. "I don't even ride the bike Jay bought me. I suck at being a biker."

"Hey." He pulled me toward him. "I heard you shoved Jay out of the room so she wouldn't get hurt and you took care of Tyler. That's pretty fucking badass if you ask me."

My cheeks heated. "She would have done the same if the roles were reversed."

"Yeah." Dale inched closer. "She would have."

I glanced down at his mouth, my tongue licking along my bottom lip. I shivered, looking away. "I'm sorry." I knew what Brogan and Coby had been through. I didn't know every dark and dirty detail but I knew it had put a strain on their relationship even though it hadn't been Coby's fault. Although I never had sex with Tyler, he still saw and touched me. It might not have been between my legs but it was enough to still make me feel violated.

"Baby." Dale took a deep breath. "I don't blame you. For anything. I'm proud of you for standing up to him and for taking him down all on your own. I understand how hard it must have been."

"You do?"

"Yes. You're right. You're not like your sisters." He leaned his forehead against mine. "You're a good girl. *My* good girl. You try to be like them but you're not. And that's why I love you."

My heart gave a start. "You do? You really love me?" I didn't want to ask. I didn't want to show any sign of doubt that I didn't believe him. I tried hard to take everything he had given me over the past couple of weeks but the hurtful words we had said to each other, still hung over my head.

Dale leaned back and brushed the back of his hand down my cheek.

My eyes fluttered closed at the soft touch.

"I know it's hard to believe me but I will spend the rest of my life showing you how much I love you. I will burn this motherfucking world down until Tyler gets what he rightfully deserves."

"I think I gave you a good head start," I said, trying to lighten the mood.

He chuckled. "Yeah, you did, kitten. I just wish I could have been there to take care of you after."

I shrugged. "It's no big deal."

He searched my face. "Yeah, it kind of is."

The events of the past couple of hours came rushing back. Every time the hospital gown slid over my skin, the burning pain reminded me of what happened and what could have happened if Jay hadn't shown up. My heart started racing, the air in my lungs shortening and coming out in small bursts of air.

Dale pulled me against him. "Let it out, baby."

A sob escaped me. Gripping his hoodie, I cried against him, letting out all the emotions I had felt for the past several months. All the hurt, anguish, anger, fear … Every damn feeling I had tried hard not to feel.

It all came out. Every single one of them rolled down my cheeks and dripped off my chin. My body ached, my muscles burning over the uncontrollable soul crushing cries.

"That's it, kitten," Dale coaxed. "Let it out."

His soothing words only made me cry harder. I wasn't my sisters. I wasn't Brogan. I couldn't do this and move on like nothing happened. I wasn't as strong as her. "I'm not strong," I whispered.

Dale cupped my face, pushing me back gently, and stared intently into my eyes. Wiping my tears away with his thumbs, he placed a soft peck on my mouth before pulling away suddenly. "I'm sorry. I know we're not … together anymore."

I gripped his arms. "No, I …" I let out a heavy sigh. "We can talk about that later. Right now, I just need you."

"Okay." He kissed my forehead. "You are the strongest person I know. My brothers and I have fought through hell. We've seen shit no human should ever have to see but even after that, you are still the strongest."

"No." I struggled out of his hold. "I'm not."

"Yes," his brows narrowed as he spoke, "you are."

Just when I was about to argue with him again, a throat cleared from the doorway.

My head whipped around. "Jay."

She smiled softly. "Can I come in?"

"Of course." I reached a hand out to her.

"I'll be out in the hall." Dale kissed my head and left the room.

When Jay sat on the bed beside me, she grabbed my hand and linked our fingers. We sat in silence, the words over what had happened floating above our heads.

"I'm sorry," I eventually said, needing to break the silence.

"You're sorry." She turned to me. "What the hell for?"

"For ..." I wasn't even sure what I was apologizing for. It wasn't my fault Tyler had attacked me. But why the hell did I feel so damn guilty?

"Listen," Jay sighed, squeezing my hand. "Tyler has always been a dick. But I underestimated him. I should be apologizing to *you*."

My eyes widened. "Why?"

She looked away, glancing down at our joined hands. "For years I tried convincing my father that Tyler had issues. He's not all right in the head. The relationship I had with him proved that. But my dad said he was good for the crew, doing whatever he could to get the answers they were looking for. Tyler had said how he would ..." She met my gaze. "How he would do anything to pay me back for leaving him." A nervous laugh left her lips. "But I didn't think he would stoop this low. But I need you to tell me something."

"What?" I asked, my heart jumping against my ribs.

"Did he rape you?"

***

(Dale)

"You killed Charles," Coby said, his voice low.

"I wish I could do it all over again," I mumbled, closing my hand into a fist. I could still feel his blood spraying my skin. I could taste the metallic liquid on my

282

lips and see the life leaving his eyes. I wanted to do it again. But this time, it would be Tyler.

"Tyler won't get away with this shit." Coby sat back in the chair beside me. "None of them will."

"He'll be in recovery for who the fuck knows how long." I shook my head. "We need someone on the inside."

Coby grinned. "I'm sure Jay's father knows someone."

"Really?" I mentally smacked myself. The guy was the president of a motorcycle club with some of the most dangerous men I have ever come across. They even made *me* nervous.

"Tyler won't get out of prison. And if I have it my way, he won't even make it out of the infirmary. If I have to do it myself" —Coby's face hardened— "he *will* pay for what he did to your girl, brother."

His words hit me square in the gut. "He didn't rape her." I had believed Max when she told me but I needed to say the words. I needed to hear them again for myself. Even though her body looked like it had been beaten down and broken, he didn't force himself inside her. My muscles vibrated. He would still pay. I would make damn sure of it.

"Have you seen what he did to her?" Coby asked, rubbing his jaw.

"No." My body tensed. "I don't know what I'll do when I see his marks on her skin." I had never become so possessive in my damn life.

"Be gentle with her." Coby clapped a hand on my shoulder. "She's not like her sisters. She's the good girl. Remember that."

***

NUMB

(Max)

"No, he didn't rape me." *But I still felt dirty and stripped bare from where he touched me.*

"I'm sorry for what he did to you," Jay muttered.

"Why did you show up? I'll be forever thankful but I don't understand how you showed up at the perfect time."

"You didn't answer your phone," she told me. "You always answer your phone. So, when I called and kept getting your voicemail, I went over to your place. The door was unlocked and I let myself in. That was when I heard your screams."

"Do you always carry your gun on you?"

She searched my face. "Yes. Angel makes damn sure of it. I know you're not like the rest of us. I get it. But I need you with me. You can step down from being the vice-president, I get that too, but I can't do this without you."

"I'm not strong enough." My voice wavered. "I can't do something like this and just move on like nothing happened."

"And you think we can?" Jay shook her head. "Look at Brogan. Her and Coby are still dealing with this shit. They probably will be for the rest of their lives. And Asher and Meeka? You remember what happened there, right?"

I nodded slowly, memories of them going undercover after trying to bring Charles down flooding my mind.

"We're human. We put on a good front but none of us do this and move on right away." Jay wrapped her arm around my shoulder. "Trust me. Tyler caused a lot of shit for Angel and me. I almost lost him. We're not as strong as you think we are."

"When will this stop?" I asked, leaning my head against hers.

"Whenever the Devil has his fill."

"You sound like Coby." I rose from the bed, stretching my arms up and over my head. The sudden onset of pain traveling down my back reminded me that Tyler was still nearby. I chewed my bottom lip, glancing at the doorway.

"He can't come in here." Jay winked. "Not like the fucker can walk anyway."

"I'm not strong enough for this." I wrapped my arms around myself for fear that I would finally once and for all lose it.

"That's just it. You *are* strong enough, Max. You're like the glue keeping us all together. You balance out the good and the bad. You're the peanut to my butter."

I laughed, wiping the lonely tear free-falling down my cheek. "I love you girls. So damn much but these past couple of months have been a right off. I think something happened though. With Dale and … Charles."

"What do you mean?"

I swallowed hard, my heart racing. "Tyler is in on this human trafficking shit, Jay."

She let out a soft sigh. "Yeah. I kind of figured."

"Really? How?"

"Tyler always needed to be in control. Not like Angel. Tyler forced me and hit me when I didn't submit to him. He always talked about having someone who would bend to his demands and hated it when I wasn't that person."

"I think that's the most you ever said about him," I told her.

"Yeah." She gave me a small smile.

"I wanted to kill him. I couldn't stop myself," I confessed, remembering Angel breaking the door to my bedroom down.

"But you did," she reminded me, reaching for my hand.

"I did." My shoulders slumped. I couldn't get the sounds of his screams out of my head. But what would forever be burned into my nightmares was the vile grin on his face. The dark evil in his eyes. Although he had been writhing in pain, he still managed to scare me. He gave a look that promised his marks on my body would be there. Forever.

"Um …" Jay shifted beside me.

"What?" I asked, her movement pulling me from my thoughts.

She met my gaze, her eyes wide with excitement and fear. "I think my water just broke."

CHAPTER THIRTY-ONE

Max

"HOW THE FUCK I let you talk me into this shit is beyond me," Jay groaned through gritted teeth and gripped her lower abdomen.

"Baby, it's not like it was planned for." Angel rubbed her lower back, a hint of amusement flashing in his gaze.

I smiled to myself, shaking my head. "Come get us when the baby is born."

Jay met my gaze. "Thank you …" She winced. "Fuck me." She let out a slow breath.

"Take care of her," I told Angel and stepped out of the room when I ran right into a hard body. A flush of heat washed over me.

"You good?" Dale asked, steadying me on my feet.

My best friend was about to give birth when I had lost my own baby a couple months back. "Yup. I'm perfect. You?"

Dale grabbed my hand and kissed my knuckles. "I'm fucking perfect as well."

My heart stuttered. "Let's go back to my room and be perfect together."

He kissed my forehead. "I like the sound of that."

We headed back to my hospital room and sat there for what felt like hours. Maybe it was. We were silent, speaking through the small touches by just holding hands. I loved this man pouring his strength into me but I hadn't told him yet. Not since the first time.

He remembered everything. All the women. Hurting me. Laughing in my face. But he still confessed his love for me anyway.

He didn't push me when he knew how I felt. It was obvious in the way he took care of me. I knew that once everything was said and done, we would have to go our separate ways. Maybe for a little bit. Maybe for good.

My eyes burned, the lump lodged in my throat threatening to choke me.

Every now and again, Dale would lift our joined hands and kiss my knuckles. That small touch sent a flutter of happiness through me. But was I allowed that? Could I allow myself to have that reprieve after everything that had happened?

As if he could sense my thoughts, Dale's brow crinkled. "Talk to me."

"In a couple of days or so, I want to go back and see … and see our daughter." I swallowed hard, breathing through the impending breakdown trying to control me.

"I'd like that, kitten." His eyes warmed. "I would like that very much."

***

(Dale)

Max wanted to run. She wanted to hide away from all the pain life had caused her. When she broke down in my arms earlier, I held her, but it wasn't enough. She went on like everything was fine but it wasn't. And she earned that right. She had every reason to feel the way she was feeling. I just wished she would open up to me.

"Let's go see her now," I suggested, the unnerving silence getting too heavy for me.

"Right now?" she sat back, staring at me through red rimmed eyes. "But what about Jay?"

"We'll come back." I sent Angel a quick text.

Max looked around the room. "Do you think they would mind?" she asked, chewing her bottom lip.

My body stirred. It wasn't the right time or place but fuck me, I enjoyed when she did that. "No," I said, my voice coming out more of a growl.

Her cheeks reddened. "Okay," she breathed. "Take me to her."

I dialed Coby's number. "Coby," I barked into the phone.

"Yeah, brother," came his short reply.

"I need your—" Coby stepped into the room and placed his keys in my hand. "Thank you." I rose from the bed, pulling Max with me.

289

"Wait," she said. "I—"

The doctor took that moment to come into the room. "Oh." He stopped suddenly when he saw me standing with her. "I was about to give you your discharge papers. You're free and clear." He placed a small jar in Max's hand. "Rub this salve on the wounds. It will ease the pain and help with the healing process. But I'm sorry to tell you that there will be scars."

Max jutted her chin out. "I'm aware," she said, her voice firm. "Thank you."

The doctor looked between us. "Okay …"

"Is there an issue?" I asked, my muscles tight.

The doctor flipped through his chart. "Tyler Bone." He glanced at Max, shifting his weight from foot to foot.

"What about him?" Max rubbed a hand down her arm, clasping her fingers around her bicep to keep from shaking.

My stomach twisted over what that fuck did to her.

"He survived the surgeries."

A forced laugh escaped Max's mouth. "Of course he did. Thank you, doctor. We'll be leaving now."

"Max," I said gently.

"I said we're leaving," she repeated, grabbing her clothes and headed to the bathroom. She came out a moment later completely dressed. "Now. Please."

I nodded, thanked the doctor again and guided Max out of the hospital.

"You need to drive," I told Max once we reached Coby's SUV.

"Okay." She didn't argue and took the keys from my hand. "Still not allowed to drive?"

"No," I grumbled. "After I drove the last time, I realized it was too soon. I have an appointment coming up and I swear if the doctor doesn't give me a clean bill of health, I'm going to shit bricks."

"Sounds painful." Max smiled softly.

My mouth turned up into a grin. "No pain no gain, baby."

Max's smile grew. Moving to the driver's side of the large SUV, she opened the door.

I did the same, standing on the passenger side.

With both of our doors opened, we stood there and stared at each other. Only a couple feet stood in our way of touching but it felt like we were miles apart. I prayed with everything in me that we could get through this. If we didn't, I wasn't sure what I would do.

***

(Max)

I love you.

Those three words were on the tip of my tongue but again, I couldn't say them.

Dale stared at me from across the passenger side of the SUV, his big body filling the door frame.

"We ..." I cleared my throat. "We should go." Jay's baby would hopefully be born soon and I didn't want to miss being there for her.

He nodded once and slid into the vehicle.

I did the same and started it up. The big machine rumbling beneath me ignited that familiar ache. I missed riding my bike but it just hadn't been the same without the other girls. I made a mental note to set something up for us to head to another town to see a sister club. Although I felt I was a crappy biker, I still enjoyed the wind whipping through my hair and the open road.

Once we reached the cemetery, my fingers tightened on the steering wheel. After I had brought Dale there weeks ago, a lot had changed in that short amount of time.

He loves me.

"Do you think we could have been happy?" Dale asked, cupping my inner thigh. "If she was born, I mean. Do you think we could have been good enough for her?"

My chest constricted. "I'd like to think so."

"Do you think we could have been enough for each other?"

My breath hitched. "I think maybe she … she died so we could find each other again. Or at least be civil." I met his gaze. "I know we need time apart. It's only been two weeks and I …"

"What?" he asked, pushing a strand of hair behind my ear.

"I miss your arms wrapped around me. I miss *you*, Dale."

"I can't be with you if you don't trust me. It's not fair to either of us."

Chewing the inside of my cheek, I looked down at his hand wrapped around my inner thigh. His knuckles were torn from whatever beating he had given Charles. Black and blue bruises marred his wrists from being bound.

"I trust you," I whispered. My tears were worth a thousand words but they still couldn't speak. "I want to trust you with everything that I am."

"Baby." Dale's voice took on a tone I didn't like hearing. It became thick with emotion, rough with pain and deep with guilt. "I … *fuck.*"

Yeah. My thoughts exactly. I left the vehicle, waiting for him to follow, and when he did, only then did I head to our daughter's grave.

Kneeling on the sun-kissed grass, my gaze landed on a single flower that had sprouted up from the grave. I wasn't sure if someone had planted it there but, either way, I took it as a sign. A sob escaped me, crashing through my body and hitting me square in the chest.

Warm arms wrapped around me. A soft mouth kissed my head over and over. The small touch repeated itself until all I felt was the love Dale had for me.

"I love you," I blurted, wiping the tears from my cheeks. "I love you so damn much, Dale." I gripped his hoodie.

He cupped my face, tilting my head to meet his mouth. "I love you too, kitten. I promise to make up for what I've done but you know we can't be together. Not yet."

He was right which made me cry even harder. God, I hated it when he was right.

"All we can do is take it a day at a time," I told him through my sobs, "but I need you to be patient with me. I trust you. I do. But when she died, a part of me died with her. Please don't push me."

"I would never push you." His brows narrowed. "But think about it, Max. Can you really trust me? After everything I've done to you?"

I searched his face, cupping his cheek. My thumb grazed over his bottom lip. My heart was full but my mind kept playing the images of him being with those women over and over in my head.

"Yeah." He pulled from my grasp. "That's what I thought."

"I didn't even say anything and you're pissed." A laugh lodged free from my throat. "I can't believe you're actually mad."

"What the fuck do you expect from me, Max? Of course I'm pissed. I've tried doing everything to make up for what I've done."

"You can't make up for it in a matter of a couple weeks, Dale," I threw back at him.

Dale crossed his arms under his chest, his jaw clenching. "We're going back and forth again. I don't see you for two weeks and then I find out Tyler attacks you. And now, after all that shit, you finally tell me you love me. Why, Max? Why the hell do you love me?"

"I can't control what my heart wants, Dale," I said, my voice rising. "I've tried leaving but every time I get on my damn bike, something calls me back to you. I can't stop it."

"Well, baby, I'll make it easy for you." He shoved his hands in his pockets and started walking down the path.

"No." I ran after him, grabbing onto the back of his hoodie. "You don't get to walk away from this. I can't move on from her death if you leave me."

"I can't be with you and deal with the judgment. I've done that for months. I can't do it anymore." He pulled from my grip. "I'd rather go back to fucking war then see the hate for me in your eyes."

"I don't hate you," I cried, stepping in front of him. "I love you. I mean that. Please don't leave me."

Dale kept his arms at his sides, no longer trying to walk away but not trying to touch me either. "I can't keep doing this."

"I don't hate you," I repeated, leaning my forehead against his chest and breathed him in. "I'm sorry for not trusting you completely. But how would you feel if it was reversed? Could you be with me if I fucked a bunch of men knowing that you loved me?"

"Yes," he said. "Because my love would be stronger than those bastards. I know how I feel. But do you?"

I swallowed hard. "We can get counseling. Talk to your doctor. Just please … I can't do this without you."

"We've moved past that, kitten." He grabbed my wrists, pulling me from him. "I love you but I refuse to be with someone who doesn't trust me."

Hot tears rolled down my cheeks. I could tell him over and over again that I did in fact trust him but both of us knew it would be a lie.

Dale was right.

And I hated him more for it.

CHAPTER THIRTY-TWO

Dale

I NEVER CRIED over relationship shit. Losing my daughter was the only thing in my life to bring me to my knees. Even as a kid, I never allowed myself to break. But hearing Max beg for me to stay with her tore at my motherfucking soul.

I had promised myself and her that I would never hurt her again and that was exactly what I was doing. It wasn't intentional. Not anymore. In the beginning, I was scared to love her, and now that I did, I had to let her go. But I didn't want to. It took everything in me not to wrap myself around her, tell her how sorry I was, and bring her home. But I couldn't.

"Please stay," she pleaded. "I'll do anything."

I grabbed her wrists, freeing her grasp from my hoodie. "That's the thing, Max." I fisted a hand through her hair. "All I want is for you to love me. That's it."

Her chin trembled. "I'm sorry."

I crushed my mouth to hers, tasting her tears on my tongue. "I'm sorry too." With my heart in my hands, I walked away. Never again would I allow myself to fall for someone like I did with her. My heart no longer beat. My soul crushed and ripped with agony. She wanted me to stay but she didn't trust me. Not completely.

I didn't blame her.

But I couldn't do that to myself.

I would rather be alone then be with a woman who couldn't believe in my feelings for her. Love could only do so much before it ruined us.

It didn't help when I couldn't forgive myself for what I did to Max but when she didn't forgive me, either, I realized then that it was finally over.

***

(Max)

"Oh, my sweet baby girl." My vision blurred. "What have I done? How could I let him walk away from me?" The tears fell, rolling off my cheeks, and dripped onto the dew-soaked grass. With shaky hands, I placed the bouquet of yellow tulips at the foot of the grave.

It had been a couple of days since Dale left. I hadn't seen him. I hadn't heard from him. No calls. No text messages. I didn't even hear from our friends how he was doing. Did he ask about me? Did he care?

NUMB

My phone chimed, interrupting my moment of self-pity.

Jay: We're leaving the hospital if you want to come visit.

She had the baby yesterday. A girl. And I didn't go see her.

I was happy for my best friend but I fell into myself. Her patience tugged me out of that dark hole.

Jay had a hard labor after her water broke, eventually needing a C-section. The baby just didn't want to leave the safety and warmth of its mother.

My feet moved before I had any idea what I was doing. It was like my body was controlled by a higher power.

This would be it. This would be the final test to see if I could move on or not.

Holding my best friend's baby in my arms.

I never thought it would come to this. We had always joked that Jay would be single forever and then she met Angel. I was happy for them. I was happy for all my friends but it didn't stop me from having my own pity party any less.

Once I pulled up to the hospital, the moment of truth awaited me.

Taking a deep breath, I tried to pull the strength from within but no matter what I did, I couldn't find it. So, I faked it.

Rubbing the grit out of my eyes, I headed into the large building and up to Jay's room. "Jay?" I gave a light knock on the open door and stepped over the threshold.

"Hey." She smiled, sitting on the edge of the bed. "I'm glad you made it. We're leaving in an hour or so."

"I'm sorry I wasn't here yesterday. I just …"

She raised her hand, stopping me. "I understand."

I nodded, giving her a soft smile. And that was when I saw something I never knew I wanted until it was taken away from me.

Angel held the tiny bundle wrapped in pink in his arms. He met my gaze, his dark eyes warming. "Do you want to hold her?"

"Yes," I whispered.

"You don't have to," Jay said gently. "No pressure." She touched Angel's arm.

He placed their baby in her arms and kissed her forehead. "I'll give you a moment." When he walked by me, he squeezed my shoulder.

My vision blurred, a heaviness settling deep in my chest but I took a step toward Jay. Ringing my hands in front of me, I stopped a couple feet away. "How did everything go?" I asked, my voice shaking.

"Good. Hard." Jay brushed a finger down her daughter's cheek. "But it was worth it. Everything …" She swallowed hard. "Was worth it."

The air was sucked from my lungs. "I went to my daughter's grave."

Jay's eyes shone. "How did that go?"

"I've been a couple times." I shrugged. "I think it will get easier. I brought her yellow tulips. I like to think they would be her favorite." I was rambling but I knew if I didn't stop, I would fall to my knees.

"I'm sure they would be." Jay cleared her throat. "Are you sure—"

"Yes." I held my arms out. "Please."

"Okay." Jay smiled softly, placing her baby in my arms. "Max, meet Angelica Maxine Rodriguez."

My head snapped up, a sob escaping my throat.

"You've been there for me." Jay's smile widened. "You've done what no one else could. You're more my sister than my own flesh and blood."

I shook my head, the tears falling free from my eyes. "I can't. I don't deserve it."

"Yes." Jay's voice was firm. "You do." She grabbed hold of my arm, gently pushing me to the chair in the corner of the room. "Take your time. Hold your niece. Pull the strength from her that I know you need."

"I can't. I'm not strong enough to move past this," I cried, my tears falling onto Angelica's forehead.

Jay sniffed, brushing her thumb over the drops. "You are the strongest person I know. We would like you to be her godmother."

"Yes, oh God, yes. I would … I would be honored." The sobs came out harder, crashing through my body and tearing into my heart. "Thank you."

Jay leaned over me and gave me a hard hug. "I love you, girl."

"I love you too," I whispered.

"Take all the time you need." She kissed Angelica's head and sat on the bed, giving me a moment with her daughter.

My goddaughter.

"Angelica Maxine," my voice wavered. "It's nice to meet you, baby girl," I whispered. "I'm your godmother and auntie. Not by blood but my friendship with your mom runs deeper." I kissed Angelica's forehead, inhaling the fresh baby scent. Memories of me kissing my own daughter's head came rushing back, hitting me square in the chest. "Why?" I let out a sob.

Angelica squirmed, lifting her tiny hand.

I wrapped my fingers around it, gently kissing her palm. "I love you too, baby girl. I will spoil you like you're mine and I'll love you even more."

I only just met her and already she had my heart. It was something I would never change or want to. With her dark hair, her tanned skin, and her bow-shaped mouth, she was my best friend's baby. And she was perfect.

CHAPTER THIRTY-THREE

Dale

"ALL RIGHT, BABY girl." I took a deep breath. "It's just you and me today." I sat beside the tombstone, placed the twelve-pack of beer in front of me and pulled the first bottle out of the case. "Here's to fucking life and how shitty it can be." I toasted the air, popped the cap and took a long swig.

The early afternoon sun beat down on my face, warming my cold heart. The only good thing that had come out of all of this was that Jay and Angel had a healthy baby girl.

My chest tightened, that familiar ache growing stronger as each second passed.

Reaching for the second beer, I swallowed half of it before glancing down at the stuffed brown bunny in my hand. My thumb brushed over its face, the piercing, brown, glass eyes stared up at me. My throat closed. Finishing the beer, I tossed it on the grass and immediately went for the third. Fourth. Fifth. And sixth before I turned to the tombstone.

Baby Stanton Michaels.

She never even stood a chance. All because of me. Her dickhead of a father.

"*Fuck.*" I rubbed the tight spot in my chest, swallowing past the lump lodged in my throat. After the tenth beer, I finally felt the numbing I craved. My feelings diminished as the alcohol enveloped me in a blanket of peace. It was fake. I knew once the buzz passed everything would go back to the way it was.

Pulling my phone out of my pocket, I scrolled to my music app and played a song that spoke all the words I could never say. I hummed along with it, the alcohol only heightening the pain I had felt.

"I'm sorry, baby girl," I whispered, dropping my head in my hands. "And I'm sorry for what I did to your mom. They say everything happens for a reason but fuck if I believe it." My eyes burned. "Shit." Alcohol flowed through my veins. The bunny stared up at me, taunting me.

"I don't deserve your mother," I told the grave, hooking an arm around the tombstone. "But I love her. I love her so fucking much." I rubbed the tension out of my temples, the beer bottle falling to the ground in front of me.

It had been almost two months since I had seen Max. I heard through rumors only that she went to stay with her grandmother for a little bit. I had no idea when she would be back or if I would even see her again. She stepped down from being vice-president of the King's Harlots but anything else? The information was locked up tight.

Trying to get any details about her from anyone was worse than bringing this organization to its fucking knees.

A small brown bunny hopped in front of me. It stopped a couple feet away. Its nose twitched, its deep brown eyes staring at me. It could have just been a coincidence, if you believed in that sort of thing, but I liked to think it was a sign. Of what, I didn't know exactly. I wasn't a religious guy, after dealing with the horror and evils of the world. It was hard to think how a higher power could allow something like mass murders and so on to happen. But this, with the stuffed bunny in my hands and the real bunny only a few feet away, I could feel a sense of peace wash over me.

"I don't know if you're trying to tell me something but I'm listening. I'll listen to you for the rest of my fucking life, just help me understand. Help me understand that we can get through this. That your mother can. I don't care about me. It's her. Baby girl, I need her to be happy. I need her in my life. Help me find her. Help us find each other. Bring her back to me. I ..." Tears burned my eyes. The bunny hopped a couple times until it stood within touching distance from me.

"I wish I could have held you. Just once." My words slid into the air, floating away with the whisper of the wind.

The bunny tilted its head, wiggled its nose, and hopped away.

Scrubbing a hand down my face, I reached for a beer when I saw that the case was empty. *"Fuck,"* I yelled, slamming my fist onto the ground.

I reached for my phone, the small screen blurring before me. My head spun, the world around me tilting on its axis. I was drunk at my baby girl's grave.

Fuck my life.

***

(Max)

Dale: I need u.

Dale: Where r u?

Dale: Text me back!

Dale: I'm drunk.

Dale: Nothing matters anymore.

There was an empty feeling in the pit of my stomach when the text messages stopped. I tried calling Dale but it only went to his voicemail. I didn't know where he was. I hadn't heard from him in weeks until now.

I went to his apartment, only to find that there was an eviction notice on the door. My heart jumped to my throat. What the hell?

When Dale was nowhere to be found, I went to the only place I suspected he might have gone. But what I didn't expect to see was him passed out by our daughter's grave with an empty case of beer beside him. And then I saw *it*. A stuffed brown bunny sat at the base of the tombstone. My eyes welled, my knees buckling beneath me.

"Oh, Dale." I knelt beside him, brushing his bangs off his forehead and kissed him softly on the cheek. When he didn't stir, I sighed. The scruff on his jaw had grown in some, wrinkles creased at the corners of his eyes like he had aged years in only a matter of weeks.

Pulling the phone from his hand, I frowned when I saw the music app on the screen. I pressed play on the last song he listened to and when the words registered in my ears, my breath hitched. The song was about losing someone and never having a chance to say goodbye. It was from a father to his child. Tears streamed down my cheeks. I kissed Dale again, letting my lips linger against his head.

"I love you, Dale, but you can't do this to yourself," I whispered. Alcohol solved nothing.

Searching through his contacts for Coby, I dialed his best friend and waited.

"Yeah. Porter," came the deep growly reply.

"Coby." I took a breath. "I need your help."

***

"I'm surprised this didn't happen sooner," Coby said, helping me put Dale in his SUV.

"Has he always drank this much?" I asked, brushing my fingers down his cheek.

"Only since everything with you went down." Coby met my gaze. "This may be hard to believe but he's loved you all of this time. He's young. That's no excuse, I understand that but after what happened …" Coby shook his head. "He didn't wake up the same person."

I knew that. Every time he touched me, I felt he had been different since before his accident. "He's not the same man I fell in love with," I confessed. "But I love him even more. Maybe … maybe I was in lust with him before his accident. I'm not sure. He's … God, Coby, I can't do this without him. But he left me."

Coby, usually withdrawn and showing any lack of emotion unless it was directed toward Brogan, smiled. He actually smiled at me. "Neither of you think you're strong enough to handle this. Look at what you've been through already."

"Yes, but losing a baby can bring the strongest man to his knees."

Coby's gaze darkened. "I lost my own baby years ago."

"You did?" My eyes widened. "I'm sorry. I had no idea."

"The only person who knows besides Brogan is the man you're in love with." Coby took a deep breath. "I got married at a young age. My wife had mental health issues. I came home one day to her lying on our bed. Dead. She was pregnant."

"Holy …" My heart reached out to the dark man. "I'm sorry."

"Don't be. I'm telling you this because I didn't think I was strong enough to get through it but with Brogan, I realized I could take on the motherfucking world."

I laughed, wiping a tear from my cheek. "She has that way."

Coby grinned. "She does." He searched my face. "Whatever happens now, just be there when Dale wakes up. I don't expect you to jump back into a relationship with him. Just be there."

I nodded.

"Let's get our boy home."

"My home," I corrected. "We're taking him to my home," I said quickly, my cheeks heating.

Coby nodded once. "Good girl."

****

(Dale)

My head pounded. My bones vibrated. My body fucking ached.

I was hungover as shit and the emotional turmoil I had put myself through didn't help. Twelve beers later and I had passed out at my baby girl's grave. What kind of man did that make me?

I woke up in Max's bed, surprised to find myself at her home instead of my own. And that was when I remembered that I was evicted. My life was turning to shit and I had just that to show for it. Shit. Everything was fucking shit.

Sitting up, my gaze landed on the stuffed bunny sitting on the nightstand. Letting out a curse, I grabbed it and ran a hand over its soft head.

"You bought that for her," Max said from the doorway. "For our daughter."

"I did." I let out a sigh and placed the bunny back on the end table. "I think she would have liked it."

"She would have." Max chewed her bottom lip. "Tell me what happened."

I shrugged. "Nothing you didn't see."

"You were evicted from your apartment."

My gaze snapped to hers. "How do you know that?"

"After your text messages, I went to check on you and found the notice on your door. So, I went to the cemetery and I found you there. Coby helped me bring you ho—here."

"Text messages." I checked my phone, finding the last texts I had sent her. *Shit.*

Max moved to the bed, sitting on the edge but careful to keep her distance.

Smart girl.

With how tight I was wound, I would lose it first before any of this was resolved. My hands itched to touch her. To brush the hair behind her ear. To just hold her. But none of that happened because she was no longer mine.

CHAPTER THIRTY-FOUR

Max

"CAN I HUG you?"

My head snapped up at his words.

Dale never asked for permission when it came to touching me.

"I … I want to but I don't think it's a good idea."

He nodded, cursing under his breath. "I'll leave and let you get back to whatever you were doing." He rose from the bed.

"Dale" I placed a hand on his arm, stopping him.

"What?" he asked, his voice rough.

"I …" I chewed my bottom lip, pulling away from him.

"Yeah." He brushed past me. "That's what I thought."

"What do you want from me?" I yelled after him, clenching my hands into fists at my side.

"What do I want from you?" he repeated, spinning on me. "I want you to fucking love me and not look at me with hate in your eyes. I want you to admit that you're not fine. That you can't do this shit on your own. That you *need* me."

"I *can't* do this on my own," I said, repeating his words.

"Don't fucking patronize me, Max." He turned for the door. "It's been a couple of months. Both of us wanted time but I don't think it's done shit."

"I love you," I breathed, swallowing past the hard lump in my throat.

"Yeah." His gaze turned dark. "And look where the fuck that's gotten us."

"I never asked you to throw me out. I never asked you to leave me. I never asked for our baby to fucking die. I never asked for any of this. I only wanted you. Excuse me for telling you how I felt and for getting pregnant. Because that's clearly all my fault." I scoffed, stomping past him when I was grabbed from behind.

Dale spun me around, slamming me up against the wall. "Don't you dare fucking walk away from me."

"Or else what, Dale?" I pushed him. "What are you going to do? You keep threatening to leave. Do it. Leave. *Leave already*," I screamed, beating my fists against his chest.

But he didn't. He only stood there, taking the punches from my hands. He didn't touch me, he didn't move, he didn't do anything, and it only made me hit him harder.

"Leave," I repeated on a sob. "I can't do this anymore. I'm done." I went to step around him when he slapped a hand against the wall beside my head, stopping me.

Dale stood right in front of me but he was so far away at the same time. I could feel him pulling away from me. He was shutting himself in between the walls of his mind.

"Tell me you're okay," he demanded, his voice gruff. "Look me in the eye and tell me you're fine."

I swallowed hard, looking away.

He pinched my chin, his fingers digging into my skin. "Tell me."

"I'm fine," I bit out, keeping my gaze locked with his.

"Fuck you, Max." He wrapped a hand around my throat. "With what we've been through, you should have enough respect for me to not stand there and lie to my face."

"I'm not lying." He was leaving, what was the point in telling him the truth? It wasn't like he was going to stay.

"Max," he shouted, punching his fist against the door beside my head. "Don't lie to me."

"I'm not." I lifted my chin, shoving past him when I was tackled from behind.

***

(Dale)

I didn't want to hurt her. I didn't want any of this. But her defiance and the fact she was lying to my face, drove this darkness inside of me to come to light. Every inch of me wanted to cover every inch of her. With my fist in her hair, I held her head down. My breathing came out ragged, the muscles beneath my skin vibrating with a need I had never felt before.

Max's eyes were dark, dilated to the point of black. She licked her bottom lip, the flush in her cheeks becoming more pronounced the more time went on.

It took everything in me not to force myself inside of her. Her sass mixed with her innocence drove me fucking crazy. This back and forth shit we were doing was going to kill us both. A part of me couldn't help but crave it and it was time I took advantage of it.

I kissed her cheek, letting my lips linger against her skin. It was a contradiction. The sweet gentle touch mixed with the hardness of my lower body. The fact I had her pinned down against her bed, trying everything in my power not to fuck her, proved just how much of an asshole I really was.

She squirmed beneath me, the flesh of her ass rubbing against my crotch.

A growl left my throat. "I'm not sure you want to keep doing that." My dick grew, pressing against the fabric of my sweatpants.

She groaned, pushing into me.

"Max," I snarled, tugging her head back. Grabbing hold of her wrists, I pulled her arms above her head and held them in one hand.

A low moan rumbled from the back of her throat.

My cock twitched, pushing into the heat of her center. *Fuck.*

Max spread her legs, chewing her bottom lip.

My body trembled above her, my heart hammering against my rib cage. Inching a hand beneath her knee, I pushed her leg to her chest and ground into her.

She gasped, arching beneath me.

A tingle hit me square in the balls. I didn't want to do this. But then I did. My body reacted to hers before my brain could comprehend what we were doing.

With Max, I had been in denial for long enough. I didn't know how we could ever get out of this hell we had fallen into.

She writhed beneath me, pushing her ass into my pelvis, rubbing her center against me.

Tightening my hold on her wrists, I inched a finger beneath her panties and pulled them down her legs. Her pussy glistened, swollen and begging for my touch.

A drop of pre-cum fell from my dick at the beautiful sight before me but all I could think about was getting my body balls deep inside of hers.

Her ass held hints of the beating she had endured from Tyler and I found it only made me want to fuck her even more. That darkness inside of me burst forth, until a hard growl left my throat.

Max whimpered, digging her nails into my hands.

Before I knew what I was doing, my hand landed against the flesh of her ass.

She yelped.

I did it again.

She cried out, pushing back into the swings of my palm.

Digging my fingers into the flesh of her rear, I lowered myself down her body and sunk my teeth into the full cheek of her ass.

Max threw her head back, a hard cry escaping her lips.

Massaging and kneading the flesh, I bit and sucked, taking the flesh into my mouth until her skin became red from my touch.

I met her gaze, my mouth turning up into a grin when I bit her again.

She gasped, licking her lips, her eyes bright with lust.

This wasn't about our love for each other. This wasn't about our feelings. We turned into a possession. It was to see who had the true power over the other. Her. It had always been her. Max controlled me. Every waking thought. My dreams. My actions. My damn soul. She was the reason I woke up from the coma. And she was the reason I would leave her.

****

(Max)

Every inch of my body tingled from Dale's mouth and hands.

He was replacing Tyler's touch with his own.

As soon as Dale had tackled me to the bed, I knew it would turn into sex. It was a given. But even more, it was needed.

Both of us were wound up tight and we needed that release before we snapped.

Dale's mouth moved over my skin. He lifted my shirt, tracing his nose along my spine and inhaled.

I shivered, arching under him.

When his lips found my neck, he thrust into me.

I cried out, scratching my nails into his hand holding my wrists.

He grunted, his hips moving painfully slow. Gripping the sheets tight, he trailed kisses down the side of my neck. "Tell me," he demanded, sinking his teeth into the soft spot beneath my ear.

"Fuck me," I breathed. "Please."

"No." Dale nipped my shoulder. "Tell me who you belong to. Tell me who you will always belong to."

"You," I whimpered. "Always you."

"That's right." Dale's fingers gripped my ass, spreading me open. He released me and pulled my top up and over my head before taking his own off.

I licked my lips.

"Are you ready for me?" he asked, towering back over me and linked our fingers.

"Yes," I whimpered.

His hips reared into my ass.

I gasped, the fullness of him stretching me.

Dale tightened his hold on my hands, keeping his mouth against my throat. "I'm not leaving until all you think about is me. Every inch of you will smell like me. Your skin will taste. Like. Me. Everything about you will scream that you were fucked by the man you love. And that's me, isn't it, Max?"

I swallowed hard, nodding.

"Tell me." He closed his teeth around my ear. "Say it. Say the fucking words."

"*Yes*," I screamed. "I love you."

"Only me." His hips sped up, thrusting hard and deep, pulling a release right from my body. "That's right, kitten. Come for me. Come so fucking hard."

My body shook, the electric wave of pleasure shooting right up my back.

"That's it, Max." He kissed my throat, thrusting hard before he growled out a release of his own. He kissed my shoulder, falling free from my body before wrapping his arms around my middle. "No man will be able to give you what I can."

Tears burned my eyes, a lump lodging its way in my throat. His words whispered over my skin, stabbing me right in the heart because they were the truth. No man could ever give me what I needed.

"Tell me you're okay," he muttered, kissing me softly on the cheek.

A sob crashed into me, squeezing my lungs.

"Tell me," he brushed a hand down my side. "Max."

"I'm not." Agony whipped around me, piercing me in the stomach. "I'm not okay."

CHAPTER THIRTY-FIVE

Dale

"*I'M NOT OKAY.*"
Placing the bouquet of yellow tulips at the foot of my baby girl's grave, I kissed my fingers before brushing them against the tombstone. I didn't want to leave but without Max at my side, there was nothing for me here.

Max's words from last night made me realize that neither of us were *okay*. Being apart but still being in the same town, didn't help. After grabbing a couple things from my apartment, I decided to just … leave. I had no idea where I was going or what laid in store for me, but I knew I needed to get away.

"I will always love you, Max. No matter what. No matter how long we're apart. My love for you will never lessen."

But I still walked out.

And she still let me.

"Can we be friends?" she asked, reaching for my hand.

I linked our fingers and kissed her knuckles. "Maybe in time."

She nodded, her eyes shining. "I love you, Dale."

Walking away from her was the hardest thing I ever had to do but we both knew our relationship wasn't healthy.

When she had finally confessed she wasn't in fact okay, I couldn't do anything but hold her. I was a pansy-assed-pussy who didn't deserve her.

"You sure this is what you want to do?" Coby asked, leaning against his SUV.

No. "Yes."

Coby nodded once, looking out at my shitty car parked by the curb. "You still got that old beater."

I grunted. "Yeah."

"What's the first thing you're going to do?" He crossed his arms under his chest, his gaze slowly meeting mine once again.

"Buy a new car." The joke meant to lighten the mood but it did shit all.

"I'll watch out for her," he told me, clapping a hand on the back of my neck. "And any fucker who comes in breathing distance of her, I'll bust their kneecaps."

All I could do was nod as the billowing ache formed in my chest.

"I love you, brother." Coby leaned his forehead against mine. "You better come back."

"I will."

"You better come back for *her.*"

"I will." I took a deep breath. "I don't want anyone else."

"Good." He kissed my head. "Fuck, Dale."

"Yeah." I rubbed the tightness out of my chest. "I agree."

***

"Where the *hell* are you going?" Angel barked as soon as I entered the King's Harlots clubhouse. His gaze zeroed in on the bag hanging off my shoulder.

"I'm not quite sure," I muttered, throwing the bag on the bench. After Coby left my place, I had driven over to Asher's, said goodbye, and made my way out of there before things got emotional again.

As I walked into the Harlot's clubhouse, I just finished sending Stone a text. The guy was nowhere to be found. He did some running for Angel few knew about. I didn't ask questions.

"Listen, brother." Angel clapped both hands on my shoulders, his brows furrowing. "You don't have to leave."

"I do."

"Why?"

"Because I love her too much to stay," I said, a flutter of relief washed over me. It had been the most honest thing I had said in months. Max's happiness meant everything to me and if she couldn't be happy with me, I would leave.

"Fuck, Dale." Angel squeezed my nape. "I love you, man. I know we've had our own shit but … fuck."

I chuckled. "Aww, Angel, are you becoming a softy now that you're a father?"

"Shut up," he grumbled, punching me gently in the shoulder.

We stayed like that for a couple minutes before he pulled away and shoved his hands in his pockets.

"I need you back here in six months. I don't give a fuck where you go. Find yourself. Sort your shit out. But be back here on October twenty-first."

"Okay ... why?"

Angel grinned. "Because that woman of mine is finally making an honest man out of me."

My eyes widened. "Fuck yeah." I tackled Angel, pulling him in for a hug. "Congratulations, brother."

"It's about damn time too," came a deep reply.

We pulled apart, finding Coby coming toward us.

He smirked, clapping a hand on Angel's shoulder.

"I thought you were heading back to the city," I said to Coby.

"This is more important right now." He handed me a beer. "Brogan understands."

"You know what this means right?" Asher stepped out from behind the bar. "Bachelor party time." Asher wrapped an arm around my neck. "Good to see you, brother," he muttered in my ear.

"Good to see you too." I shoved out of his grip before hooking an arm around his shoulders and kissed his cheek.

"Fuck, Dale." He pushed me away, slapping me across the head. "Why the hell do you do that?"

"You love me." I blew him a kiss.

Asher shook his head. "It's about damn time you got your humor back."

My smile faltered. It was fake. All of it was damn fake. But they didn't need to know that or that I had left the woman I loved. I was sure they could take a guess as to what had happened but there was no way I would discuss it.

Not then. Maybe not ever.

The light banter went back and forth between us.

Friends. Brothers.

We ended up moving to one of the booths, joking and picking fights like old times. It was how it used to be.

Before we met the King's Harlots.

Before I fell in love.

Before I met Max.

CHAPTER THIRTY-SIX

Max

6 months later...

MY CHEEKS HURT. I had never smiled so much in such a short amount of time. Hell, I hadn't smiled like this in a year. It was a nice change but that never-ending nagging feeling that I shouldn't be happy still poked at my heart. I ignored it like my counselor had suggested.

Angelica shifted in my arms, cooing around the soother in her mouth. I kissed her cheek, inhaling deep, the sweet scent of her skin easing all the nerves racing through me.

I was going to see Dale.

It had been over six months since I last saw him. He never told me where he was going. He never made contact.

My stomach did flips that we were in the same building but hadn't run into each other yet.

Jay and Angel's wedding was supposed to be small but half the town had shown up.

I still hadn't seen Dale. But I felt him.

Through the whole ceremony, I could feel his eyes burning into my skin.

But he never did make an appearance.

I sighed, kissing my God daughter's cheek again.

"All right, baby girl, let's go find your parents." I walked through the crowd at the back of the clubhouse in search of the newly married couple. Finding them standing by Asher and Meeka at the door, I kissed Angelica's cheek before handing her to Meeka. "You leaving already?" I asked her.

"We are," Asher answered for her, hooking his arm around his girlfriend's neck. "Gotta get my girls home to bed."

"Or boys." She winked, a slight flush spreading up her neck.

"What?" I screeched.

"Are you fucking kidding me right now?" Jay cried. "And you're only just telling us this now? Twins?"

Meeka nodded, a small smile splaying on her lips.

"I'm the twin and I only get one," Jay pouted, brushing her hand down her daughter's cheek.

"Hey, I'm all for making another one." Angel patted her lightly on the butt. "You know. Since it is our wedding night and all."

"I'm getting drunk. I pumped enough breastmilk to last Angelica a lifetime. You're going to have to peel me off the floor, remember?" She poked her husband in the ribs. "I *need* to get drunk," she repeated slowly, jabbing him with her finger after each word.

Angel grabbed her hand and kissed her knuckles. "My wife is so demanding." He shook his head.

She let out a dramatic sigh, her eyes twinkling with mischief.

We all laughed.

"Congratulations," I told Meeka, pulling her in for a hug.

"I'm happy to see you smiling again," she whispered, returning the embrace.

My heart thumped.

"Are you sure you don't mind watching Angelica for the night?" Jay asked, hopping from foot to foot.

Meeka laughed. "You're antsy. Get a drink. And no, we definitely don't mind. It's good practice."

Jay patted Angel's chest. "Get me a drink, my husband? Pretty please?"

He grinned, placing a hard peck on her mouth.

Clearing my throat, I kissed Angelica on the head and left them to their goodbyes.

"Max," someone called out. "Great reception, girl."

I waved, smiling at the compliment but that smile only went so far. It stretched across my skin, turning my lips up at the corners but it never reached my heart. A smile meant you were happy but in my case, it meant I was fake.

I put on a good show but that was just it. It was all just a damn show.

"Max."

My heart jumped to my throat, my feet stumbling over themselves. Just when I was about to land on my ass, Dale stood in front of me with his hand wrapped around my arm.

"Steady." He smiled, helping me regain my balance.

"Thank you." I pulled from his grasp and stared up at him. Somehow, he looked different. A light smattering of scruff covered his strong jaw. His hair had grown in. But, it wasn't that. He looked … happy. Refreshed. Looked like the time apart did him some good. That made one of us.

My stomach sunk to my feet. Maybe he had met someone.

"How are you doing, kitten?" he asked, pushing a strand of hair behind my ear.

"I'm …" I swayed toward him when he pulled his hand away. *Shit.*

A wicked grin spread across his face. "I see I still have the magic touch."

Oh, God, yes, the voice inside my head screamed. Clearing my throat, I composed myself and stood taller. "I'm doing well. How about you? How was your trip?"

He grunted, leaning against the wall. "It was lonely at times but it was needed."

"Where did you go?"

"I had no intention of going anywhere specific but the next thing I knew, I was at the airport. I backpacked through Europe." He shrugged. "It was fun and enlightening but I would have preferred to do it with someone."

I looked away, my cheeks heating. "I'd love to hear about it sometime," I blurted. As soon as the words left me, I snapped my mouth closed. "I mean … if you want to."

A cheesy grin spread across his face. "Yeah, I want to."

"Okay." A breath left me on a whoosh. "Well, it was nice seeing you." As soon as I took a step forward, rough fingers wrapped around my arm, pulling me back into the darkness behind the building.

"It was nice seeing me, Max?" Dale asked, brushing his nose just under the soft spot beneath my ear.

"Yeah." I leaned against him. "It was."

He spun me around and cupped my face. "It was nice seeing me," he repeated.

"Yes." I pulled from his grasp. "What did you expect me to say?"

"How about something more than that shit, Max? Maybe, I've missed you and I can't sleep or eat or … fuck if I know, but it's nice seeing me is a fucking lie and you know it."

"I don't know what the hell you want me to say." I placed my hands on my hips, jabbing a finger in his chest. "You left me, remember?"

He grabbed my hand, pulling me against him. "Yeah and I haven't been able to sleep since. I've missed you. I've missed everything about you. I have to force myself to do anything. I try not to think about you but I can't stop myself."

"What are you telling me?"

"I'm …"

"Dale," I whispered.

"Do you know what today is?" he asked, searching my face.

My eyes widened. "What … wait … do you?"

"Yes." He kissed my forehead, my nose and then the corner of my mouth before brushing his lips over the shell of my ear. "It's been a year and a half since we conceived her. I missed the official anniversary but I thought of you. I thought of you so damn hard."

My eyes burned, the back of my throat tightening. "How can you remember that?" I gripped his arms. "No man would ever remember that."

"I did the math, baby." His eyes shone. "I know we have our issues but it's been six long months without you."

"I can't …" I swallowed hard but I needed to know something. "Has there been anyone else?" I whispered, looking down at my feet.

His finger pinched my chin, tilting my head to meet the soft impact of his mouth. "No. It's always only been you. I know I was a dick, an asshole and I can never make up for what I did but there has been no other woman for me."

My eyes welled. "There's been no other man for me."

A cheesy grin spread across his face. "It's been a long six months without your warmth wrapped around me, baby."

"Way too damn long," my breath hitched. "I can't believe you remember."

"How the hell can I not remember?" his hand curled around the back of my neck. "I remember everything about you. Every moment we've shared. Every word we've said."

"Oh, God, Dale. The time apart has been awful but I realize now that it was needed." I wrapped my arms around his waist. "Please don't leave me again. Stay with me."

"I'm never leaving. Not again. We can work on this now. Tomorrow. The next day. Fifty years from now. I don't give a fuck. I'm not leaving you. I'd rather be in a toxic relationship with the woman I love then to be alone and miserable."

A sob escaped me. "You want to do this?" I asked him, looking up at him through unshed tears.

"Fuck yes." He crushed his mouth to mine, lifting me in his arms.

I laughed against his lips, wrapping my legs around his waist. "God, I love you, Dale. I love you so damn hard."

"Good." He kissed me repeatedly, placing tiny pecks all over my face. "Love me even harder, kitten, because I'm sure as fuck not going anywhere."

***

(Dale)

Her giggle was what I lived for. Making her laugh was my sole purpose in life. I loved this woman with her arms wrapped around my neck and the look of adoration in her beautiful eyes. She looked at me like I was a hero. *Her* hero.

"You're not mad?" I asked, sitting on the picnic bench and pulled her down beside me.

"Mad about what?" she kept a firm grasp on my hands.

"Me leaving and then coming back after all this time. Come on, Max. Most women would have kicked my ass long ago." I didn't want to fight but I didn't want her to go into this with any intention of leaving. Ever. Again.

329

She chewed her bottom lip. "Maybe so." She smiled up at me. "Although I *have* kicked your ass in the bedroom."

Fuck me. My body stirred.

Her smile widened. "I don't know." She let out a slow breath. "You leaving made me realize something else."

"What?" I asked, my heart jumping.

"That I need you. Angelica showed me that. I love that little girl like my own and I am honored Jay and Angel asked me to be her godmother. Getting to know her has shown me how life is too damn short. You hurt me, yes. You hurt me so damn much, Dale, but you've also loved me. You showed that when you walked away so I could be happy." A lonely tear strolled down her cheek.

I itched to kiss her, taking her tears on my tongue but I didn't. Not yet.

"I love you," she whispered.

I pulled her into my arms, pushing my face into the crook of her neck.

"I love you, Max."

We sat like that for a while. I leaned my forehead against hers, holding her hands between us and kissed her knuckles and fingertips.

"I'm not perfect. We both know that. I ..." I swallowed hard. "Fuck. I'm not good at this shit."

She laughed lightly. "Just be honest."

I took a breath and said the first words that came to mind, "The only thing I've ever been good at is loving you."

EPILOGUE

"I LOVED YOU before I even knew what love was. I loved you when you hated me. I loved you when you pushed me away. Every time you smiled for me, I realized that my sole purpose in life is making you happy.

"We had a long road between us and we still have a long way to go but I'm willing to work for it. I'm willing to keep those smiles on your face.

"I look forward to growing old with you. To have our friends by our sides. Our children, our grandchildren, everyone we love close by as we live out our days. Together.

"I love you, Maxine Stanton. And nothing is going to get in my way of showing you just how much I do, in fact, love you."

Max's eyes shone as tears fell down her rosy cheeks. Her smile had never been so bright as she stared up at me on our wedding day.

A year later and I was professing my love for this woman in front of our friends and family. We still had so much to work through but as each day passed, it only got easier.

Max grabbed my hands, not waiting for instructions from the priest. "I love you, Dale. I love you so damn much. You fought for me even though I pushed you away. You never gave up on my love for you. You knew how I felt before I was brave enough to admit to those feelings myself. When I hated you, you loved me. When I yelled and screamed at you, you spoke to me with gentleness in your voice. Not always, of course." She winked. "You were patient. So damn patient, I didn't deserve it. But I love you more for it. I understand now. After everything we have been through. I get it. I …" Her breath hitched. "I …"

Not waiting for the priest, I pulled her into my arms and crushed my mouth to hers.

I heard him say that we were now man and wife and that only made me kiss this woman harder.

Slipping my tongue between her lips, I swallowed her moan.

Cheers and hollers sounded around us followed by clapping.

I had let my love for Max be known in front of all our friends and family and now I was staking my claim.

I cupped her cheeks, pulling back a bit, and placed kisses all over her face.

She giggled, smiling up at me through unshed tears.

"I love you, kitten. So fucking much."

Her smile grew. "And I love you."

Wrapping my arms around her, I pushed my face into the crook of her neck and inhaled. The scent of vanilla and roses wafted into my nose.

She smelled delicious.

She was beautiful.

She was perfect.

And she was *mine*.

***

Many years later…

The first time I met you was when I looked into our mom's eyes. I saw pain, anguish, and worst of all, fear. She was terrified to let you go. Scared she would forget you if she opened her heart again.

You were the first. The one who got away.

I pleaded for them to love me just the same but you took that from me.

This was what I thought even though none of it was true. I didn't understand. I probably never will.

You have always been a part of me. That little piece that would stick with me for the rest of my life. You were a dark cloud for most of my childhood. Hovering over my head and threatening to explode into a thunderous roar if I wasn't careful. You were the pain and heartache. The suffering my parents went through.

But I reassure you, our parents are happy now. They had a long road and travel it together hand in hand every single day. They were honest with me about everything. They brought me to see you when I was just a small girl. I knew from that moment that if you were alive, we would be friends more than sisters. You would be my best friend. A girl I could count on and trust. We would gossip, do girly things together, and drive our parents nuts.

It would have been perfect.

Without you leaving, our parents never would have found each other and I can't help but be grateful to you.

You brought them back together again.

I no longer resent you.

I'm thankful to you.

And for that, you will always be a part of me. But I can't come back. As much as I want to visit you again, it can't happen.

I love you,
Your sister

Brushing my fingers over the stone, I said my goodbyes and headed down the middle of the graveyard.

A sense of calm had washed over me. I felt no regrets. No resentment. It was all taken from me the moment I finished reading my letter to my sister.

"You good?"

The deep voice pulled me from my thoughts. I smiled at my boyfriend. "Yeah," I said, sliding onto the bike behind him and wrapped my arms around his waist.

He grabbed hold of my hand and kissed my knuckles. The scruff on his jaw scratched at my skin, sending a hot shiver racing through my body.

He winked, his deep blue eyes twinkling in the midafternoon sun. "Ready, baby?"

"I am." I held onto him and brushed my fingers over the patch etched into his leather jacket.

Knowing we would probably never be back, a lonely tear rolled down my cheek. But this was it. I could finally move on.

I could be with this man and be free. Be us.

Thanks to her.

THE END

Grab Numb (King's Harlots, #5):
https://www.aboutjmwalker.com/rust

ABOUT

J.M. Walker is an Amazon bestselling author who also hit USA Today with Wanted: An Outlaw Anthology. She loves all things books, pigs and lip gloss. She is happily married to the man who inspires all of her Heroes and continues to make her weak in the knees every single day.

"Above all, be the HEROINE of your own life..." ~ Nora Ephron

Website: http://www.aboutjmwalker.com/
Facebook: https://www.facebook.com/jm.walker.author
Reader Group:
https://www.facebook.com/jm.walker.author/
Twitter: https://twitter.com/jmwlkr
Instagram: https://www.instagram.com/jmwlkr/
Goodreads: https://www.goodreads.com/author/show/51
32169.J_M_Walker
BookBub: https://www.bookbub.com/authors/j-m-walker
Amazon: https://tinyurl.com/y7dpjkud
Newsletter: https://tinyurl.com/ya9hycak

Want more? Head on over to my website for my

complete backlist!

https://www.aboutjmwalker.com/books

www.ingramcontent.com/pod-product-compliance
Lightning Source LLC
Chambersburg PA
CBHW071347300726
48976CB00006B/1801